RYAN'S BED

TIJAN

Edited: Jessica Royer Ocken
Proofread: Paige Smith, Kara Hildebrand,
Chris O'Neil Parece, AW Editing
Formatting: Elaine York, Allusion Graphics, LLC
www.allusiongraphics.com
Cover image: Depositphotos 15561905

RYAN'S BED

THIS IS FOR ALL THOSE HURTING FROM PAIN SO DEEP
AND SO DARK THAT YOU DON'T THINK YOU'LL EVER
BE RID OF IT. THIS IS FOR THOSE WHO SUFFER WHILE
WATCHING THEIR LOVED ONES SUFFER AND FEEL
HELPLESS TO TAKE THAT PAIN AWAY.

A NOTE TO READER THAT ALL
TOWNS AND LOCATIONS ARE FICTIONAL.

CHAPTER ONE

The first time I snuck into Ryan Jensen's bed was an accident. I'd been lying in bed next to this girl I'd been introduced to twelve hours earlier at a company picnic. My family had just moved to Portside, Oregon, from Schilling, Arizona, because of my dad's promotion, so the whole picnic had been new faces, new names, and that feeling of being the newbie on the scene. Portside wasn't huge, but it wasn't small either—maybe around twenty thousand people lived in this suburb outside of Merridell.

Robbie would know. My brother could spit out statistics because he was the family genius. Willow was the family artist. She excelled at almost everything creative, or it seemed that way. Piano. Dance. Painting. Once, she made a six-foot papier-mâché dragon that won a state competition.

Trust me. That was a big deal. She was on the local news.

Maybe that was when it started. Maybe she felt as if she had to compete with Robbie.

I'd found empty bottles of laxatives in our shared bathroom, smelled the dried puke in the toilet, and a couple of times, I'd woken up to find her exercising in the middle of the night. We were the only two sisters, so it made sense we shared a bathroom. We'd shared the bedroom too until our pre-teen years, and then we got *freeeee-dom!* (I'm saying that in the best *Braveheart* yell I can muster.)

I didn't know why she felt she had to compete with Robbie.

No one could compete with that kid. He was a walking, talking, and eating computer. Robbie wasn't ever going to be normal, but Willow and me—we were. Or I was.

1

I wasn't the best at anything.

Willow had been popular in Arizona. I hadn't.

Well, I hadn't *not* been popular. I wasn't in the top tier of the social hierarchy, but I was liked. Everyone knew me. Everyone was nice to me, though, thinking back, that might've been because of Willow. If someone came at me, they came at her. And she was *not* one to be messed with.

Same thing with grades. I did okay. My B+ average made me beam with pride. Not Willow. It was A+ or the end of the world. There'd been talk at our old school about raising our GPA from a 4.0 to a 4.2 scale. Willow was all for it.

Not me. That meant I'd have to try harder. No way.

Maybe that was my role in the family. I was the slacker.

Yes. I liked that. I'd been the slacker in the family—or maybe I was the lazy one. There was a difference between being a slacker and being lazy. One slacks, and the other excels at slacking. That seemed to fit better.

Yes, that was me, and I had been once again fulfilling my role when I missed Peach's door and tiptoed into the wrong room. I went in search of a glass of water and got lost trying to find her room again. It was easy to do. The place was a mansion.

I didn't realize it at the time. Both bedrooms were cool, with fans forming a breeze, and large, comfortable beds. These people were rich.

Wait, not rich.

They were wealthy. According to my sister, there was a difference.

I'd met Ryan and Peach at the company picnic—or, rather, I met Peach. I assumed she was nicknamed for her fuzzy red hair. Freckles all over her face. Blue eyes. Blending. That was what she did, just like me. I blended into the crowd, whereas Willow never did. It was the same with Peach and Ryan. She blended, and her brother didn't.

I wasn't actually introduced to Ryan, but he didn't need it. I noticed him anyway. He was that kind of guy. People noticed him, even adults.

Golden brown hair long enough that it flipped over his face and still looked adorably rumpled, hazel eyes, a square jaw, and a dimple in his right cheek—Ryan had a face girls sighed over. Even with him sitting at a picnic table, it had been apparent he was tall with a lean build and wide shoulders. Since his shirt had flattened against his arm, it was also obvious that there was good muscle definition underneath.

The guy worked out.

And judging by the look on his face, he'd been bored out of his mind.

He'd been sitting on a picnic table with two friends, not doing anything. He wasn't talking or shouting or waving his arms around. He was literally just sitting with his feet resting where people would normally sit, and he'd drawn attention. His elbows had been braced on his legs, and there was an air around him. He'd exuded a nonchalant charisma.

I wasn't the type of girl to notice a guy and stalk him from afar. No, no, I was the type to notice a guy and then notice the hot dog stand beyond him. Willow would go for the guy, and I would go for the hot dog.

Priorities, right?

But even though I hadn't talked to Ryan earlier, I knew he was popular. A person just knew, and my hunch was confirmed when two girls walked past him. They'd paused, hands in front of their faces, and whispered to each other. One of Ryan's friends had tapped his leg and gestured to the girls. He'd looked, and the girls had erupted in giggles before running away, their faces flaming red.

Meanwhile, Willow refused to come so I was on my own, sitting at my own table, feeling like a loser while I stared at all the other kids there.

They'd all seemed beautiful or remarkable in some way. And they'd all managed to find each other, like with my little brother. He'd been at a table with two other boys and a girl. All were focused on their iPads. I was pretty sure they were speaking nerd language, and if I'd walked over, the conversation between the eleven-year-olds would've gone over my head.

Again, I was the slacker of the family. I should be able to communicate with an eleven-year-old, but no. I'd been to other outings with Robbie. I knew the routine. He'd found his crowd, and I could tell he was happy.

Then again, Robbie never endured what another genius eleven-year-old might.

He was never bullied because he was smart. He was almost worshiped. People thought he was going to be the next Steve Jobs, and his classmates had caught on, already sucking up to him. Yeah, maybe there was a jealous kid every once in a while, but Robbie never talked about it. If he was picked on, I wondered if he was even aware of it.

I wondered how things would be for him . . . after. Robbie had always seemed happy. Would some of that be gone? I hoped not—stop.

Mind, back up here. Mental reverse, and back to Ryan again.

I should've known something was different from the minute my head hit the pillow in his room. I felt warm, at ease, and my body relaxed. It shouldn't have. I should've remained awake like I had been while I was in Peach's bed. They said I'd be 'better off' not being alone that night so I'd been in a stranger's bed. I was tense and gripping the sheet with white-knuckled hands, replaying in my head what had happened at my new house earlier over and over and over.

But not in Ryan's bed.

He was as surprised as I was when we woke the next morning.

He jerked upright. "What?" he asked, his mouth gaping open at me.

I grabbed for the covers, made sure they were pulled tightly over me, and I gawked back at him. That was it, really. My body was still relaxed. Only my mind was alarmed, but then my mind lost the battle. There was other shit up there that I didn't want to stir and think about, so I gave in and let my eyelids droop again.

"I must've gotten lost," I murmured.

Ryan and I hadn't talked—not at the picnic earlier when our parents greeted each other, and not when Robbie and I were ushered into their home that night. Everything was hush-hush when we got there. Mrs. Jensen had whispered something to Peach, and she gasped, her hand covering her mouth as her eyes filled with tears.

I looked away at that point. My chin had started to tremble, and I didn't want to start. If I started, I didn't know if I could stop.

So there in the darkness was the first time Ryan and I talked, and it wasn't really a conversation. He looked to the door like he should tell someone, but I said, "Please don't. I couldn't sleep until I came in here. I don't know why, but I can now. I just want to sleep."

His eyebrows pinched together. His dimple disappeared, and slowly he lay back down. He didn't say anything. A minute passed, and I realized he wasn't going to. He was going to let me sleep, and thankfully, that was exactly what happened.

I slept.

"I don't know, Mom. I woke up and she was there."

I could hear Ryan on the other side of the door.

"Well, I don't get it."

"I don't either," he grumbled.

"I thought it was weird when she didn't come back last night." A sigh.

I recognized Peach's voice, but I couldn't place where it came from. Then it didn't matter. I was asleep again.

The bed shifted under me, and I heard a whispered, "Mackenzie." A hand touched my arm and shook. "Hey. Are you awake?"

It was Robbie. I rolled over and opened one eye. "What?"

He'd been crying. The tears were dried on his face, and I could see two fresh ones clinging to his eyelashes.

He wiped at one, embarrassed. "Are you going to sleep all day?"

"If I'm lucky."

He frowned and then glanced to the door. "I don't want to be out there alone. I don't know these people."

I scooted back until I felt the wall, flipped back the bedcover, and patted the place next to me. "Scootch in."

He looked to the door again, indecision on his face, and then let out a small breath. His tiny shoulders slumped as if he'd lost what little fight he had. He sank into the bed, clasping the covers tight over his shoulder, and looked at me, lying on his side. I moved closer, mirroring him so our foreheads almost touched.

We didn't talk, but a fresh tear welled, pooling on the bridge of his nose. I reached over and smoothed it away.

"Mom and Dad are going to be gone all day today. I checked their phone calendar."

How Robbie could do that, I had no idea, but I wasn't surprised.

"Why aren't you crying?" he whispered.

"I can't."

He nodded as if this made perfect sense. "I wish I were like you sometimes. You're the strong one, Kenz."

Strong? Was that my role in the family?

I tried to muster a smile, but I knew I failed. I probably looked like the Joker instead. "Can you sleep?"

"I'll try. Can we stay here all day?"

"I'm going to try."

That seemed okay with him. He closed his eyes and a settled look came over him, one that resembled peace. But I knew it was a lie. There was no peace. Not anymore.

"Hey, Kenz," he whispered a minute later.

"Yeah?"

"Happy birthday."

It was dark when I woke again, and Robbie was gone. The door was open, and I could hear the sound of silverware scraping against plates. The smell of food must've woken me, and for a moment, I was cross.

They could've closed the door. But then the fog left my brain, and I realized it was probably Robbie who'd left it open. He had a habit of doing that, and it always annoyed Willow.

Willow . . .

The small grin that had tugged at the corner of my mouth fell away.

God.

I drew in a rasping breath, and this time, I knew I couldn't keep the thoughts at bay.

It had been a weird smell. A rich, rusty smell, like wet metal. It made my stomach cramp, and I'd been biting my lip even before I opened the bathroom door. Willow's arm had gotten scraped earlier when we were moving boxes around the house. If she'd opened her bandage and dumped it onto the counter, I was going to be pissed. She was always yelling at me for leaving my toothbrush and paste on the counter. Everything had a place in her world, and for the life of her, she couldn't understand why I didn't remember that.

My answer was always the same: because I wasn't an anal, obsessive control freak. That usually angered her, but this time, I was going to be the one to explode. Willow wouldn't know what was coming her way. I was going to wave my arms in the air, stomp my feet, and yell like I just didn't care.

She knew how much I hated blood.

But then I was there, pushing the door open.

I don't remember when I realized what I was seeing. I suppose I felt something, because they told me later that I went into shock. My body shut down, and I left it. They said this could happen when a person experienced a traumatic event, but all I knew was that I watched from the doorway as my body fell to its knees.

My hand covered my mouth, and my shoulders jerked like I was throwing up. I learned later I'd been screaming.

Then I was shaking her, sliding on the blood on the floor, because it was everywhere. Thinking about it, I could feel it on my hands again. *Warm.* Liquids were supposed to be refreshing and cool. This was heavy. It felt no different from my own body temperature. I didn't like that. It should've felt different. Because it was Willow's, it should've felt perfect.

I stood in the doorway as I watched myself. And I kept screaming, until suddenly, I stopped. I choked on a sob, and like that, I was back in my body.

My face: dark eyes, golden blonde hair, heart-shaped chin.

My body: slender arms, long legs, and petite frame.

My heart: beautiful, broken, bleeding.

All of it on the bathroom floor in a bloodied pile.

Feeling a weird serenity, I gasped on a breath and moved next to Willow. I sat on the tile the blood hadn't touched yet. But it would. It was seeping out of her.

I knew she was already gone. Her eyes were vacant, but I wanted one more moment. My sister and me.

I lay down, just like her.

On my stomach.

My face turned toward hers.

My hand on the floor, palm up, mirroring her.

I watched over my sister one last time before we were discovered.

There was a flash of light. Someone was coming in through my bedroom—Mom. I didn't look up at her. I couldn't hear much. A dense cloud came over me, dulling my senses, but I heard her screaming, as if she were far away.

She was shaking Willow.

Time sped ahead. Time slowed to a crawl. Time was all over the place, in patches.

When I noticed the sirens, the flash of red and white outside my bedroom window, I reached over and held Willow's hand.

My face. My body. My heart—it all went with her, because she was me.

My twin sister killed herself on June twenty-ninth.

We would've been eighteen the next day.

CHAPTER TWO

"Uh. Hey."

It was nearing eleven the next night. Robbie and I had been there almost twenty-four hours. I hadn't left Ryan's room except to visit the bathroom, and I was currently sitting on his bed, book in hand. He edged into the room, his hands in his pockets and his shoulders hunched forward.

I should've felt all sorts of weirdness, but I was at the point where I'd sit on the roof and not give a flying fuck what anyone had to say. Keeping my finger between the pages, I closed the book and waited.

"Um . . ." He paused, staring right at me.

He had no idea what to say. I could see the floundering on his face, but he shook it clear and a small smile showed. His dimple winked at me. He raked a hand through his hair, leaving it as rumpled as it was yesterday. I knew why those two girls had squealed. He was all sorts of dreaminess.

I waited for the spark to flicker in me. I should blush? Giggle? Sigh?

No. Nothing.

I felt nothing, and then I remembered how it felt to lay in his bed, and I knew that wasn't true. I felt some peace around him for some reason.

He scooted farther inside, glancing back at the door before leaning against his closet. "The whole my-bed thing . . ." He motioned to where I was sitting. "Did you want the bed again tonight?"

I looked down. I didn't want to see his eyes when I asked this question. "Are my parents coming back?"

There was silence, and it stretched past the point of not having an answer. He had one. He just didn't want to say it.

I shook my head, letting the book fall to the bed. Wrapping my arms around myself, I turned away. "Never mind."

He cleared his throat. "For the record, I'm not supposed to know about your folks."

I looked back. "But you do?"

The hesitancy and fear I'd seen on his face melted away to reveal the sorrow, and he nodded. "Yeah. I eavesdropped on the call. They're at a hotel. I guess your grandparents are coming tomorrow."

"Oh. Okay." I cleared my throat. "Thank you."

"Yeah." He sighed. "You don't have to thank me for anything, but I do have to know about the bed. I was trying to tell my mom maybe it was me—like, you could sleep when you were around me because of my teenage pheromones or something."

I cracked a grin. "That's a new theory."

"Hey, not all of us are child Einsteins like your brother."

"Touché, and neither am I. I'm the only normal one in my family."

But I wasn't normal anymore.

"Yeah."

Maybe he thought the same thing because another silence descended over us. It felt like a sullen quiet too, as if maybe we'd both realized the true travesty of this situation. My remark-able quality had gone from being the slacker to the surviving twin.

"Well, fuck." I breathed.

He'd been picking at his jeans but looked up. "What?"

"Nothing. Yes, I'd like to sleep in your bed, if that's okay with you."

"It's fine with me." He grinned. "It was kinda nice, waking up to find a hot chick in bed with me. My friends will get a kick out of that—"

"You aren't going to tell them!"

10

His eyes widened. "No. I know, I wouldn't, I mean—I'm not that kind of guy, but my sister has a crush on one of my friends. She already told him. I overheard that phone call too."

"What are you? A male Veronica Mars?"

He scoffed, but that dimple was flirting with me.

"I get bored easily," he said. "I shoot hoops to keep busy. You know, like restless leg syndrome? I have that, but it's my entire body and brain. It doesn't turn off sometimes."

"Oh."

"Anyway, Mom said I couldn't play today. She was worried some of my friends would show up, and she didn't want anything to get out." He snorted, rolling his eyes. "I'll get blamed for it, but it's always Peach who tells. She never gets in trouble."

Robbie was beloved. Willow was perfect. And I guess I was the one who got in trouble, like him.

"It's the same for me," I offered faintly.

I got blamed for the laxatives. I was the one they thought had an eating disorder. They ignored the bowl of Cheetos in front of me during the "intervention" talk.

"Mackenzie, your father and I want you to know that we love you a great deal. Looks do not define our self-worth . . ."

There'd been other times, like when Willow wanted me to ask for a treadmill. They didn't see her on it during the day, only me. She ran in the park during the day and then used the treadmill at night. I did the normal thirty minutes Coach Ellerson required from us during the off-season for soccer. I should've done more, but Cheetos and being lazy were a lot more fun.

"So . . ." Ryan pulled me from my thoughts.

I almost sagged with relief. No more memories.

He tugged at one of his sleeves. "Do you, uh, want me to stay with you? Or, I mean, do you want to sleep alone?" He rushed out, "I can do either, that's cool. You just let me know."

"What?" Someone knocked on the door. One quick, hard tap.

He groaned. "My mom said it's fine, but she's going to put the nanny cam on us. So, you know, no messing around." His head shot up. "Not that that's what I have in mind. I mean, you're hot, but you're grieving. You lost your sister, so . . . you know . . ." He flinched, cursing under his breath. "Sorry. I shouldn't have said that last part. I—sorry. I'm shutting up before I say any more shit."

"What?" I asked, hoping the upward curl of my lips resembled a grin, or better yet, something cool and maybe even seductive. "You mean you've never been asked to pretend you're a grief counselor?"

He barked out a laugh. Then his eyes darkened. "I lost a friend almost two years ago, so I kinda know what you're going through. Kinda. Not really. I mean, he wasn't my brother or my twin or anything, so it isn't the same. But . . ." He stopped himself, closing his eyes for a moment.

Loss was loss, as far as I was concerned. Yeah, there could be different degrees of it, but it was the same emotion. The only thing that differentiated was whether it came suddenly or slowly. But I kept that to myself because honestly, who the hell wanted to talk about that?

I pointed to his television and video console. "You have Warcraft?"

"Yeah." He brightened up. "You play?"

"Got a sudden urge to learn."

"All right." He grabbed a controller from his desk, found the other next to the bed, then climbed up next to me. Leaning back against the wall, his leg next to mine, he taught me how to play. His arm and hand brushed against mine randomly, and every time they did, I felt a small but warm tingle.

We played Warcraft most of the night. Robbie played with us too, until I convinced him to go to bed. Ryan and I only turned out the light when his mom stuck her head around the door.

"It's after two," she told us. "Time to sleep." She gave me a soft smile. "I hope you can sleep okay, Mackenzie."

Me too.

She gave Ryan a pointed look, jerking her eyes to a stuffed rhino on his desk. A red light blinked in its nose.

He ran a hand through his hair. "Yeah, yeah, Mom."

"Good night, both of you."

The next morning, I ventured to the kitchen for the first time and found it filled with an uncomfortable tension. They could have been sitting in silence *before* I showed up, but I doubted it. I didn't need Robbie to decipher who'd been the subject of conversation two seconds before my arrival. It was one of those scenes where you walk in and know they were talking about you.

Mrs. Jensen was at the counter, making coffee. Peach sat at the table, and a middle-aged lady—I assumed their maid or something—placed Cheerios in front of her. I had to stop and take that in. A maid. And she was wearing a blue dress with a white apron over the top of it.

These people didn't just have house staff; they had house staff in uniform. That was, like, a whole other level. *Wealthy* rich. That was what Willow would've said, and she was right. She was always right.

"Mackenzie." Mrs. Jensen sounded breathless. Her cheeks flushed a little, and she smoothed a hand down her hair. "How are you? You slept well?"

I had, and I glanced over at Ryan, who was coming in from outside. A warm breeze came with him. Seeing me, he paused with his hand still on the door's handle. His mouth formed an O, and he gripped a basketball in his other hand.

"Hey!"

Peach made a sound. I registered it in the back of my mind, but I ignored it. I could hear the disapproval in her voice, and I already knew who Peach's friends would be at school. She'd run with the snooty girls—mean, catty, and looking down their noses at peeps beneath them. Those types of girls. And in other words, most definitely *not* my type.

"Hey." I gave a brief wave, glancing to the side.

Robbie sat next to Peach, and he lifted his hand to wave before it dropped back to his lap. I noticed the toast in front of him, how it was untouched. My gaze skirted away. I didn't want to see the sadness or bags under my little brother's eyes. I didn't want to remember why.

"Uh, how about a seat, Mackenzie?" Mrs. Jensen extended an arm to a chair across from Peach.

I took the chair next to that, across from my brother instead.

She cleared her throat, holding a cup of coffee tightly right in front of her chest as if it were protecting her. "Toast, Mackenzie? Rose could get you some."

In the next moment, I had a piece of buttered toast in front of me, but I couldn't touch it. Peach circled her spoon in her bowl of Cheerios. She was glaring at me with a hint of confusion.

I lifted an eyebrow. "Yes?"

She dropped her gaze but still circled her spoon around her bowl.

Ryan dropped into the chair at the end of the table between my brother and me so he was facing the kitchen.

Both Mrs. Jensen and Rose fussed over him. What kind of cereal did he want? Oh, he didn't want cereal. Toast? Bacon? Wait, Rose could whip up some pancakes. Not pancakes? French toast, then? After the fifth question, Ryan got up and poured his own bowl of cereal, rolling his eyes as he started back to his chair.

"Mil—" His mom started to suggest, but he'd already grabbed it and poured a hefty glug into his bowl.

"Knock it off, Mom," he grumbled, hunching over his bowl. "Fuss over Peach. She actually likes it."

"I do not."

He shot her a look, his spoon poised in front of him. "You do too. The whole spoiled thing works for you. You love it."

She transferred her glare to him, giving me a respite. "You're such a jerk sometimes."

A cocky grin spread over his face. "Sometimes? I heard you on the phone with Erin. I thought it was *always*?"

Her eyes got big, and she slammed a hand down on the table. "Stop listening to my calls!" Her head whipped around. "Mom!"

Ryan shrugged. "Not my fault your voice carries through the entire house. Close your door next time." He rolled his eyes. "Might help, genius."

"Okay, you two. Stop it." Their mother decided to wade in, sitting at the head of the table. Her coffee remained gripped with both hands. A frozen yet polite smile appeared as she turned to me. "Mackenzie, you and Ryan are in the same grade. You're a senior, right?"

Miracles did happen, after all.

I nodded.

Peach's eyes were narrowed on me, watching for a reaction. I kept my face straight, but I was doing somersaults inside.

Mrs. Jensen cleared her throat. "Your grandparents are going to arrive today. They'll be picking you and your brother up and taking you back to the house . . . or . . . a hotel. I'm not sure where you're going, actually, but I know they're eager to see you."

"Grams is coming?" Robbie's head popped up.

I shot him a look. "Didn't see that on the calendar, huh?"

He rolled his eyes, but one corner of his mouth lifted. He leaned back against his seat. "I can't check everything."

"What?" I teased him. "How is that possible?"

He shrugged, but anything he would've said was cut short.

Mrs. Jensen exuded a relieved and forced laugh. "Brian told me one of Phillip's children was brilliant. That must be you, Robert."

Robert. I almost scoffed at the name no one called him except Grams.

Mrs. Jensen kept going, leaning forward to beam at Robbie. "Portside has an advanced program for gifted children like yourself. I think you'll really like it. I know sometimes the exceptional children can be outcast by their peers in other places, but rest assured—" Her voice was so cheery. "That isn't the case in Portside."

She paused, waiting for Robbie to say something.

He looked at her and then to me. His little hand fisted around a fork, and a tear welled up in his eyes. He looked away.

"Oh." The corner of her mouth turned down. "Dear."

Shit. It was time to do my big-sisterly duty. I coughed and scooted back my chair. "Thank you for breakfast, Mrs. Jensen."

She had paled, but she tried to muster another smile for me. "Yes, well, you should thank Rose. She does most of our meals. We wouldn't know what to do without her." She turned toward Rose, who paused at the sink. "Right, Rose? The entire household would fall apart if it weren't for you."

"Yes, Mrs. Jensen. Yes."

Mrs. Jensen laughed, and I tried not to wince at how fake it sounded. Her hand came to rest on her chest. "Well, I brought up school before because Peach is having a few of her friends over at the end of the week. If you wanted—"

Ryan groaned.

She showed no sign of hearing him. "—to come and meet some of them. Her friends are so well-behaved, and they're good girls. They're the type you'd want to be friends with. Right, Peach? You and your friends seem like the popular girls in your class, even though Mackenzie is a grade above you."

"Mom!" She was horrified too. "Shut up."

"Mom," Ryan drawled. "She doesn't want to hang out with strangers right now."

"Mmmm?"

I could only sit there and watch this unfold in front of me. Mrs. Jensen seemed oblivious, sipping at her coffee as if it were an IV filled with morphine. I frowned, scanning the back of the kitchen for a hint that maybe she put something else in there besides coffee. Then I felt Robbie's foot pressing into the top of my knee. He was pushed right up against the table, holding on as he stretched his leg all the way to me.

I thought I'd done my sisterly duty before, getting the attention off him, and I lifted an eyebrow at him.

He mouthed the word *bathroom*.

I nodded. "Can we be excused from the table?"

"We?" Mrs. Jensen looked from me to my brother. "Oh. Yes. Of course." Her eyes fell to our plates. "Neither of you has eaten. Okay, Rose? Can we make sure there's food left out in case they want to grab a bite later? We could order bagels if we don't have any on hand."

God. Bagels. I felt whiplash at that word.

"Willow, you aren't hungry?"

My mom never knew. Right? It wasn't that she didn't *want* to know. Right?

"Well, we have bagels, Willow. Make sure to grab one, okay? You need to start the morning off right. Snack on it during the day if you need to."

Tears threatened to spill, but nope, I would not cry. No way.

Robbie's chair scraped against the floor. He pushed it back and stood there, a look of surprise on his face, as if he didn't realize what he'd done. "Um . . ." His mouth opened—nothing. It closed. Then opened. Still nothing.

I said softly, "Bathroom."

"Oh yeah." He darted around the table, around Ryan, and hurried up the stairs.

Another uncomfortable silence descended.

I looked down at my lap because, honestly, why would I want to see their pity? I'd had to remind my little brother why he stood from the table. That wasn't normal, and nothing about our visit was. We weren't friends with these people. We barely knew them. We had no other friends or family here. I mean, I was pretty sure I was sort of friends with Ryan, but we weren't there for a fun visit.

I could feel their attention. I hated it.

Willow had wanted attention. She and Robbie. But it was on me, and not in the way I'd always gotten it before. I was the laid-back one. The one who could joke. The one in the background. The one who everyone always forgot about. I was the steady one. That kind of attention—or lack of attention—was what I liked. This attention, I loathed.

It wasn't mine to have. It had been forced on me.

Clearing my throat, I had to get out of there. I turned to Ryan. "Warcraft till my grandparents show up?"

He stood right away. "Hell yes."

He was as happy as I was to leave that kitchen. I should've wondered why, but I didn't.

We spent the rest of the day in his room, Robbie too, until the doorbell rang around seven that night.

CHAPTER THREE

S hit got real once Grams and Grandpa Bill arrived.

There were tears. Hugs. Patting on the back, a lot of it. And that was between the adults.

"Have they met each other before?" Robbie asked me in a whisper. Once they turned to us, he stuck to my side. Still, he was almost mauled by Grams.

Ryan, who was leaning against the wall next to me, snorted but coughed to cover it when his sister shot him a dark look. It transferred to me before she seemed to remember why I was there. Her head hung, and she kicked at the floor. I couldn't really blame Peach. I suppose I wasn't like the other girls she knew. I mean, I wasn't crying. I'd left her bed and had stuck like glue to her brother, and the few times she'd talked to me, I hadn't been the most receptive. I wasn't rude. But I didn't respond to her the way she was clearly used to. That was Willow's role. She'd been the social one, the engaging one.

The perfect one.

I folded my arms over Robbie, pulling him back against me, and rested my chin on top of his head. "No. I think Grandma needs to cry. That's all."

Robbie found my hands and held tight. "Grandpa looks like he wants to cry too."

Standing off to the side, Grandpa Bill clutched a white cloth handkerchief in his hand. He always had one in his pocket, Grams insisted on it, but I'd never seen him use it before today. As Grams talked with Mr. and Mrs. Jensen, Grandpa Bill scrunched his nose, blinked a few times, and turned to the side. His hand came up before he turned back, and he blinked his eyes a couple more times. At the end he lifted his shoulders and rolled them back, as if he had to keep reminding himself to stand tall.

The conversation started to dwindle, and that was my cue to get ready.

I knew Grams's questions for me would start soon.

Had I known? Did Willow say anything before it happened? Could anyone have done something to stop it? Did something happen that day? I sucked in my breath, already feeling the slap of each inquiry.

"Ouch, Kenz." Robbie wiggled out of my hold. "You're hurting my hands."

I released him immediately, seeing white imprints where I'd been holding on to him. A wave of disgust rolled over me, and I replicated Grandpa Bill. Blink. Blink. Turn. *I will not cry. I will not cry.* Blink. Blink. *I'm okay.*

Lift your head.

Stand tall.

I can do this.

Robbie touched my hand, and his sympathy almost undid everything I'd shoved back. I was the strong one, that was what he said.

Head high.

I couldn't cry. Not yet.

I gave Robbie a little smile, pretending to hit his shoulder. "Ready for the adult melodramatics?"

"Mackenzie!"

Grams had heard me.

"How crass and insensitive of you! Your sister died two days ago. Melodramatic? That's what you call a grieving grandmother?"

I cleared my throat. "You're right, Grams. How insensitive of me." Willow hadn't been her twin sister, her other half, her partner from the womb. How thoughtless I was.

"Mom?" Ryan straightened. "Are you guys going to talk for a while more?"

"Uh . . ." Mrs. Jensen glanced to Grams, the question in her eyes.

"Charlotte and Phillip were hoping we could talk about the children before we went to the hotel," Grams said.

"Of course." Mrs. Jensen touched Grams's arm, and both couples turned down the hallway.

When they were out of earshot, Ryan said, "They're heading for the formal dining room. That's where Mom takes all our guests, unless she really wants to impress them. They'd go to the formal living room then. We can go back to the kitchen if you wanted to eat something."

I hadn't eaten all day.

That was odd. Was I trying to be like Willow? Was I trying to be close to her, or had I lost my appetite?

Robbie's stomach grumbled, and I squeezed his shoulders gently. "Looks like we have an answer."

Rose was in there, and it was as if she'd read Robbie's mind. A packet of pizza rolls appeared, and it wasn't long before my brother was stuffing them into his mouth. I lifted an eyebrow. "Didn't you eat today?"

He paused mid-stuff and shrugged as he swallowed a bunch of them all at once. "You didn't. I wasn't sure if I should or not."

Definitely not like Willow. I knew then. "You can eat any time you want. I didn't have an appetite today."

"Ryan, why are you acting like this?"

Peach's question came from left field. She was almost glowering in her seat at the kitchen table. She'd followed us in and locked her gaze on her brother.

He frowned. "What do you mean?"

"You never act like this." She gestured to us with a brisk motion. "All hostess and stuff. You usually can't wait to get away from guests. You're acting like she's your girlfriend or something. She isn't."

"Shut up, P. Seriously. I'm being nice, and the reason I usually leave when we have guests is because I don't like the guests."

"You didn't care when Erin came over on Sunday."

He lifted his eyebrow. "I ate a pizza at the same table with you two, and then I left. Don't make it something it isn't."

Her face got red, and if possible, her glower went up a notch. "Whatever. You're being weird."

"What does it matter?"

Robbie was on his second handful of pizza rolls. He was nearly through them all, and Rose must've noticed because she pulled out a second package. Once they were cooked, they all went on a single plate. Just for him.

"It doesn't. It's . . ." Peach cast me a look, chewing on her bottom lip. "It doesn't. Never mind."

Ryan looked as confused as I felt when he met my gaze. He shook his head, and for a moment, it was just the two of us. I knew the others were there, but they all melted away and an invisible, unbearable weight lifted from my chest. It was over as soon as it happened, but I was already yearning for the next time.

"Okay." Mr. Jensen came into the room, rubbing his hands together. He swept a look over all of us, lingering on Robbie before falling to me. "Your grandparents are going to take you with them. I guess your mother packed some bags for you two. It's all waiting at the suite."

"Are my mom and dad going to be there?"

My throat burned, and I was glad Robbie had asked the question. I couldn't bring myself to voice the words.

"Uh . . ."

And like his son the night before, Mr. Jensen gave me the answer without saying a word.

Shoving back my seat, I avoided his gaze and said to Robbie, "Come on. We gotta be strong for Grams now."

"I don't want to be."

I whipped around to face him. "Robbie! Just . . . come on."

His lip started to tremble, and I experienced instant self-hate. Taking his hand, I pulled him with me. "If you're still hungry, we can make Grandpa stop at a drive-thru somewhere."

I wanted to stay.

I didn't want to have to be strong for Grams either. I didn't want to see Grandpa struggle to keep from crying, because he too had to be strong for Grams, and I really didn't want to think about how the last time I'd seen my mother, she'd seemed all too relieved to see me go.

I held tight to Robbie's hand until I heard him hiss. I relaxed my hold. "Sorry."

"It's okay."

But it wasn't. Nothing was okay anymore.

We were halfway to the car when Ryan called my name. I looked back, stopping as Robbie kept going. Ryan was coming down the sidewalk, the house door closed behind him. Everyone else had stayed inside. Glancing over my shoulder, I could see Robbie settling into the car. Grams was already seated, and Grandpa headed to the driver's side. He'd left the back door open for me.

"Hey," I said.

Ryan stopped, and a flurry of expressions flashed over his face. Doubt. Confusion. Then wariness. He started to rake his hand through his hair, but he realized what he was doing and stopped.

He laughed shortly. "I do that all the time. My hair's always a mess."

"It suits you. You look cute."

His eyes widened. "Oh. Thanks."

I shrugged. It was the truth. Well, it made him hot, not cute. But I kept that to myself.

He looked back at his house, like he was deciding whether to say whatever he'd come out to say. He slid his hands into his pockets. "Are you going to be able to sleep okay?"

Ah. The bed. "Are you going to miss me?"

His dimple winked at me, teasing. "Maybe." The other side of his mouth curved up, and I realized he had a second dimple. "For real, though. Are you going to be okay? Your Grams doesn't seem the most soothing type, you know?"

"Oh boy. I know." I tried to grin but failed. Ignoring his question, I said, "Thank you."

"For sleeping with you?"

"That too. Thanks for spending time with me. I know I'm . . . not really myself."

"With reason."

"Yeah." I had to get going. I probably had three more seconds before Grams would be lowering her window to call for me. "Look—"

"My sister isn't that bad," he said.

"What?"

"My sister." He pointed over his shoulder toward his house. "I could tell you thought she was a spoiled bitch, and yeah, she can be that. But she isn't always. I think she wanted to be friends with you."

"Why?"

Ryan looked as if he was trying not to laugh. "You're kidding, right?"

I wasn't. I didn't know what he meant. Two seconds. I was already bracing to hear Grams's voice. "I should go."

"Nolesrock at gmail. You can email me if you want. It goes right to my phone, and I'll get an alert. I can call you if you want."

I opened my mouth, but I heard the car window coming down and swallowed my thanks. Before Grams could say anything, I remembered I didn't have my phone. I'd dropped it when I saw Willow.

Willow . . .

"I'll email you," I said quickly before hurrying into the car.

I wanted to look back to see if Ryan had stayed to watch us go. But I didn't. I didn't know why. And as soon as we got one block away, I regretted it. I wished I had looked, but again, I couldn't explain why. I just did.

Then Robbie said what I was thinking. "Ryan's cool."

Yes. Yes, he was.

COUNSELING SESSION ONE

"Hello, Mackenzie. My name is Naomi. Your parents thought it was a good idea if you had someone to talk to during this time, but I want to help you in any way you need. So, why don't you tell me where you'd like to start?"
"I want to leave."
And I did.

CHAPTER FOUR

One month later

"Counseling isn't working," my father said. "She won't go to most of the sessions, and it's been a month. What about Arizona? Should she go back home?"

I shouldn't have been eavesdropping, but the temptation was too great. They'd been in the kitchen talking about what to do with me for the last twenty minutes, and I finally gave in, moving from my room to sit at the top of the stairs.

And no shit, Sherlock.

The whole push for counseling had started right away. It was Grams's idea, and everyone except me agreed with it. I'd fought hard, but nothing I said made a difference. So, I resorted to some stupid-shit tricks. And I say stupid shit, because it was as basic as I could get. I didn't go. Literally. If they dropped me off, I went in and left once the car moved ahead. If they parked and waited the whole hour, I went out through a back door.

The only way I would've stayed the entire hour was if one of my parents went in with me, and I knew that wasn't happening. Deep down, they were about as fond of counseling as I was. So, no, it wasn't working. After a few missed appointments, the counselor called my parents, and I don't know what they discussed, but something shifted. I bargained down to one session every other month. That was the most I'd agree to, and anyone who thought it wasn't enough could suck it. It wasn't their twin who died.

"Nan Jensen was telling me about the Portside Country Club," my mom replied. "They have programs that Mackenzie could attend. Her daughter goes to them with her friends. She says they're very beneficial for her daughter, teaches her respect and how to act like a lady."

My dad's snort told me his thoughts on that suggestion. "What about back home? That'd be more beneficial, wouldn't it?"

"You want to fly her back and forth the rest of summer? I don't think that would be helpful. Besides, you can't push her Arizona friends like that. I talked to Emily and Amanda."

"Who are Emily and Amanda?"

"You know, Emily Christopherson and Amanda Green. Their daughters are Mackenzie's friends in Arizona—"

"The ladies you had your wine walks with?"

I almost smiled as I imagined Mom bristling. Dad thought the wine walks were stupid. Mom thought they were the next best thing to going to church.

"Yes. Those ladies." Her voice dipped low, almost a growl. "But I talked to them about Zoe and Gianna. They said they want to be there for Mackenzie, but you know how it is. Teenagers don't know what to say, so they hold off."

"Isn't that the same with adults?" Dad griped. "We haven't heard from Tony and Danielle since the funeral."

Silence.

A sniffle. "Well, we're talking about Mackenzie's friends right now—"

"If they don't want to support their friend, then that's on them. We have to deal with the here and now, and getting her into some form of activity is the best idea. She needs to be busy. She needs to be . . ."

I leaned forward, my hand wrapping tight around one of the stair posts. What was he about to say?

"What?" More sniffling, but she sniped back. "She needs to be gone? Away from us?"

"Tell me who Nan is again." He was resigned.

This was fight number I'd-lost-count. This was what they did. They thought Robbie and I were sleeping, so the checkered flag dropped, and off they raced. They couldn't get to fighting fast enough.

They assumed too much.

While they made sure Robbie was tucked in bed with his lights off, I got only a gentle tap on the door and a "You in bed, honey?" The term of endearment was on a rotating schedule. Every fifth night was *honey*. Others were *sweetheart, baby girl, my sweet daughter*, and *Kenzilicious*, and to answer their question, I never was. My light was always on, but they left after I replied with a loud and clear yes.

I shouldn't complain. We'd spent a week with Grams and Grandpa, and it was a week too long. Our parents had been busy while we were away.

I didn't know the specifics, but they got a new house. Then there was the funeral. It was in Portland because they'd buried Willow where we could visit her. We flew back to Arizona for a memorial service, though. It was more for everyone there— Willow's friends, my friends, our parents' friends, and relatives.

When we came back, we'd gone straight to the new house. I called it the new-new house since it was the second one we'd had in this town. Everything was already there for us, which was weird. In the new-new house, I didn't share a bathroom with anyone. There were four bedrooms. My and Robbie's were upstairs, and we each had our own bathroom. Our parents' room was on the main floor, and we had a guest room in the basement.

There was no room for Willow.

She'd been the only one who'd already decorated her room in the first new house. No one else had completely unpacked.

Willow . . .

An image of Willow in her casket flashed in my head—no, I wasn't going there.

My phone beeped.

I grabbed for it, silencing it so my parents didn't know I was eavesdropping. Again.

Unlocking the screen, I saw the text was from Ryan. A warm fluttery feeling spread in my chest.

Ryan: **Going to the movies with friends tonight. Want to come?**

Movies? I checked the time. It was after nine. I typed back.

Me: **Late movie?**

Ryan: **Yes.**

Me: **What movie?**

Ryan: **It's the new superhero one. You in?**

I didn't care about the movie.

Me: **Yes.**

I wanted to see Ryan, even if I had to sneak out.

We'd emailed at first. That had progressed to him calling our hotel room. Once I got a new phone, we texted daily.

He mostly asked how Robbie was. I asked how Warcraft was. He'd asked twice if I could sleep okay. I never answered. The answer was always no, but that was depressing. I didn't want my conversations with Ryan to be sad. Everything else was steeped in sadness, but I didn't want it to touch him. Not anything to do with him. We'd seen him and Peach once. They came to the hotel to go swimming, but that'd been it. Robbie and I had been holed up in the new-new house for weeks.

Ryan: **Sweet. Pick you up in ten minutes.**

Ten minutes? Wait.

Me: **You know where I live?**

Ryan: **Yeah. My friend lives next door. Be there in ten.**

For the first time in a month and one day, I hoped my parents would keep fighting. I sneaked back to my room and dressed. My light was off, but to be safe, I did the whole pillow-acting-like-a-human-body under my covers.

Slipping out, I didn't need to worry about going to the back door. The fight was still fully engaged. My parents never saw me on the stairs, and I headed out the front door. I was waiting on the curb when a car pulled up in front of me.

"Hey!" Ryan rolled the passenger window down and gestured to the back seat.

Another guy was driving, bobbing his head up and down in rhythm with the bass blaring from the radio. He watched me where I stood, faint curiosity in his eyes.

"We gotta pick up one more. Then we're good to go," Ryan told me as I got in.

Once I'd settled, the driver started off, and Ryan twisted around. He pointed to the guy next to me, who held up a hand. "This is Tom Sanderson and Nick Lumoz."

Nick was the driver, and he held up a hand but didn't look back. "Yo."

Tom nodded again, a friendly smile on his face. Both guys looked gangly. Each had their hair spiked like Ryan's and wore Portside High School shirts.

"Is this the chick who—"

Ryan cut Tom off. "Yeah, so shut up."

I caught the regret and sympathy that flashed in Tom's eyes. They knew about my sister.

"Tom's the guy Peach likes," Ryan explained.

"Ah, man." Tom groaned, slinking down in his seat. He'd been tapping his hands on his legs but moved to cross his arms. "It isn't something that's supposed to be acknowledged. It's the thing no one talks about, you know? Why'd you have to say something?"

"Because it's wrong. All sorts of wrong."

Nick snorted. "You didn't think that way when my sister liked you last year."

Ryan turned sideways, facing the driver. "Because that was last year, and your sister's hot." His eyes flicked to mine, and he amended, "Not that I was interested in her."

Tom snorted. "Right. Because that's why." He turned to me. "Nick's parents split, and his sister went with her mom. He stayed with their dad because of basketball, and us." He patted Nick's seat. "Right? You couldn't leave us. That's why you didn't go with your mom."

Nick scowled in the rearview mirror. "Thanks for blasting my personal shit. No offense," he added, looking at me.

Tom guffawed. "Whatever, man. And I said my thing because we know something personal about her. I felt it was fair."

"Fine." Nick leveled him with another look. "Then I'll tell her how you'd really like to date Peach, but you don't because of Ryan. You're too worried about losing him as a friend. How's that feel, buddy?"

"You do?" Ryan turned fully around.

Tom closed his eyes and heaved a deep sigh. "Oh God. This sucks."

Ryan frowned. "You actually want to date my sister? Since when?"

"Since never now," Tom grumbled under his breath.

"Since May," Nick said. "Since Parker's party where they kissed."

"You kissed my sister?"

"Shut up, Nick! You made your point. I'll never share another thing about you unless I have your written approval."

"Good. Glad we're clear."

"Crystal," Tom snapped.

Ryan sat back, waiting for the exchange to conclude and then turned to me. "My friends are idiots. They aren't usually like this."

"Yeah, we are," Nick and Tom interjected at the same time.

Ryan nodded. "Okay. They are. But . . ." He raised his voice, giving both a meaningful look. "Maybe *they* can simmer down? At least for the night or until after the movie?"

I shook my head. "Please. Keep going. I'm enjoying this."

Tom held up a hand, and Ryan narrowed his eyes. "Don't think I'll forget hearing about you and my sister. I know you talk on the phone, but kissing her is a whole other thing."

"They kissed twice."

"Shut up, Nick!" Tom yelled.

"Okay." A satisfied smile stretched over Nick's face. "Now I'm done."

"You're such an asshole."

Nick lifted a shoulder as if to say *meh* before slowing the car and pulling into a driveway. I assumed another guy was coming out, so I was surprised when a girl came out the front door instead. Long, beautiful brown hair bounced behind her as she hurried down the sidewalk. Ryan stepped out as she approached.

"You got shotgun," he told her. "I'll sit in the back."

"What?" Then she got in and saw me. Understanding dawned as Ryan sat next to me. "Oh."

"Cora, this is Mackenzie." Ryan gestured between us. "Mackenzie, Cora."

"Hi." I waited, tensing slightly. You never knew what would happen if you encroached on another girl's territory. I was the new girl, and I was ready for the bitchy comment, but nothing came.

Only a tiny bit of hurt flashed in her very aqua eyes before she tucked her hair behind her ear and looked down. "Hey." The word was a soft mumble.

I felt bad. I didn't need to be Robbie to know what that look meant. She liked Ryan. And judging by the way Ryan shut his door and said, "Ready to go!" he had no clue about her feelings.

The other two were quiet, watching Cora.

They cared about her, and she cared about Ryan.

I'd stepped into something. I let out a soft sigh.

"You okay?" Ryan asked, lowering his voice.

Nick had pulled out of the driveway and turned the music up louder. Cora looked over and mouthed *thank you*.

We drove with the music surrounding us for a while. Nick wasn't talking. Cora wasn't either, and Tom had settled back, looking out his window.

I turned to Ryan, unsure of my place. "Are you meeting any other friends at the theater?"

He shook his head. "Nah. Just us." He gave me a thoughtful look. "I wasn't sure if I should ask you about the movie. Tom said the lights have been shutting off early. Since you guys hadn't come over again, I thought maybe you were on lockdown."

The knot in my stomach—the one that was always sitting there—loosened a small bit. I'd forgotten. This is how it had been with him before. And he wasn't going to ask about the memorial service. He wasn't going to ask how awful it had been to sit with my friends, who suddenly didn't know what to say to me. I wouldn't have to explain how they'd either stop crying or cry even harder when I walked into a room. He wasn't going to ask about Willow's boyfriend and how Duke couldn't look at me, how *no one* could look at me.

I was there—the face they wanted but not the person they wanted.

With Ryan, in this car, I wasn't Willow's surviving sister. I was just Mackenzie.

I nodded. "Kind of. I think my mom wants me to get out of the house and do more stuff."

"That's perfect. We're doing shit all the time. You can hang with us."

As Ryan said that, I caught Cora watching us from the corner of her eye. Her lips tightened a bit at his suggestion.

"Uh, yeah. Maybe."

"We're hitting up a party later tonight, if you want to come to that."

The invite came from Tom.

I lifted a shoulder. Old Mackenzie wouldn't have gone—that was more of a Willow thing to do—but everything was different.

A party sounded like the best thing ever. "I would, actually."

Cora lifted her head, giving Ryan a wolfish grin. "Erin's going to freak."

The other two guys started laughing.

I frowned. "Peach's friend Erin?"

Ryan hardened. "Yeah, but she's kind of an ex of mine too." He leaned forward, raising his voice, "And I can do whatever I want."

Peach's friend who was also Ryan's ex, and she was going to freak because I was going to a party with him. This was the second situation I'd stepped into.

Lovely.

Cora glanced back at us. "She even has a hard time with me, and Ryan and I have been friends since second grade."

My lips thinned. "Let me guess. She's popular at school?"

Cora's eyebrows lowered. "She's one of the most popular girls in school, even though she's a junior this year. Stephanie Witts is the one from our grade."

I raised an eyebrow. "Is she coming tonight too?"

Cora shook her head. "No, just Erin."

Nick spoke up. "Erin's included because of Peach and . . ." His eyes darted to Ryan, and he shut his mouth.

Coughing, Tom said quickly, "But she isn't the hottest." He was smiling at me like he wanted to reassure me. "Don't worry. You're way hotter than she is."

Cora squeaked.

My knot tightened back up.

"Tom." Ryan glared at him. "Shut the fuck up."

"What?" Tom gazed around, blinking. "What'd I say?"

Cora shook her head, trying not to laugh. "You honestly need to get a clue one of these days."

Tom looked mystified. "Huh?"

Nick pulled into the movie theater's parking lot. We all piled out of the car, and the guys headed in first. Cora fell back to walk next to me. She looked up, tucked some hair behind her ear again, and dropped her gaze to the cement.

Her hand touched the back of mine lightly. "Can you hold back a second?"

I stopped.

Ryan and the guys were going inside, and he glanced toward us. Holding the door open, he stood there, waiting.

I saw the question in his eyes and had to pull my gaze away. Cora was saying something. It seemed like something I needed to pay attention to, but all I wanted was to be next to Ryan. I didn't care about this Erin girl. I probably should've. My brain was telling me to be smart. I was entering high school drama. Ryan was wanted, but I wasn't surprised. He had *that* look—dark molten eyes, broad shoulders, trim waist. Both of those dimples. Lean, but muscled. His shirt rode up once, and I saw the six-pack there.

I'd noticed all this on day one.

He was going to have girls after him. Of course.

Willow would've been after him.

I blinked a few times, shocked at that thought. Yes. She would've. And I would've done nothing. After seeing that she'd claimed him, I would've melted into the background, found my own group of friends, and I would've had no problem in school. All these issues—Cora and the ex—these would've been Willow's battles.

Was I taking her stuff on?

"So, you know." Cora had finished whatever she was saying.

I cringed, but I had to ask. "Sorry. I spaced for a bit there."

"Oh." She frowned. "You lost your sister, right?"

I nodded.

"Look, maybe it isn't my place, and I know we just met, but people have been talking about you. They don't know about your sister. I mean, I haven't heard any of that. Ryan made us all promise not to say anything, and I'm guessing he threatened Peach too. She has a big mouth, so if it got out, it would be from her. But anyway, she told Erin you slept in Ryan's bed when you were there, and Erin freaked." She rolled her eyes. "Erin could be inside, which is why I'm saying all this to you now. Ryan doesn't think things through sometimes. He doesn't think Erin's as bad as she is, but she's evil incarnate. I swear."

"Does she come at you sideways or straight on?"

"What?"

I wasn't a fighter, but an eerie calm settled over me. "I need to know how to fight her, so how does she fight? Usual catty-bitch way? You know, saying shit behind my back and verbal jabs. Or is she a face-on bully kind of girl? There are all different sorts now."

"Um . . ." Cora looked at the sky, her hands sliding inside her back pockets. "She has bleached blonde hair, and she'll be surrounded by a whole bunch of girls. They all look the same. Glitter on their face, something pink. If she sees you inside, don't go to the bathroom. She has a gang. They'll come at you and try to hurt you but make it look like it was an accident."

She was the type to sic her friends on me. I nodded. "Got it."

"Wait."

I had turned to go but looked back.

Cora seemed surprised. "Aren't you scared?"

An image of Willow lying on the floor, her blood pooling around her, flashed in my head. "Not a goddamn bit."

I started off. I was looking forward to this.

CHAPTER FIVE

I knew instantly which one was Erin.

She was the tall drink of water trying to cling to Ryan as they waited in line for tickets. She kept putting her hand on his arm, and he'd move it out of the way, shrugging off her touch.

It wasn't working.

He was irritated, and he wanted her away, but his scowl and the way he kept messing his hair up were having the opposite effect on her. The blonde could-be-a-model only stood closer each time he rebuffed her.

Nick and Tom were already in line for snacks, along with a group of girls. I didn't need two guesses to know they were Erin's friends. Cora was right. They all looked the same—with tight jeans and different shades of pink sweaters, glitter all over their faces and necks.

Cora came up next to me. "That's her."

There was a mix of envy, fear, and caution in her voice. It hit me in the chest. This girl was reacting to the ex the same way she would've reacted to Willow. Willow *was* Erin. I couldn't believe it, but it was true. The way she was standing, the way she whispered in Ryan's ear—that was how Willow had been with her last boyfriend, and how she'd intimidated his previous girlfriend. She'd been scared of Willow the same way Cora feared Erin.

For some reason, that pissed me off.

Then Ryan saw me, and with his wave, the beast saw me too.

Her demeanor changed. Gone was the seductress. Her eyes grew cold, and her lips formed a sneer.

Hello, cold-hearted bully.

I fought against grinning. This girl was trying to intimidate me.

It was working on Cora, who shied away from her place beside me. She actually took two steps away, and I looked at her, meeting her gaze so she knew I knew.

I grunted. Well, screw it. I'd take Erin on alone.

I turned back to regard the ex again.

She was smug under a layer of frostiness. She assumed I would be afraid of her.

Her mistake.

Something came over me. It'd been itching at me since I heard about this Erin girl, but right then, it was like a blanket wrapped around me. It wasn't a supporting or warm blanket. I wasn't being enveloped like that. It was eagerness. It was anticipation. It was . . . I had a target.

This girl wanted to make *me* the target, but no, honey. It wasn't going to work that way. Even if she knew about my sister, I wouldn't have cared. I was fast feeling the first peak of adrenaline.

I had an outlet, and I went straight at her. No hesitation. No lagging. I wanted this fight, consequences be damned. I had nothing left to lose.

Surprise flared in her eyes, but then the authoritative look returned to her face. She expected me to bow down to her.

My lip curled. She had another thing coming.

"Hey."

Even Ryan was cautious around this girl. I was beginning to wonder what powers she had tucked away for this reaction.

"I got you a ticket," he added. He glanced at Erin before handing it to me. "Here you go. I wasn't sure if you had money or not."

I gestured behind me. "Give it to Cora."

If he was scared of this bitch, then fine. I'd buy my own ticket. He hadn't asked me on a date. He'd asked if I wanted to go to the movies. But instead of pulling out some cash, I continued staring at Erin.

She narrowed her eyes. "Do you have a staring problem?"

"Move." I loved that simple command, and I stepped even closer. I was almost in her personal space. "You're in my way."

My voice was strong and clear. No break. No trembling. No softness. And I wasn't being aggressive. I wasn't tense. She *was* in the way. The ticket guy was right behind her.

"Oh." She moved aside, but only barely. Folding her arms over her chest, she was still in the way. There was enough space for me to move forward, but I'd have to hunch to the side, stand awkwardly, and feel her breathing down my neck to get the ticket.

Fuck that.

I stepped right up to the counter, my arm jabbing into her.

She cried out.

I turned to look her right in the eye, our faces inches apart. "Then *fucking* move."

She gasped, but I ignored her and bought my movie ticket.

After I pocketed my ticket, I turned to her. I was an inch taller, but I had to give her credit. Cora said Erin could've been a model, and she was right. The funny thing was—so could I and so could have Willow.

I'd never cared for our height. Sometimes I hated it during soccer, but I almost reveled in it while I stood toe to toe with Erin.

There were other people behind us, waiting to get their tickets, but I wasn't going to be the first to move. No way. I couldn't. She'd made this a pissing contest, and I wasn't going to be the one to falter.

So there we were, standing ridiculously close, staring at each other. Her eyes were heated, her sneer reinforced, and I was dead inside. I had no problem showing her that.

You can't battle someone who's lost everything.

Erin broke first. She whipped around and left, her hair flicking over her shoulder.

As soon as she did, I moved to the side so the next person could get a ticket. Her friends flanked her immediately, and she paused to glare at me. I stared back. I couldn't look away first. She had to do that too. This was her home turf. Not mine. I had to win both battles to have even footing.

Cora moved beside me. Ryan was off to the side, frowning.

"That was unexpected," Cora said, moving closer. "No one's been able to out-Erin Erin before."

She was impressed. I felt nothing inside.

Tom and Nick headed our way, their hands full of soda and popcorn.

"What'd we miss?" Tom sounded damn chipper.

Ryan studied me a moment before glancing to where Erin had disappeared, but all he said was, "Are we ready for the movie?"

"Let me take one of those." Cora took a soda, leaving with Tom for the theater. Nick held back, giving Ryan and me a look before turning, popping a kernel of popcorn in his mouth, and following at a more sedate pace.

Ryan stayed with me. As soon as they were out of earshot he said, "I'm sorry about Erin." I felt him move a little closer, his arm brushing against mine.

I waved that off. I didn't even care about his ex-girlfriend. "It isn't a problem," I assured him. "Really."

"I knew she could be a bitch, but I haven't seen it like that in a long while. I can talk to her—"

"No!" I grabbed his shirt, and my hand formed a fist in it. "Don't."

He frowned. "She can't be a bitch. It isn't right."

Was he clueless about how girls worked? I shook my head. "Let it go. I can handle myself, but word to the wise." I nodded in the direction his friends had gone. "I've got a feeling she's been a bitch behind your back to Cora."

His head moved back a centimeter. "You serious?" His mouth pressed in a hard, flat line.

Good. I liked that he cared about his friend.

It was good that he cared, and that look told me so much.

He'd do something about it.

He was like Willow in that regard. If she saw an injustice, she did something. Unless *she* was the injustice.

My stomach twisted.

I had been that friend, the one who wouldn't do anything. I never had to. Willow fought our fights for us.

I felt nauseated thinking about that, and I suddenly, didn't want to think about it. I didn't want to think at all anymore. I didn't want to have memories in my head, making me feel things I couldn't handle.

I was ashamed. I should've been this person before . . .

No. Stop thinking. Stop feeling. "Let's go watch the movie."

Ryan gazed at me a moment longer and then nodded. "Okay."

Once we sat, once the lights turned off, once the move started, I let the first tear fall.

CHAPTER
SIX

I passed on the party after the movie. No one protested when Nick took me back to my house, and I suppose it was partly because they all had the same survival instinct as I did. No shock there. Heads would roll if I went to that party, and I wasn't sure if it'd be mine or Erin's first.

Ryan crawled out right behind me, and I turned around. "Wha—"

He ignored me, shutting the door, and tapped twice on top of the car.

Nick rolled his window down, but before he said anything, Ryan leaned close and smirked. "Don't be reckless, kids. Use safe drinking protocols. You know, lick the salt *before* you shoot the tequila. And no backwashing."

Nick flashed us two fingers. "Peace." His eyes slid me up and down. "Use a condom, children."

Tom started laughing, and the car shot forward.

Cora was in the back, her face resembling a sad owl's as she watched us until they turned onto the next street.

"That one is Tom's house." Ryan pointed to the house to the left of mine. A lamp was still on inside. "We were all out at Nick's, and Tom told me about his new neighbor, asked if you were the same girl who'd crawled in my bed." His hands slid into his pockets, and he hunched his shoulders forward. His shirt strained against his form, showing off those muscles again. "I'm glad you came to the movie. I thought it was a shot in the dark."

I was glad he'd texted too. And I was surprised at that, but I was. Even dealing with the ex was a good distraction.

41

I tilted my head to the side. "Did you really not know how mean your ex is? She seems like the resident bully."

He hesitated before letting loose a long sigh. "Guys don't see that stuff. I'm not using that as an excuse, but we usually focus on the good stuff about chicks. Boobs, you know. Other stuff." He gave me a half-grin. "I've heard rumors, and Peach told me a few things, but seeing how she was with you tonight—and how you handled it—that was eye opening." He chuckled softly. "It's the same with girls, you know. You don't see the shit guys do to each other."

"Is that supposed to make it better?"

He shrugged. "No. Just the way it is. And for what it's worth, I feel like an asshole for not knowing how bad Erin is."

A brief flicker of anger had sparked, but it fanned out, and I shrugged. "I think I was spoiling for a fight. I can't take it out on my parents like a normal teenager. They're in this thing called mourning."

I bit back a grin, but Ryan saw it. His right dimple showed.

"Did you want to come in?" I gestured to my house. It was completely silent and dark.

The other dimple winked at me. "I was hoping. If you don't want to go in right away, we could sneak into Tom's house. His parents are in San Diego, and he's staying at Nick's tonight."

I eyed Tom's house. "He's okay with you sneaking in there?"

"Yeah. We've done it before, use someone's house if it's empty, you know."

I suddenly didn't want to know any more. "You know how to get in there?"

He nodded, watching me. He was waiting.

The thought of going somewhere that was not my home had my mouth watering. And that place was empty. No parents. No Peach to stare at me weirdly. No crazy ex girlfriend. No little brother in the room where my sister wasn't. No worrying if he'd hear me crying when I couldn't sleep at night.

"Let's go." Decision made.

"Yeah?" he asked.

I nodded.

"Sounds good. We should go to the back. It's easier not to set off the alarm there."

Ryan led me to the backyard and pulled the hidden key from under a plant. Unlocking the door, he keyed in the code and returned the key a second later. I slipped inside, and he turned the system back on.

I rolled my eyes. "Tom's parents must be geniuses."

"Eh. They're no Robbie Malcolm, but I'm sure they do okay." He gestured to a picture where a couple stood with one of the older living former presidents. "They go golfing with that guy."

And I was reminded that Portside was not Schilling, Arizona. Cripe's sakes. They knew one of the presidents.

Yeah. *So* not Schilling, Arizona.

Ryan chuckled. "We aren't any better. We use the fake frog, though the alarm system is the real backup."

"Yeah." I joked. "Remind me tomorrow to tell my parents to install infrared security system. I'm thinking we could use a handprint machine. Fuck the fake frog."

He laughed, leading the way inside.

As we walked toward the kitchen, a different feeling settled over me. We were alone. I'd wanted to get away, but maybe I hadn't thought this through.

I hadn't been thinking anything through, not for a whole month.

Ryan nodded toward the kitchen. "You want a drink? I know where they keep the good stuff."

My stomach rumbled.

He heard and flashed me a grin. "Or something to eat?"

"You know where they keep that stuff too?" I teased.

"I can make an educated guess."

I ended up sitting on a stool by the island while Ryan scored leftover pizza. He popped the pieces into the microwave and pulled out two glasses.

I lifted an eyebrow. "You and Tom must be close." He acted as if this were his house.

"Since second grade." He ducked down to pull out a bottle of whiskey. "He won't care. Trust me."

"You bring girls to his house often?"

He laughed, pouring some lemonade to mix with it. He took a sip before pushing it my way. "No, but he brought a girl to my place once. More than once. My family was on vacation, and he asked, so since then, it's a given. If one of us has an empty house, it's an open invitation if we want to use it."

"You've done that before?"

"I haven't, no." He looked at me, his eyes darkening.

Our gazes caught and held, and I felt a tickle at the bottom of my stomach. It was a good feeling, a thrilling one, and I held my breath for a moment because I didn't want it to go away. The knot next to it relaxed, and maybe this was what I'd wanted since Ryan texted. I wanted to be around him. I could sleep.

I could feel normal, just for a while.

He took his glass and gestured to mine, the pizza in his other hand. "Let's head downstairs. Feels weird going anywhere else."

I followed him down to a large sectional couch that formed half a square. It looked like one large bed, and Ryan crawled onto it, scooting to the rear. He placed his glass on the back of the couch, which looked like it had been made for that purpose. I hesitated, but he patted the spot next to him, picking up the remote.

"I can grab us blankets and pillows too, in case."

It felt so weird, but it also felt so right, and that made it even more jarring. For whatever reason, I was becoming addicted to this boy.

When I still hesitated, he lowered the remote. "What's wrong?"

"This."

"Us?"

I shrugged. Yes, but I felt stupid saying it. "I don't know."

He frowned and tilted his head to the side. "We're hanging out."

Okay. I nodded. I could do that. Hanging out. "You're right."

"That's it."

I nodded again. "Yeah."

"So." He looked at the spot next to him, and I climbed onto the couch, scooting to sit beside him.

After that, no words were needed.

It wasn't that I didn't want to talk, but Ryan put on a movie and seemed content to eat his pizza, watch the show, and sip his drink. When mine was emptied, he went upstairs for refills, but the same thing happened. He returned to the couch, scooted back, and started the movie again.

It was my second movie of the night, but I couldn't remember either of them. The only thing I remembered was relaxing. That was it. Willow, my family—they were all pushed to the back of my mind, and I felt everything start to unravel inside me.

I fell asleep during the movie, scooting down to lay next to Ryan. And at some point, I felt him get up, but he came back. He placed a blanket over me, and I curled into it, once again falling asleep.

When I woke, he was on his back beside me, one of his hands on my side.

He had fallen asleep like that, like he was protecting me.

CHAPTER SEVEN

"Mackenzie."

I woke to Ryan saying my name and gently shaking my shoulder. "Wake up. We gotta go."

"What's wrong?" My eyelids were freaking heavy, but I sat up. A big ass yawn on my lips.

"Tom's parents are home."

"What?"

"We gotta go. Quick." He scrambled off the couch, and I could hear footsteps above us.

"Was Tom here last night?" a woman's voice asked. "I thought he was at Nick's."

More footsteps, and a man's voice rumbled, a murmur through the ceiling.

I hurried after Ryan. He led me up some back stairs and then circled through the garage and to a side door. A door was open between the main floor and garage, and I heard the woman ask, "Was he drinking?"

The male voice grew louder. He was coming toward us. That was when I saw the car doors still open. They were unpacking.

"He had the pizza. The whiskey's out, but I can't tell if he drank any of it."

"We'll definitely have a talk with him," the man replied.

He was right there, almost to the doorway.

Ryan slipped out the side door, and I pushed him the rest of the way. We clicked the door shut moments before we heard heavy footsteps from the garage.

Ryan shot me a look, letting out a deep breath. "That was close."

"Too close."

"I'll call Tom. He'll cover for us."

"We'll owe him one."

"No." Ryan shook his head. "I'll owe him one."

I didn't agree with that, but he looked determined.

We moved out of the yard and headed up the driveway to my house. I couldn't hear or see movement inside, but I knew my parents were probably having coffee. That was what they liked to do since Willow. Before, they would've been rushing through the kitchen, yelling at us. We all would've been rushing around, whether it was a weekend, weekday, or summer day. There were always activities to go to.

The quiet creeped me out.

"Are you going in?" Ryan asked.

I twisted around. I'd been standing on the front steps, staring at the door. I must've looked whacked out, like some space cadet who couldn't sleep by herself, couldn't handle being around her family, and couldn't even bring myself to walk up to the porch.

"You're too nice to me."

"What?" Ryan stepped closer.

I saw that he had his phone in hand. "Are you going to call Tom?"

"Yeah. I'll let him know what happened last night so he's prepared in case they call when they're done unpacking the car."

I nodded. Yes, that would be soon. It didn't look like they had much more to do. "I suppose you should call now."

"Yeah."

But he wasn't. And I wasn't leaving.

We stood there. I watched my front door. He watched me. We sounded normal. We probably even looked normal, but one of us was very much not normal.

"Why are you doing this?" I asked.

An irritated huff came from him. "Is this the same thing as last night? You and me?"

"You and me, you being nice to me, doing this. Are you going to get in trouble?"

"The only one who might get in trouble is you. Tom will cover, say he stopped by earlier for food and that's it. Trust me. This isn't our first rodeo."

But why was he being nice to me? Why was he going out of his way to help me? We didn't even kiss, so he wasn't doing it for an easy hookup. He was just sleeping next to me.

"Stop. Okay? Stop." He touched both of my arms, coming to stand in front of me. "I can see the wheels going in there. Stop."

"But why—"

He cut me off, his hands squeezing once before falling away. He stepped back. "Because I want to."

"But why do—"

"I don't know, okay? I don't know either. I . . . I don't know either. It is what it is. I don't want to think about it any more than that."

And that was the end of it. The questions plaguing me went away as if he'd silenced them. We didn't have a formal goodbye. I nodded and slipped inside my house. The door was unlocked and the alarm off, so one of my parents had already been outside this morning. Once I was inside, I went to the living room window and watched. Ryan continued to stand in our driveway a moment longer before heading back down the road.

"Good morning, honey." My mom sailed past me on her way to the kitchen.

No, "Oh, you're up," or "Where were you last night?" or "When did you get home?" Just "Good morning, honey."

I followed her to the kitchen and stared. She never looked at me—not while she filled her coffee cup, not while she put a piece of bread in the toaster, not while she poured some orange juice in a glass. Her head remained down as she buttered the toast.

"Would you like some breakfast?" she asked. "I'm making some for Robbie. I can put more bread in the machine for you."

My stomach had rumbled last night, so I said, "Sure. Yeah."

And she did, putting two pieces in before pushing the lever down. Then she picked up the plate with Robbie's toast and the orange juice.

"Be right back for my coffee," she said over her shoulder as she left.

She took him *his* food. She was coming back for *her* coffee, and me? I buttered my own toast.

"I know you snuck out last night. I saw you."

My door was open an inch, and Robbie was there. I would've teased him about being a creeper except for the sadness, yearning, and caution that filled his eyes.

"Hey, kiddo." I was at my desk and slid the chair over enough to toe open the door. "You come around these parts often?"

A soft giggle was my reward, and he came in, bouncing to a seat on the bed. His eyes calmed.

"So you caught me, huh?" I smiled, leaning back in my chair. "What do I owe you? You didn't rat me out to Mom and Dad."

He rested his hands next to his legs and lifted his shoulders. "You were with Ryan. I knew you were safe."

"Yeah?"

His cheeks pinked, and he looked down at his lap. "Ryan's cool."

"I agree."

"Did you sleep together again?"

For a moment, I had no words. It sounded wrong, that sentence coming from my eleven-year-old brother.

"Uh . . . what?"

"Sleeping next to him helps you sleep. I overheard at the Jensens' house, and I assumed there was a reason you were in his bed." He lifted his hands, folding them in his lap. "Is that why you left last night? So you could sleep?"

He thought I left to sleep. Then again, maybe he was right. It wasn't about seeing Ryan or sneaking out and giving a silent middle finger to my parents. I sighed. Robbie was too young to deal with any of this—with Willow's decisions or mine.

"Forget about me. How're you doing?"

He'd been kicking his feet back and forth, but he paused at my question. He looked away. "I'm fine."

"Hey." I scooted my chair closer and tapped on his knee. "I mean it. How are you?"

He looked back, and my heart was almost ripped out. Unshed tears hung on his lashes.

"I'm fine." His voice trembled.

We'd been there for each other before the funeral, during the funeral, and I'd like to say afterward, but I couldn't. Since we'd come back to Portside, I'd shut down. Literally. Going to see Ryan last night had been almost the first thing I'd done besides going from my bedroom to the kitchen or bathroom. Seeing his tears made me want to curse myself.

"Hey." I gentled my voice even more. "If you need anything, you can come to me. You know that, right?"

"Where'd you go?"

"We went to the movies."

"Where'd you sleep? At Ryan's?"

"I . . ." The words were stuck in my mouth. He looked at me, completely innocent and vulnerable, and I contemplated lying to him. That was what it was. Not telling the truth was a lie.

I shook my head. "We came home. I was going to come in, but we snuck into his friend's house. He lives next door to us."

"And you slept there?"

I nodded.

"Good. You look better today. And I didn't hear you crying last night."

"I didn't know you could hear me."

He bobbed his head and jumped up from my bed. I could see his mind whirling. He was already thinking about whatever he would do next in his room, and he headed for the door.

"You cry every night. I'm glad you didn't last night." He pulled open my door. "You should do that every night." And then he was gone.

I could've looked down to see my beating heart at my feet. He'd ripped me open. Again.

COUNSELING SESSION TWO

"Hello, Mackenzie. It's been a while since our last meeting. Would you like to talk today?"

"No."

CHAPTER EIGHT

It was almost another month before I saw Ryan again. He traveled with his family and then went to New York to see his grandparents. He was all over, including a wilderness camp. We texted back and forth, but when he was finally home, my parents shipped me off to Arizona. It was supposed to be four days where I'd heal with my friends, but some major miscommunication happened somewhere between the parents. They set it up, but the friends I used to cry with, laugh with, and who I thought had my back didn't show up. Strangers did.

Zoe and Gianna spent most of the time talking to each other, laughing over someone's tweet, and they forgot I was there. No joke. I was watching television in Gianna's basement when I heard the door shut upstairs, and the house was quiet. They'd gone. I checked on social media and saw they were at the community pool, but I wasn't going to get mad. I mean, seriously. Fighting with Erin was fun. She was someone I hadn't known since second grade. She was someone I hadn't shared chain letters with or plotted with on how to get even with Mia Gillespie in fourth grade when she stole Zoe's boyfriend.

Erin was easy. There was nothing emotional there, but my two old best friends—too much history.

Instead, I booked my own flight back home and ordered a car.

It was close to midnight when I texted Ryan, telling him I was outside his house. The driver's taillights were disappearing when he came out the front door.

"Hey." Dressed in lounge pants and a soft shirt, he folded his arms over his chest, tucking his hands under his arms. He eyed my small suitcase. "You really came straight from the airport?"

"Was this stupid?" A normal girl might've had that thought in her head. But my head? There wasn't enough room for second thoughts in there. I gestured to his house. "Should I go home?"

"No." He'd hunched over a little but straightened and shook his head. "No. It's fine. Seriously." He went back to eyeing my luggage. "I thought you were joking about the airport. I could've picked you up."

"Oh." That meant a lot. "No, this is fine. Simple. No fuss. That's how I roll these days."

He fought back a grin. "Except when we break into my buddy's house to spend the night, right?"

I laughed. "Except for that."

"Come on." He jerked his head toward the house before reaching for my suitcase. "My mom has book club tonight, which is aka wine night, and Peach is at Erin's house."

"Your dad?" I had to admit it felt nice as I stepped inside, warm and cozy. I hadn't known how cold I was until then.

Ryan closed the door behind me, locking it. "He's downstairs watching the baseball game. He DVR-ed it, and trust me, by the time it's done, he'll be a full case in. He'll either sleep down there or head straight to bed. I've had friends over before when it's a baseball night for him, and he had no clue." He stepped around me, moving quietly. "You want something before heading up?"

I fought back the smile this time. "Going right to it, huh?"

He glanced back, and his eyes darkened. "You know what I mean."

"I do." I shook my head. "And I'm good." My stomach rumbled, which makes Ryan's eyebrows rise. "You sure? Your stomach says otherwise."

Thinking about it, I didn't know when I'd last eaten.

I ate breakfast Thursday morning. My mom drove me to the airport two hours later. There was a meal offered on the plane, but I didn't eat it. Gianna's mom picked me up, and we went to a pizza place. I picked at a slice, but I couldn't bring myself to chew it and digest it.

Zoe and Gianna had eaten popcorn that night while we watched movies. They'd laughed. I'd curled in a blanket and tried to sleep.

Then this morning, I had orange juice and coffee. That was right. Zoe and Gianna went to the coffee shop and brought back bagels and lattes. I had one of the lattes. Lunch was licorice for them, which Gianna's mom didn't approve of. She made a big salad, and the other two nibbled on it, but they were too full from licorice.

And this afternoon they'd left me.

I hadn't eaten on the plane again, so it had been almost two days.

I shrugged. "Maybe a drink?"

He clipped his head in a nod. "Got it." We went upstairs first, and he stowed my luggage in his room before returning to the kitchen. I went into his bathroom, grateful it was attached to his room, and by the time I'd cleaned up and felt a little refreshed, he was back, carrying a glass in each hand and a bag of chips in his mouth.

"Here." I started to take the bag, but he shook his head and held up one of the glasses. I took that instead, and as soon as I did, he opened his mouth.

The bag of chips fell to the bed and he took a sip from his own glass. "Mmmm . . ." He winked. "Rum and Coke. Good stuff, right?" He clinked his glass to mine and then settled on his bed, moving back to rest against the wall. The chips went on the stand next to him, along with his drink after a second good sip.

He had a loveseat against the other wall in his room, and I perched there. Fuck. This drink was good. I craned my head back, staring at it. "I could down this whole thing in two seconds."

"So do it." He opened the chips and popped a couple in his mouth. Grinning at me, he added, "Not to tread where you might not want me, but I'd think you'd want to pass this year in a drunken haze. I would."

Yeah. I drank a third of it before leaning back against the couch. "It isn't my style."

It would've been Willow's, though. She would've drank, partied, and become a nympho if I'd been the one . . .

My throat burned, and I took another long drink. Shit. This really was good. Two more sips, and I'd need a refill.

I eyed Ryan over the top. "You aren't the type to take advantage of me, are you?"

He chuckled. "Nah." He winked. "But I might graze the side of your boob when we're sleeping later."

I laughed and stopped immediately.

Shit. The last time I'd laughed, the last time I'd smiled, had been with him—not my old friends—or ex friends—and not anyone else. Just Ryan.

"Does it get better?" The question was out before I could take it back.

Ryan was quiet, holding my gaze across the room, and then he sighed. "I think it has to, at some point."

God. I hoped so.

Pain I didn't want to feel or acknowledge rose in my throat. It threatened to choke me, but I sat there. I waited, and it passed. I could breathe again a second later.

I finished my drink.

Ryan scooted forward, handing his glass over. "Here, take mine."

"It's yours."

He shrugged, eating more chips. "I'll down a beer later, maybe. Trust me. It's fine."

I took the glass, feeling his fingers on mine for a moment, and a warm and cozy sensation settled over me. It was the same tingle I'd felt when I had stepped into his home. Everything else was flat, black and white, gray, dull, cold, and then I went to him, and it felt like color was turned on.

I could feel hunger again, thirst again. I remembered it was normal to feel warmth.

Feeling the choking come back up my throat, I turned off my thoughts. Life was easier that way.

"You're staying here tonight, right?" Ryan asked.

"Hmmm?" My shoulders sagged in relief. Thank you, Distraction.

He gazed around his room. "You're sleeping here. That's why you came, right?"

I nodded. "If that's okay with you?"

A slow and wicked grin spread over his face. His eyes darkened, falling to my lips. "I'm a nice guy and all, but I'm not *that* nice, and especially lately, so trust me when I say this. You can sleep here any time you want." His head leaned forward, his eyes almost digging into me. "That offer doesn't go to anyone except you."

The back of my neck warmed. I almost felt tongue-tied. "Thank you, and yes, that's the plan."

"But what about your folks? Won't your friends or their parents say something when they realize you skipped town?"

I shook my head, feeling the booze loosening me up. "I left a note for Gi's parents, but that was it. I doubt they'll even notice till tomorrow morning."

"You serious?"

I nodded. I should've felt sad about that. I felt relief.

"Gi and Zoe didn't want me there. I knew it. They knew it. The parents didn't care, but my friends have moved on. They have new lives."

"That's bullshit."

Maybe. I drank half of Ryan's drink instead of caring. "They loved Willow too. They were my best friends, but Willow and I were a package deal. I was friends with her friends." I gestured to my face. "You weren't at the funeral. It's easier to forget Willow than to mourn her." I remembered the disgust I saw on Duke's face. "Her boyfriend couldn't get out of there fast enough. He had his hands all over Serena, Willow's best friend."

"Yeah. Well . . ." Ryan balled up the bag of chips and tossed it across the room. It landed on the desk next to me. "People suck. Trust me. I get it." He stood, pointing to my glass. "I'll bring the ingredients. We can mix drinks till we pass out, huh?"

He left, so he didn't see my response.

I was smiling so damn hard, and I wasn't even sure why. All I knew was that I was happy when he came back. I could relax in this room with him, and I laughed until we did exactly what he said.

We passed out around three in the morning, after I drank myself into oblivion.

It was the best night I'd had in a long while.

CHAPTER NINE

I woke the next morning around eight.

I would've freaked, but Ryan rolled over, put his arm over me, and tugged me in for a side-hug. "No one's here," he murmured. "Trust me. We're good."

He was right. Even two hours later, the latest I allowed us to sleep, no one was around.

"My dad golfs on Saturdays."

"What about your mom? Peach?"

He yawned, raking a hand through his hair as he padded to the bathroom. "Mom's probably sleeping. Her book club doesn't mess around. When they drink, they drink." I heard the shower turn on, and he yelled over it, "And gossip. They wine hard and gossip hard."

I stood, edging to the opened door. I almost gulped, but he didn't seem to care. This was a different level of intimacy. Then again, maybe it was because we'd slept together. Yeah. That was it. Either way, I was feeling nerves and flutters in my stomach that I didn't recognize. I'd never felt like that. Ever.

"What about your sister?" I asked, not moving inside the bathroom.

Ryan looked over, his hair getting mashed down from the water, and he gave me a side-grin.

God. A whole new level of flutters exploded in my gut at that sight.

The shower doors were frosted, so I couldn't see anything from his chest down. But I could see the silhouette of his body, and I think that was enough. My whole neck and face were getting warm now.

"She won't be back till this afternoon, or even tonight," he drawled. "She might stay till tomorrow too. We could hang out all day, if you wanted."

I perked up at that suggestion—no home, no angry or absent parents. But also no brother who I knew needed me.

I shook my head. "I can't." But wait—I remembered a conversation. Robbie was going somewhere today. "Wait. Maybe I can."

"Yeah?" He was shampooing his hair, and I tried not to watch as the suds fell down his body, his nice lean body, the body that felt so strong when he held me.

I tore my gaze away. Was I becoming like Willow? Was that what was going on? I couldn't see her, talk to her, be with her, and so I was starting to *become* her?

I grabbed my phone and sent a text.

The shower turned off, and I kept my head down as Ryan stepped out and began toweling off. He came back to the bedroom, going to his closet as my phone pinged a response.

Robbie: **Mom and Dad are taking me to a school. I thought you knew? Where are you?**

"What?" I typed back a response.

Me: **What school? I'm coming back early.**

"What's wrong?" Ryan came to sit next to me. He had jeans on and bent over to pull on socks and shoes. He was close enough that I felt the brush of his shirt before he sat up and leaned backward on his bed.

"Robbie's going to some school today."

"Oh." Ryan snapped his fingers, pointing at my phone. "There's a private place not far from here. All sorts of gifted and smart kids go there."

I twisted around to face him square. "You're joking." My stomach took a nosedive. I wanted him to be joking. This school was made up, a figment of his imagination.

"What?"

He wasn't. This had become my new nightmare. My phone pinged another response from Robbie, but it almost fell from my hands.

They were taking him away. I knew it. I could feel it.

Willow had left, and they were taking away Robbie.

Who was next?

"What's wrong?" Ryan leaned forward again, his voice soft. He took the phone from me, reading Robbie's message aloud. "It's fine. I want to go. I'll see you tonight. Love you, sis."

He handed my phone back, but I almost didn't want it. And seeing that, he put the phone on the bed, tossing it by his pillow.

His shoulder nudged mine gently. "You okay?"

No. I was *so* not fine. I didn't know if I ever would be again.

But all I said was, "I'm down to hang out today."

Sometime between grabbing an early lunch—where Ryan ordered food for me and didn't give me a say in the matter—and returning to the house, our plans changed.

We walked in and heard shouts and laughter coming from the backyard.

"What?" Ryan frowned, tossing our bag of food onto the counter and going to the back door.

Peach ran in, opening and shutting the door behind her. She didn't see me but greeted Ryan with a wide smile. "I call pool party today!"

"What? No."

"What?" She mocked him, fluttering her eyelashes. "Yes. And get ready, douchebag. Your friends are coming over. I called 'em. And some people from your grade. Stephanie Witts and her friends are already here."

"Mom and Dad okay this?"

Peach didn't answer. She'd spotted me, and I watched the life drain out of her. "Oh. You."

I rolled my eyes, but Ryan beat me, saying, "She's a friend. Back the fuck off, Peach."

Her mouth snapped shut. His growl worked wonders.

The doorbell rang, and the door opened. "Yo, Ryan!"

Tom, Nick, and another guy barreled in. They stopped short when they saw me.

They didn't give Peach a second look. It shouldn't have pleased me, but it did.

Tom's eyes went wide. "Hey, Mackenzie. I didn't know you'd be here."

Nick added, "Yeah, long time no see. You ditched us after movie night."

The third guy pointed to me. "This her?"

The back of my neck got hot. "Are you asking about my sister?"

"Sister?" the guy echoed.

"No. Erin, man," Tom told me. "You took her down. You're infamous."

Nick rolled his eyes. "He means you're a big deal in our group. At least among the girls." His eyes went to Peach then, who still stood watching the exchange. "Hey, Ryan's little sister." He tossed a smirk at Tom, who seemed flustered.

Tom went into the kitchen, and Nick lounged back against the wall, his eyes sliding from Peach to the rest of us.

Ryan ignored all of it, asking around a clenched jaw, "You guys knew about this?" He nodded to the backyard, and I turned to inspect what was happening.

A bunch of girls stood around the pool, clad in bikinis, and there were a few other guys with them. I recognized Erin and assumed those were her friends, but there was a separation out there. Some girls were in the pool and playing a game with a bunch of guys while Erin and her friends stood on the sidelines.

"Yeah. Your sis put the word out. Pool party at the Jensen household. Everyone's coming." Nick was still salivating over Peach's uncomfortableness.

She looked down at her fingers, picking a nail.

I felt Ryan's gaze and looked over, meeting his eyes. I saw the apology there and knew our hangout had been replaced with a party with a bunch of his friends. I shrugged, trying to give him a small smile to let him know I was okay.

I didn't want to be there with them, but I wanted to be there with him. I'd take it how I could get it. This was better than an empty house, and I wasn't going to turn my phone on. An hour ago, Gianna had sent me a text asking why I left, but she was almost twenty-four hours too late for me to respond.

"So," Nick said. His grin was wicked. "Peach. Do anything fun last night?"

She turned and fled.

As soon as she closed the patio door, Tom was across the room and punching Nick in the arm. "You're such an ass!"

"What?" Nick laughed, rubbing at his arm as he moved down the wall, closer to where Ryan and I stood. "It isn't my fault you were texting with your buddy's little sister."

Ryan's eyes clamped shut, and his hands moved through his hair. He pulled them out, leaving his hair sticking up in an adorable mess. Swinging stormy eyes over his friends, he grabbed Tom and shoved him against the wall. "You're into my sister?"

"No!"

Nick snorted. Even I knew that protest was too much.

Tom's shoulders slumped down. "I don't know. We were texting last night. She asked where you were, if you were hanging with us, and it kept going from there."

"He texted with her for three hours. I heard the damn phone beeping the whole fucking game."

Tom shot Nick a glare. "There's no way you could hear my phone. We went to the summer league basketball game. The entire gym was loud as hell."

Nick shrugged, his wicked grin still there. "I stand by what I say." His eyes were hard. "It's wrong, and you know it."

Ryan rolled his eyes. "Whatever." He pushed Tom back against the wall again, but there wasn't much heat in the action.

"Don't fuck with Peach unless you're going to marry her. Got it?" He tapped Tom's cheek and then swung his gaze my way.

The third friend grunted, his hand in the air. "Uh . . ." He cleared his throat. "You're insanely hot."

Tom and Nick grinned, and the tense moment was gone.

"Hands off. Ryan laid claim long ago," Nick said.

Ryan pointed between the newcomer and me. "Pete, Mackenzie. Mackenzie, Pete." He added, "Pete's Nick's cousin. He visits when he wants to get high."

"Yeah," Nick drawled, throwing his arm around his cousin's shoulder. "He comes to the cool table then."

Pete shrugged off his arm. "Hate to break it to you, cousin, but Ryan's the cool table. He's the basketball star. Not you. You aren't good enough"—he began edging backward, his arms already in the air as if to ward off a hit—"at anything!"

"Shut it." Nick went after him, delivering two quick punches to Pete's side. The two wrestled before Nick ended up pinning Pete. Only then he flicked him the forehead and got up. "Loser."

"Asshole." But Pete was grinning.

They were both grinning, and when both were on their feet, I waved to Pete.

"Nice to meet you."

"You too, and I go to Frisberg. It's a few hours away, so I'm not around that much, but if I do show up, it isn't just to get high, Ryan."

Ryan only grunted in response. He didn't seem to care too much.

Nick added, "We call him Peepee sometimes. Feel free."

"Hey!"

Peepee rounded on Nick, and soon insults were flying back and forth. But Nick eased up on the jabs at Tom.

After everyone raided Ryan's kitchen, we headed upstairs, drinks and snacks in our arms. I was thankful we'd made the bed before leaving, and I was doubly glad I hadn't left anything behind, putting my suitcase in Ryan's truck, where it still was. No questions, just the way I liked it. And finally, I was glad the guys continued giving each other shit as they sat to play Warcraft.

They weren't watching me because of Willow, and unlike the movie night, as I sat in Ryan's room and listened to his friends joke, I felt normal. It was small. And I knew it'd be gone soon, but I felt it, and I savored it.

"Hey! Fuck no, man!"

"Ah!"

Tom and Nick had the video controllers, and as Tom bent to the side, trying to get his car to turn all the way left, Nick jumped up and down. He bit his lip. His eyebrows were furrowed in concentration, and I knew at any moment the room would explode in cheers or curses—probably both.

I glanced to the door and saw Ryan watching me. He gestured with his head to follow him out, and I scooted off the bed as Nick won the race.

He dropped the controller and thrust his arms in the air in victory. "YES!"

"NO!" Tom shook his head.

Pete stuffed a handful of chips in his mouth and reached for Tom's controller. He mumbled around a mouthful, "My turn."

I slipped out of the room.

Ryan waited at the end of the hallway, nodding for me to keep following him.

I trailed behind. He led me down a back way to the basement. We could hear footsteps above, along with giggling.

I arched an eyebrow. "Let me guess, the female brigade is above us?"

Ryan ducked his head as he opened a refrigerator. "We're out of drinks in the room, and I know my parents keep more booze down here. The guys will want more to drink. Peach and her friends can have the main floor."

I gazed around, noting the more casual-looking décor. It was one large room with a living area on one side and a kitchen on the other. There was a pool table in the back, along with a basketball game, two couches, and three super-sized beanbags in front of a large television screen. Two wooden tables sat in the kitchen area.

It looked like every teenager's dream apartment. The only things missing were a movie projector, a popcorn machine, and maybe a stage for karaoke.

Willow would've salivated over the room.

Ryan pulled out some more rum, and I slid onto one of the barstools.

"Is this where you guys really hang out?"

He nodded. "Tom's too." He looked at me. "Well, you know that."

"Is Cora coming over?"

Ryan was done with the drinks. He moved to the cupboard and pulled out bags of chips and cookies. Then he slid some Cheetos toward me.

"That's a negative on Cora."

My eyebrows went up. "What do you mean?"

"She tends to avoid anywhere Erin might be." He paused and amended, "Usually."

Ah. I nodded. "Doesn't want to get thrown to the wolves, huh?"

He pressed his lips together, closing the cupboard and leaning against the counter. He seemed to be choosing his words carefully. "Cora's never liked to go anywhere Erin is. We didn't know why. I knew it had to do with Erin, but Cora never explained it. I did shoot her a text, though." He pulled out his phone from his pocket and showed me her response.

Cora: **If Erin is there, hell no.**

"She's never said it so clearly like that before." His eyes seemed to soften. "I think it's because of what you did. I would've listened to her before. She just never thought I would."

"You seemed oblivious to Erin's bullying, so I don't blame Cora."

"I know." His hands gripped the counter. "Erin and I didn't really have a relationship. We just fooled around during a time last year, but it's on me. I should've paid more attention."

Well, that made me feel bad. I shrugged. "Give yourself a break."

His hands relaxed.

"Most guys are idiots," I added. "They don't see past the boobs and smile."

He groaned, his eyes sparking. "Thanks for that." He began to gather the drinks and snacks.

I took what was left and slid off the stool. "No problem. I believe in realism. I like to keep my friends grounded. The more realistic they are, the more humble they seem to be."

"You mean you squash their egos into the floor."

"That too."

As we headed back, Ryan turned around to use his back to open the door. Our eyes met and held, and I felt an instant sensation. It was us. No sister problems. No exes. No bullying. Nothing. Just him and me, and I let out a soft sigh before I realized it.

His eyes warmed.

I'd had this feeling before, but it was stronger this time.

I coughed, lifting my foot. "You caught me at a disadvantage today. I like to really grind my friends' egos into the ground with heels. The sharper the better."

He grinned, shifting back a step. "Thanks for that. I needed it."

"Always here for you. Call me Ego Crusher."

He barked out a laugh, and his hand touched the small of my back.

It was a tiny gesture, a silent touch, but it wiped away my amusement. I'd started to laugh, and then it was gone, transformed into something else. My body warmed like it had last night, and the feeling intensified, as if it were supposed to be the two of us, as if everyone else was the outsider and not wanted.

I suddenly didn't want to leave that basement, didn't want to deal with everything that lay beyond these walls. My breath caught in my throat, and my eyes watered. I blinked rapidly. A surge of grief rose up, but I stuffed it down. It was too strong, too threatening. I couldn't handle it.

"You okay?"

No.

I never would be again. Didn't he know?

I sighed. "You're having a pool party. You ready to par-tay?"

He shook his head. "That's right."

CHAPTER
TEN

The guys decided they should be "social" after another hour of playing video games. Should be. Yes. Because they wanted to be polite not because they wanted to drool over girls in bikinis. It had nothing to do with all the bare skin running around Ryan's backyard.

I joined, but I was the non-social one. I was fine to pop in my music and hang on my own. The booze had simmered me out. Ryan checked on me a few times, but I reassured him I was good, and he finally went over to his friends, laughing and doing what was expected of him. Erin was there too, her friends in tow. They all basked before her, as if they were trying to catch whatever sunglow she had in excess. Peach kept shooting her nervous looks.

From my vantage point—on a lounge chair in the corner—I saw again what I'd noticed earlier. There were two groups of girls—Erin's group and another clique. I assumed they belonged to the infamous Stephanie Witts. A couple of them were in the water with some other guys, playing a new game of dunk basketball.

As I watched, one of the girls caught the basketball but turned and glared at Erin.

One of the girls from that group walked by me, and I asked her, "What grade are you?"

She stopped, seeming surprised by my question. "Senior." Then her lip curved up and she sneered at me.

Silly me. She was a popular senior. Who was I to talk to her?

I ignored my desire to flick her my middle finger and lay back down. With my sunglasses in place, I resumed the antisocial role.

I plugged my earbuds back in and "Glory" from Dermot Kennedy filled my ears. I filled my lungs. Sitting there, with all these strangers around me, in a social scene I didn't care about, I was having a come-to-Willow moment.

What was I doing there?

This wasn't my scene, not even if Willow had been with me.

I would've been home. I would've been with my soccer friends, and if they'd wanted to go and scrimmage, I would've tried to talk them out of it. Seriously. Netflix and junk food were way more appealing.

This was Willow's scene.

She cared about popular girls, about popular guys. She would've already scoped out who to maim, who to kill, whose ass to kiss, and who to fuck.

Her world whirled around me.

Their laughter sounded like kids playing on a playground as it filtered through the music. I was in a self-assigned tornado, and everyone else seemed fine.

Why couldn't I be normal?

Why didn't I even want to try?

I felt tears fall from my eyes, trickling down behind my sunglasses, and I didn't care. I never moved. I didn't wipe my eyes. I wasn't going to stop them, but I also wasn't going to keel over in sobbing hiccups. That wasn't me either.

I didn't even remember the last time I'd cried before Willow.

She was the sobbing, melodramatic twin. Everything was ending if she got dumped, if she did the dumping. If a friend betrayed her, God forbid, her life was over . . .

Bad choice of words there.

I thumbed over to the music, hitting the next one. I needed a change of tempo if I was going to stick with socially appropriate behavior.

"I Need My Girl" by The National was next.

Oh, for fuck's sake.

I hit forward again.

"Sleep Baby Sleep" by Broods.

Shit.

I should hit it again, and my thumb lingered over the button, but I couldn't.

The words made me remember that night.

She had been on the floor. Her eyes had been vacant, open. The blood had pooled around her.

I had laid down, my head next to hers, my hands in the same position. Her blood surrounded me, and it had felt like mine.

We would lay together. She would tell me a secret. I would pretend to be excited to hear it.

That's what we did before, and I pretended that's what was happening that night as I had lain there.

God.

Fuck.

Shit.

My tears had tripled into a steady flow, and though I hadn't moved, I knew people would eventually notice.

Letting my music blast, I got up and went inside.

The world was better this way. Having tunes in my ears, I could handle the looks, the questions, the vibes people sent my way. The music protected me. I was in my own world. I didn't have to feel their shit, whatever it was. It was me and the music—and somehow Willow.

I felt her everywhere.

I'd planned to go upstairs to Ryan's room, but I glanced back.

He and his friends were in the pool playing with the others. That same girl who'd sneered at me was hanging on Ryan, attempting to dislodge the ball from his hand. Erin's group watched from the lounge chairs I'd vacated. Their heads were bent together as they glared at the other girls. Still others were tanning and or laughing on the sidelines.

They were all normal.

I was not.

And I felt her with me.

Suddenly, like she had pulled me there, a blast of anger rose in me.

I wasn't going to take on her life. That wasn't my role.

"Fuck you, Willow," I whispered under my breath as I turned my back on them. I hurried upstairs.

I wanted to grab anything I'd left up there and leave because that *was* me.

"Hey."

I turned to find Ryan standing in his doorway, his hair wet and water dripping down his chest. He frowned. "You're leaving?"

Another round of *fuck, shit, damn* ran through my head. Let's say it again, folks.

I scowled, flicking away a tear. "Yeah." I wanted to say more, but my throat wasn't working.

"Why?"

Let's go for broke. All the religious swear words flared in my mind before I could speak. "It's, uh . . ." I gestured behind me, in the direction of the pool. "I shouldn't be here."

He repeated, "Why?" His frown turned to a scowl.

"Why do you think?"

He blinked, and his face changed. A sheepish look came over him, and his shoulders hunched forward. "I wasn't thinking."

"Hanging with you is different from taking on the full social scene down there." Another pointless hand gesture. "I thought I was fine, and I like your close friends, but this is too much." I looked out the window. "I think I'm just going to go home."

"Let's go."

"What?"

His hand was in his hair as if he'd spoken before thinking. He blinked a couple of times and nodded. "Yeah." His shoulders lifted. "I'll go with you. Your suitcase is in my truck anyway."

"Ryan—"

"Look, you don't really say much, and I've got a feeling I'm the only one you *are* talking to, but I know things at your house are sad. And that's reasonable, but when you feel like shutting the world out, you don't have to do that to me. I'm not everyone else."

My heart had been ripped out of my chest, and he was putting it back together.

I laughed but felt my chest growing tight. "Willow would've been all over you."

I hadn't meant to say that.

His eyes grew keen. "Yeah?"

God. What was I saying? I wasn't Miss Talky-Shary, but this guy? I shook my head. "Why do you affect me so much?"

"I affect you in a good way, right?"

I bobbed my head. He already knew he did.

"I'll sneak in."

I lifted my head. "What?"

"So you can sleep." He nodded to himself again. "I know where you live, and your room's on the west side? I'll sneak in, every night if you want me to."

"Second floor."

"I can climb up. You have that big tree by your window."

"You won't get in trouble?" He could sneak in and stay until I fell asleep. "If you get caught?"

He shrugged that off, a cocky smirk tugging at his lips. He tucked a hand in his swimming shorts' pocket. "We can improvise, but my mom never checks my room after midnight. I'll come over after, climb in, sleep. I can set an alarm and slip out before anyone knows. As long as I'm back in my room by seven, I'm good."

A few hours would be nice.

"Okay." I was still unsure, but I needed sleep. If I became a zombie, the world was in trouble.

There was a stampede up the stairs.

"Dude!" Tom, Nick, and Pete rushed in, breathless. "Man! We—oh."

They saw me, and it was like they'd hit an invisible wall.

Tom gave me a nod. "Hey, Mackenzie. How's it going?"

Pete rubbed his forehead.

Nick rolled his eyes to the ceiling.

Tom frowned, glancing at them. "What?"

Ryan took two steps toward him and punched him in the shoulder. "You're being weird. Don't be weird."

"Ouch!" Tom rubbed where he'd gotten hit. "What was that for?"

"We were talking." Ryan wasn't messing around. He glared at Tom. "What do you want?"

Nick and Pete began snickering.

Tom shot them a look, his hand falling away from his shoulder. "We got a text. Mullaly is having a party, and the girls are going over there." His eyes lit up again, and he turned toward me. "You want to go, Mackenzie?"

But before I could answer, he was looking back at Ryan. "We were rushing up here because Nick's brother said he'd get us booze, but we gotta go now. He's heading to Lakeville for a college party—"

"Let's go to the college party." I winced. The words were out of my mouth before I realized what I was saying. What the hell was going on with me?

This was not me. I didn't care about college parties. If I'd been to one before, it was because someone forced me or tricked me into going. I would've needed to be promised Taco Bell on the way home, and maybe I would've tried to go in my pajamas. A good fluffy robe was hella sexy.

Ryan's eyes snapped to mine.

Tom's eyes went round. "What?"

Ryan studied me a moment, as if he were looking for something I wasn't sure was there. I don't know whether he found it or not, but he turned to Nick. "Would that be okay with Ben, if we went with them?"

"Um . . ." Nick's lip twisted.

"Let me ask him," I suggested. *Okay, then.* I was throwing all caution to the wind.

The guys glanced at each other, and another round of: *what the fuck am I doing?* circulated my head.

I didn't even think Willow would've done this, or maybe she would have. Maybe she wouldn't have been happy with tackling the seniors. She might've moved on to college guys. I knew she'd started talking to one before we moved. Duke didn't know it, but he'd been about to be dumped. *Sorry, Duke.*

I wanted . . . something different.

Apparently, a college party was it for me.

"Nah. Um . . ." Nick frowned. "I'll text him quick." He glanced at Ryan before adding more quietly, "I can tell him you're coming."

Ryan's jaw clenched, and he jerked up a shoulder. "That's fine."

I glanced between the two, noticing how quiet everyone else got. "Uh, what's going on?"

They all looked at Ryan, who shook his head briefly. "It's nothing. Ben's a big b-ball fan. He'll want to shoot the shit with me for a bit."

"Oh." There was more. I could tell, but after a quick scan, I could tell no one would speak on it. Some unspoken situation had just materialized, and I wasn't in on it.

Nick's phone beeped a second later.

"Yeah." He looked around the room. "He said we could go, but we gotta move now."

The guys flew around, preparing to change from their trunks to their regular clothes. They forgot I was in the room until Ryan snapped at them. Tom and Nick's hands were pushing their swim shorts down, and they froze.

I threw up a hand and looked at the floor. "I'm good. I'll grab some clothes and get ready downstairs."

"Hey." Ryan followed me into the hallway, making sure his door was shut. "You sure about this?"

I jerked up a shoulder. "I think it's safe to say I'm up for anything right about now."

Robbie was going to his new school this week. I'd be going to mine.

Who the fuck cared? Right?

"Mackenzie . . ."

I clipped my head to the side. "I'll be ready in a few minutes."

"If you're sure." His eyes were heavy with concern, and the look warmed me, but he was talking to me like I was normal.

Normal died in my twin sister's puddle of blood.

I slipped away, grabbing some clothes from my suitcase in his truck. I'd planned on using a random downstairs bathroom, but the entire first floor was crowded. The guys were still in Ryan's room, so I looked around, seeing Peach's door open.

Sorry, Peach, but I'm about to use your shit.

I ducked in. After dressing, I went to her bathroom. She could sue me; I didn't give a rat's ass. I used some of her stuff, putting product in my hair, and I went through her makeup too.

We were going to a college party. I had to look the part.

When I finished, I'd aged five years. Heavy eyeliner and eye shadow helped the image.

I pulled on a pair of jean shorts, and I undid one button to shimmy them down an inch on my hips. There. That completed the look.

Ryan and his friends were at the front door, and when Ryan caught sight of me, his eyes rounded, darkening.

"Whoa." Pete actually took a step toward me. "You're fucking hot, Mackenzie."

Nick snorted and hit him in the arm. "Real smooth, Peepee."

"Shut up—and what?" Pete gestured to me. "She is."

"You have to say it in a nice way, a way that doesn't make us think you're creeping on Ryan's girl."

Pete looked from Ryan to me, his brows furrowing. "Um . . ."

Ryan only raised an eyebrow; his lips remained shut.

Pete's face reddened, and he coughed. "Mackenzie, you are—"

I snorted, waving at him. "Please stop. We all look good. Let's leave it at that."

A satisfied smile settled on his face.

I looked at Nick and narrowed my eyes. "You, on the other hand . . ." He called me Ryan's girl. I should correct him, but after a quick glance at Ryan, I didn't want to. He was staring steadily at me, his eyes heated.

Yep. He was totally affecting me, and I coughed. "Are we ready?"

The guys took off out the front door.

Ryan held back till they were gone. Without saying a word, he took my hand. He threaded our fingers together as we headed after them, and I tried to ignore the little flutter in my chest.

CHAPTER
ELEVEN

Red Solo cup in hand, rap music blaring, slight buzz started—I was there. And we'd been embraced as if none of us were losers. Hell yeah. We'd turned down a high school party to be at a college one.

I was damn right succeeding in life.

Willow would've been fucking green with jealousy.

A mean streak raced through my insides, causing my stomach to twist around. I raised my cup, looking at the sky from where I stood in some college dumbass' backyard.

You up there, Wills? Or are you right next to me?

I hated her. She wasn't supposed to be either of those places. She was supposed to be there, not me. She was supposed to be yelling at our parents, telling them they couldn't send Robbie away. She was supposed to be stressing about school, making sure I got my locker number, and only she knew what else. I had no fucking clue.

It was Saturday night. I had one more day, and then I was going to the new school—just me. It wasn't supposed to be just me.

She was my partner in crime. No matter how much she pissed me off, made my blood boil, annoyed the crap out of me, she was my other half.

"You okay?"

I didn't know the girl who spoke to me, and maybe that was why I was honest. "I'm going crazy."

She'd been passing by, empty cup in hand, but did a double take.

I waved her on, a nice fake smile on my face. "I'm good. You?"

"Oh." Her head tilted to the side. I could've been a green alien, and she would've looked at me the same way. "Okay. Good then." She edged away.

Run, little girl. Run from the crazy, pissed-off psycho drunk.

No, scratch that. I was the crazy, pissed-off psycho buzzed chick. The little buzz I'd had before faded on the drive there. I was playing catch-up. Two more beers, and I'd be in the drunk stage. And that was something I needed to address.

I swung around, looking to follow that girl, but Ryan was there. He grabbed my arms as I walked into him, and he took away my cup.

"No." He tossed it to the side, turned me around, and began walking me away from the beer.

I pointed behind us. "I have to go that way."

He shook his head, still walking behind me. "We're going this way, away from the keg."

I pointed again. "But the keg is that way."

"Exactly."

"I want to go toward the keg."

"I don't."

I dug in my feet and crossed my arms over my chest. We were about to have a difference of opinion, but Ryan didn't care. He kept pushing me ahead, and when I locked my legs in place, his arm wrapped around my waist, and he lifted me.

"Oooh!" I squeaked. I hadn't been expecting that.

Two points for him.

He carried me until we were far away from everyone with some trees to our right, lawn to the left, and a creek crossing both. I ignored the full moon above us. I'd already looked up as I talked to Willow. The sky and anything else up there were cut off from my attention. She didn't deserve it anymore.

"Sit."

Ryan's hand went to my shoulders as if he were going to push me down, but I shrugged off his touch and moved farther away.

Wrapping my arms around myself, I warded off a chill that wasn't in the air.

"Mac."

I waved a hand at him. "I'm good. I won't drink anymore."

"That isn't why I stopped you."

I looked up, frowning. "Why did you?"

He shrugged, cocking his head to the side. "You looked upset. Okay, and yeah"—his eyes flicked upwards—"maybe it was to stop you from drinking. Getting drunk when it's just me is one thing. Getting drunk around strangers . . . I don't know." He looked back at where we'd come from. The bass thumped softly in the background. A few laughing shrieks rang out. "I didn't like how some of the guys were looking at you," Ryan confessed.

"Oh." I'd already forgotten how Nick's older brother had gaped at me. I'd gotten that a lot since Willow. I blocked it out. "Don't worry." I shot him a grin. "I won't sleep with any of them. I think the magical sleeping aid exists only with you." And remembering how Nick's brother and then his other friends had fawned over Ryan when we arrived, I nudged him with my elbow. "I'm not sure if I liked how they were looking at you either."

He smiled and seemed to relax. "Sit with me?"

I nodded. It was stupid, but I liked that he asked. This time I wasn't told where to go. I wasn't taken somewhere. I wasn't given a rule.

As I folded down next to him, he asked, "What?"

"What?" I looked over.

"You sighed. You okay?"

I frowned for a second. "It's weird. My parents don't really watch me, but in some ways, that's all they do."

"What do you mean?"

"I don't know." And I didn't.

I didn't know a lot lately, but maybe, that was to be expected. A person's always trying to make sense of things, and probably more so in a time like this.

I let out a breath. "Everything's fucked up."

His knees came up, and he put his arms around them, resting his chin atop. "Yeah. I can imagine."

I looked at him, hearing the knowing tone from him. "Your friend died."

"It isn't the same as a sister."

"You still know a little."

"Yeah." His eyes found mine, warming and holding mine captive. "I know a little."

"Is that why you're being so nice?"

He groaned, his head tipping back. His arms moved behind him, and he stretched out his legs. "We've been over this."

"You said you didn't know. You just were.'" I used his words.

He laughed under his breath. "You know, most girls would jump at the chance to sleep in my bed."

"Yeah?" I hid a grin as my eyebrows went up.

"Yeah. I'm hot stuff. If you weren't in mourning, I'd think you were blind. Check me out." He waved a hand over his chest. "Hot shit. I'm a basketball star too, if you didn't notice my greeting tonight."

"Oh, I noticed." He'd been heralded like a celebrity, but I also knew he didn't want to talk about it. He was polite to them, but after a bit, his friends stepped in and had been shielding him the rest of the night. And he was hiding with me. I laughed. Maybe I was hiding with him. I needed this banter. An invisible weight on my chest lifted a little. "Thank you." I raised my knees and rested my cheek on them, turning to peer at him. "And you *are* super duper cute."

"Super duper?" He sat up, wincing. "Are you serious? You couldn't go with something more manly?"

"You're still a boy. We're only in high school."

He shook his head. "See? That's where you're wrong. We're on the edge of adulthood. One more year for us, and that's it. Off we go."

"Like a little bird kept protected," I teased. "They're letting you fly."

"Exactly." He flinched. "I think. Or an eagle. Not a little bird. I'm an eagle. I'm lethal."

I laughed. "Go for a vulture. I think they're bigger."

"But they're ugly." He winked at me. "They aren't beautiful like eagles."

"You're beautiful?"

"Fuck yeah." He puffed his chest out again. "I could be in magazines, I'm so pretty."

He wasn't lying. Give him some high-fashion runway threads, and the guy could go to Paris.

As if sensing my thoughts, his eyes grew serious—or maybe he was reading from me.

Was this . . .

He leaned toward me.

I was almost tipping because my arms were still wrapped around my knees, and like all the other times, it was like he knew exactly what was happening with me. He touched my shoulder, steadying me, and I closed my eyes.

No guy should make me feel like I needed his touch to be anchored in place, but it had happened. Somehow, whether he wanted it or not, Ryan had become that anchor. I was starting to wonder if I could go on without his presence. I was spinning, but then his hand switched, moving toward my head, and his thumb came to rest against my cheek.

He was so close, his eyes lingering on my lips.

Were we going to do this?

And then, his lips were on mine.

They felt like home, as if I'd been kissing him forever already.

I let out a sigh, and my mouth opened. He moved forward, his mouth answering mine, and I felt his tongue slip against mine.

I wasn't going to think. I was feeling, and I felt him pull me closer.

I'd kissed a few guys back home. And I'd had one boyfriend, but it wasn't serious. Some heavy petting—that'd been it—and it hadn't felt like this. Somehow, I wasn't surprised one bit.

We lay back in the grass, his mouth still fused with mine. He was tasting, kissing, nipping, teasing me. Someone moaned, and I could feel his hands around my face, as if he were cradling me literally in the palm of his hand. I suddenly tasted salt.

They were tears. My tears.

I was kissing Ryan and crying at the same time.

He paused, lifting his head. "Are you—"

"Oh God." I rolled away, curling in on myself. What was I doing? Seriously? Fucking crying as I was making out with a guy? "Um . . ."

"I'm so sorry, Ryan." I couldn't look at him. The tears wouldn't stop. I brushed at them, and they kept rolling. "I have no idea—" Nope. We both knew. Everyone knew.

I was mortified.

Then, instead of leaving awkward silence, he laughed.

Laughed.

I looked up, and his head hung between his knees. His shoulders were shaking.

"What . . ."

"I'm sorry." He shook his head but more chuckles rang out. "I'm—this is every guy's worst nightmare, to make a chick start bawling when you're putting the moves on her."

Oh. "You know why I'm crying," I said gently. "It has nothing to do with you. You know that, right?"

"Yeah. Yeah, but still." He gazed at me again. "Telling someone this story?"

He had a point.

My mouth twitched. "I'm so sorry."

"I can hear the jokes. You kissed her so bad, she broke out into sobs. You kiss so sad, you literally made the girl cry." He shook his head, his laughter subsiding. "No one can hear about this. No one."

"Got it."

"No one, Mac. I have a reputation to uphold."

It was the second time he'd called me Mac. A rush of pleasure went through me.

I liked hearing that nickname from him.

But he was still waiting, and I nodded. "Got it. Not a word that I broke down in tears."

"You can be crying. That's fine, but I was out here consoling you—not putting the moves on you. That's key."

He seemed so serious, but like before, I could see dark humor lurking behind his eyes. I nodded. "Got it. I'm a crybaby, not a whore."

"Well . . ."

I laughed, shaking my head. "I'm kidding." And because I couldn't help myself, I leaned forward and whispered, "But you have no worries. You're a damn good kisser." My lips met his again as I closed my eyes.

Someone groaned—maybe both of us—and he pulled me on top of him this time. He fell back, cradling me in his arms. And we kissed. Then we kissed some more.

CHAPTER
TWELVE

I was a hussy.

It had been almost dawn when Ryan and his friends dropped me off after the party.

I snuck in, but if I'd been expecting any big confrontation with my folks, I would've been disappointed. They hadn't started moving around the house until around nine this morning, and when I got up, there was a note on the kitchen table for me. Robbie had liked the school yesterday—so much so that they were taking him back. For good.

That was that.

I got no say in the matter.

Ryan came over in the afternoon, and we hung out in my room most of the time. There was kissing, but also video games, cookie dough, pizza, and sneaking some wine. Okay, lots of wine and lots of kissing, and I ended up putting a note on my door telling my folks I was sleeping before I snuggled up with Ryan the rest of the night.

And kissing. There was still more of that, but there wasn't anything heavy.

When I woke Monday morning, I glanced at the clock. Six AM.

Ryan was already on the edge of the bed, bent over. His shirt was on, but it wasn't pulled all the way down. He was fixing his shoes.

I sat up, tugging his shirt into place and letting my fingers skim his back as I did.

He glanced at me, his eyes darkening, the look of lust there that I'd started to recognize from Saturday night and yesterday.

"Morning," he murmured. Leaning over, he kissed me.

"Hmmm." I pulled back, scrunching my nose. "I have morning breath."

He laughed, grabbing my arm and tugging me back to him. "You're fine." And he showed me, his lips finding mine again and not letting me move away.

I was panting in a second, feeling all sorts of tingles in my chest when he groaned, pulling away.

He rested his forehead on mine. "I gotta head home to change and get ready." He sat up again, his eyes holding mine. "First day of school. You want a ride?"

I opened my mouth, figuring my parents would take me, and then I remembered they were probably headed to work already.

"Yeah."

"Okay." He nodded, opening my window. "I'll be back around seven thirty."

"Okay."

His lips curved in a crooked grin before he was out the window and down the tree. I heard his truck start up a moment later. As it turned down the street, I lay back in bed and stared upward. I wasn't looking at the ceiling. I wasn't really looking at anything.

I was . . . I didn't know.

We didn't have sex last night, but our shirts had come off and jeans were unsnapped. I got up halfway through the night to put on pajama pants and a sleeping tank top. Shortly after that, the top was pulled off and pants pushed down a bit. Ryan had shucked his jeans off, but he kept his boxer briefs on. He held me, chest to chest, and I slept.

He was gone, and my limbs felt heavy, my lips swollen. I could easily sleep the rest of the day away. I felt content until I heard the floor creak outside my door. There was a knock, and I sat up.

"Honey?" My mom.

Whoa. I reached for my sleeping tank and tugged it on. "I thought you were gone already?"

"We're leaving in a few, but are you going to be okay to get to school? Do you need a ride?"

"No. I'll be fine."

She didn't ask if I wanted to talk about Robbie. I shouldn't have been surprised. My biggest battle had been the counseling sessions. After that, it was like they'd learned not to even give me a chance to voice my opinion.

I listened to them move around the house.

I'd been with them for eighteen years. I knew their routine. My dad made the coffee. My mom made the toast. My dad would eat that and a yogurt, and then they'd finish getting dressed. They'd take the coffee with them. I heard keys jingling while they discussed who would come to say goodbye.

My mom must've won because my dad's heavy footsteps came up the stairs.

A slight knock. His voice was muffled through the door. "We're heading out. You'll call if you need anything."

It wasn't a question. He wasn't asking, and he didn't wait for a reply.

Again, no word about Robbie. Did they not think I'd be affected by that? Then again, I didn't know what was going on in my dad's head anymore.

Did he leave feeling as if he'd fulfilled his good-father role? Or did he go off not thinking about me at all? As if checking on me were another part of their routine for the morning? Because it was. They'd always checked on Robbie and Willow . . . and there was usually something happening there that kept their attention. A few times they'd gotten to me, but the focus was usually with Willow.

My phone sprang to life, and I scooted to the edge of my bed. Bracing my elbows on my legs, I cradled my head in my hands for two seconds.

The ringing didn't stop, so with a groan, I grabbed for it. "Hello?"

A soft and tentative voice. "Is this Mackenzie?"

I stood. "Who is this?"

"Cora."

Ryan's friend. No, correct that, the girl who had a crush on Ryan—the guy I kissed last night.

I bit my lip. What was my role?

"Uh, hey. Yeah. It's Mackenzie."

"Oh, thank God." She laughed. "I swiped your number from Ryan's phone. There's another Mackenzie in our class who likes him, so I wasn't sure if I got the right one or not."

Another one? I frowned. "No, this is me. That other girl, does she text him too?"

"What?" She sounded distracted. "No, no. Well, yes. She texts him, but I don't think he responds."

Relief. Phew.

Seriously, how many girls were after him?

"Okay."

And then silence.

I waited a beat. She called me.

"Um, so okay, I called to see if you needed a ride to school, or if, like, you wanted to meet me somewhere in school? I could be your guide through classes, you know?"

Well, fuck.

She was going the friend route, which meant I'd have to adhere to the friend code. So hands off Ryan, but I'd already violated that rule. And because I didn't have the energy to worry about this, I blurted out, "Look, I have to tell you . . ."

I paused for a breath. She started to break in, but nope, I *was* doing this. She probably knew what I was going to say and wanted to put up a roadblock. But I had to say this because I didn't know her when I met Ryan. But I'd begun to depend on him since June twenty-ninth.

I spoke over her. "Ryan and I are something."

"What?"

I groaned inwardly. She sounded like she wanted to cry.

"I'm sorry, I—"

"Oh, that's okay. Just don't do it again, you know?"

"No. You aren't listening to me. I'm sorry you're hurting, but I can't step back. I wanted you to know this before we even think about becoming friends." I took a breath. "And if you don't want to anymore, I understand."

Ryan wasn't into her. I knew that, and she knew it too. She also knew he was into me.

Maybe if Willow were still alive, I wouldn't need Ryan and I'd really like Cora. Maybe then, I would have been able to step back, but I wasn't in that place.

I gentled my tone. "I'm sorry, Cora. I know you like him."

She sniffled on her end. "Then why are you pursuing him?"

It wasn't like that, but . . .

"Because I need him right now."

More sniffling. I heard her blow her nose.

"I always thought maybe, you know?" she finally said, her voice resigned. "He seemed disgusted with Erin the last time we saw her, and I had hope. Like I had a chance, finally."

Sadness weighed in my chest, but my need to get through this shitstorm outweighed that. Call me a bitch. Call me a whore. Call me whatever negative thing you want, but in that moment, I was just a survivor.

My phone beeped again.

Ryan: **Leaving in thirty. You want coffee?**

Crap. I had to get dressed.

"Cora," I said into the phone. "I gotta get going, but I'll see you at school."

I hung up, typed out a quick "yes" to Ryan, tossed my phone onto the bed, and hurried into the shower. I didn't have time to wait for her answer.

CHAPTER THIRTEEN

Two things didn't happen later that morning:

I didn't tell Ryan about Cora's phone call. If she wanted to mention any part of the conversation to him, that would be her decision.

And my arrival at school in Ryan's truck did not go unnoticed.

Heads turned and people were starting over to him when I got out. Their mouths dropped, and everything erupted in chaos.

That was an exaggeration, but with my fragile sense of reality lately, it seemed like chaos. The girls who had been walking toward him turned and hightailed it back to their friends. I could hear the whispers.

It didn't get any better when we got inside. Someone tripped as she tried to veer around us to get to her gossiping friends, squeaking as she fell. When she scrambled to her feet, her face was flaming red. She pushed all the way into her group of friends for cover.

Ryan's eyebrows went up at that one, and when he turned to me, I saw the apology in his eyes before he said anything.

I shook my head. "Trust me. In the grand scheme of my life, this doesn't factor at all. I don't care."

He gave me a small smile, but I knew he didn't believe me.

He should've. I'd rather have this attention than the other kind. The Willow's sister kind. Then again, they didn't know Willow. She was only that girl who'd killed herself.

If they even knew that. Common sense told me the news had to have gotten out, but Ryan was adamant that he and his friends didn't talk. I was still waiting for it to come out of Erin's mouth

88

one day, and when that happened, I was prepared for my first jail time.

It wasn't that I was hoping or planning for it, but I had to be realistic. I was probably going to punch the girl.

Pure agony tore through my chest as I missed Willow more than I thought possible in that instant. I faltered a moment. I felt suspended in hell. I forced myself to exhale and then fill my lungs and bring my head up. My neck felt as if it was lifting cement, and I had to break concrete to resume walking.

One step. Two. Three.

The agony was still there, but it wasn't bone crushing.

Four, five, six, and I didn't feel like I was going blind.

"You okay?" Ryan looked toward me as we walked.

He'd noticed. Of course he had.

I forced a nod—God, that hurt—and cleared my throat. "I'm going to the office, get my schedule and everything."

"You sure you're okay?"

There was no appropriate answer to that. I didn't know when there would be, so I ignored it. "I'll check in with you later."

"Okay." I felt him watching me as I continued down the hallway. I didn't stop feeling his eyes until I turned the corner and found the school's office.

The interest in me waned once I hit the second hallway, which meant the school gossip train must not have traveled as fast as I'd thought. Nearing the office door, I saw Cora lingering outside of it. As I approached, she pushed off from the wall, adjusting her hold on a textbook and notebook.

Her eyes slid to the floor, but then she straightened and her little chin firmed in determination as she looked at me again.

She reminded me of a wounded bird. I was the eagle who'd torn her wing, but for some idiotic reason, she wanted to befriend the eagle. No, wait—Ryan was the eagle. I'd be the vulture in our little scenario.

"Hey."

I paused, nodding to her in greeting.

She picked at some imaginary threads on her shirt before

rushing out, "IknowRyanlikesyouandI'msorryforwhatIdidbutI wanttobefriendsifthatscoolwithyou?" Her cheeks pinked so she had to stop. Smoothing out her shirt, she asked, "Would you?"

"Yeah." There were no hard feelings. She should be the one pissed at me anyway. "I'd like that. Thank you."

The office door opened, and I stepped back, clearing the way for some students headed out. I stepped inside, and Cora followed. The office was full of activity—teachers going in and out and three ladies working behind the desk. One waved me over with a harried expression on her face.

"Name?"

I gave her my info and slid over the papers my mom had left on the counter for me this morning.

"People are already talking about you," Cora murmured.

The lady interrupted, asking, "Mackenzie Malcolm?"

"Yes."

She went back to typing at her computer.

I glanced at Cora, who edged closer, looking over her shoulder. I saw the two girls standing in line behind us, both watching as they talked to each other. I only hoped the gossip was Ryan-centered. I could handle that.

They looked vaguely familiar. One had auburn hair grazing the top of her shoulders. The other had darker hair that was styled the same. Pink sweaters. Blue jeans. And glitter. They all seemed to wear glitter.

"They popular?" I asked Cora.

"They're friends of Erin's."

Aha. So they would've been at the Jensens' on Saturday. "Gotcha."

"Okay, Miss Malcolm." The lady reached for the printer behind her and then extended the papers to me. "Here's your class schedule, locker number, and combination, and you'll have to stop in the nurse's office. She'll have a form to give to your parents to sign, giving us permission to give you pain pills or Band-Aids, things like that." She plastered a nice smile on her face, one she'd probably used twenty other times this morning already. "Is your sister coming in?"

Cora gasped.

She didn't know . . .

The lady froze, noting my reaction and Cora's. She was thinking, but I could tell she couldn't figure it out. She cleared her throat, and when she spoke again, there was an authoritative and slightly condescending tone to her voice, as if we were wasting her time.

"Your sister, Willow Malcolm? If she's absent today, she'll need a note. I only received the information for you, my dear."

I couldn't say it. The words were stuck in my throat, and I hushed Cora before she could explain.

My fingers were clumsy as I grabbed a pen and piece of paper off the lady's desk.

She died June 29th, I wrote. **Not coming.**

I folded the paper over and then folded it again.

Sliding it to her, I grabbed my stuff and hurried out of there. I didn't want to be anywhere near her when she read it.

I failed.

I heard her gasp as the office door closed behind me.

"The records must not be updated. Or the records at your old school weren't updated. I don't know." Cora was right next to me, holding her books close to her chest.

I was walking blind, no idea where I was going, and it took a moment before I regrouped.

Locker. I needed to find my locker.

Glancing down at the number, I realized I was in the wrong hallway. I'd have to walk back in front of the office again, and there was no way I wanted to do that.

I read my first class and showed Cora the classroom number. "Where is this?"

She bit her lip, tugging at her shirtsleeve. "It's down the hallway."

That was welcome news, and I nodded. "I'm going to class."

"We still have twenty minutes—"

I was already off. I called over my shoulder, "That's fine with me."

I'd find my locker later.

When I got to the room, the teacher wasn't in, so I couldn't ask if there would be assigned seating. I slid into the seat in the back row and farthest from the door. I still had my book bag with me, but I didn't care. I pulled out a notebook and pencil, and I put my phone in my lap, making sure it was on silent. Then I looked out the window as everyone came in.

Conversations slowed as people filled in around where I was sitting.

I felt them watching me. I didn't look. I couldn't. A few tears slipped down, and I willed them to stop. I was doing a great impersonation of a statue.

Perhaps that was what I'd be for Halloween.

"Okay, everyone." The teacher paused when the door opened.

I finally looked around, surprised at who sat beside me. Before I could process that, a student darted into the classroom and handed a note to the teacher.

As he stopped and read it, a weird déjà vu came over me.

I knew. I knew what he was going to do next.

The teacher stiffened, looking up. His eyes moved over the students, landing on me.

Remorse flared in his eyes before he coughed, handed the student back the note, and murmured, "Maybe let the next teacher know as well. All of them, in fact." He said it quietly, but I heard him in the back of the room.

The school didn't want teachers to make the same mistake as the office lady, so news of my sister's death was circulating, room to room. No teacher would read the attendance sheet and ask for Willow Malcolm. No one would ask if we were sisters and where she was.

It was a nice gesture, but I felt stripped raw anyway.

I had a strong feeling the teacher wouldn't call my name

during attendance, and I was right. He named every other student in the room.

When he called on Ryan's friends—Nick and Tom—they replied "Here" from the seats around me, and I was grateful. I wasn't sure if this was where they normally would've sat, but I'd take it.

Their presence shielded me.

CHAPTER FOURTEEN

I was brave enough to sneak past the office after my second class. It was ridiculous. I was sandwiched inside a group of students, but I swear I felt the office lady watching me. I knew it couldn't be true.

Ryan came over as I was closing my locker to go to my fourth period. We had one more class before lunch, one more hour before goddamn freedom.

"How's it going?"

And cue the other form of attention. I rested against my locker, looking down, but I could see from under my eyelashes. Oh yes, everyone was dying to know about Ryan and the mystery girl.

"What are you? The Greek god of dating?"

He smirked. "Hot shit. Did you already forget?"

"Right. Eagle of hotness."

"Um, yeah." His grin turned wicked, and he glanced around and saw all the attention too. Leaning closer, he dropped his voice. "For real. How are you? Cora told me about Margaret."

I took a leap and figured Margaret was the front desk lady. "I don't really want to talk about it."

"Okay." He gestured to the hallway. "What's your next class?"

"*Espanol. Y tu?*"

"*Si, si.*" He nodded. "Come on. You can be my table partner."

I shot him a dry look, which he returned.

Once we got there, I realized it wasn't a seniors-only class. Erin and Peach were in one corner, and I couldn't stop my groan. Ryan snorted. His hand came to the small of my back, and he urged me forward. We walked to the back of the class and the very last table

94

in the room. A guy after my own heart. We both slid in, and as if they dropped out of midair, Tom and Nick came to occupy the table in front of us.

"Hey, man." Tom leaned over after the class started and worksheets were handed out. He did a fist-bumping thing with Ryan. Nick followed suit. Both looked at me, saw my face, and waved instead.

"You made it out of first period unscathed," Nick noted.

"I did. Thanks for sitting by me."

He shrugged. "It's cool. That's where we sit anyway. Seemed fitting you were there already."

That was true.

They began talking to Ryan about classes, a party already in the works, and girls. I felt their glances, but I tuned them out.

I wished I cared. I really did, but I didn't.

I felt her everywhere.

Sitting next to me.

Standing with me.

Walking beside me.

She was me, but I wasn't her anymore.

I glanced at Ryan from the corner of my eye.

I'd latched on to him. He was a bandage over my wounds—covering them but not really healing them. They were still raw and open, but I was hoping to move fast enough that my insides wouldn't spill out everywhere.

I was no longer a part of any of this, any of these people. I was on the outside, and I was the only one who really understood that.

No one else around me could claim to be a twinless twin. But that was my new identity.

I could almost hear Willow yelling at me, *Those girls need to be taught a lesson. They aren't the queens anymore. We rule now. You and me, Mac. The Willow Mac Attack. That's you and me.*

"Mac?"

I drew in a ragged breath. I could fucking hear her.

Her hand touched my arm. "Mac?"

I screamed, lurching out of my chair. Scrambling backward, my back hit the wall, and I gaped at where I'd been sitting.

Everyone was watching me.

Ryan's hand stretched out toward where I'd been sitting. He slowly closed it into a fist and turned around in his chair toward me. He bent forward, resting his hands on his legs. "Mackenzie?"

God. It wasn't her. Ryan had touched me. Ryan had only used her nickname for me.

"I . . ."

"What's wrong with her?" Tom whispered.

Nick threw him a disgusted look, slamming his elbow into his chest.

"Ouch."

As the teacher rounded the tables, heading toward me, Ryan stood and got between us. He blocked me from the rest of the class at the same time.

"What's the problem?" the teacher asked.

I heard chairs scrape against the floor, and soon Tom and Nick were standing in front of me as well. All three of them shielded me. The gesture was so sweet, so kind, that I almost lost it again.

I reached out, grabbing Ryan's shirt, and he sucked in his breath at the touch.

His voice came out a little strained. "She, uh—she needs a minute."

I bent my head forward, my forehead resting against Ryan's back.

"Well, take her outside," the teacher added softly. "I know about—"

"Will do," Ryan cut him off.

He swept his arm backward, sliding it around my waist, and pulled me with him. Twisting against his chest, I walked with him toward the door.

"My stuff," I mumbled.

"Tom and Nick will grab it for us."

Then we were out in the hallway, but Ryan didn't pause. He let go of my waist and threaded our fingers together. Tugging me behind him, he stopped at his locker, grabbed his bag and keys, and took me to mine.

"Combo." He pointed to it.

I didn't want to let go of his hand, but I did, unlocking my locker.

Grabbing my backpack and some of my books, he paused. "You have your phone?"

I nodded before reaching to get it.

Then he shut my door.

Slinging both backpacks over his shoulder, he threaded our fingers again, and we walked to the parking lot. We were skipping school. Only a few students were in the hallway, but all of them watched us go, their eyes on our hands. No one stopped us.

We were pushing out the doors as a guy in a black bomber jacket came in the opposite way. He had long black hair, dark eyes, and a sneer that turned into a frown when he saw Ryan.

"Hey, man." He stopped, his hand catching the door as Ryan let it go. "Where are you going?"

Ryan's hand tightened over mine. His jaw clenched. "The fuck? You're back here now?"

They knew each other; that was obvious. But there was something else there.

Cousins, maybe? Maybe they were family?

The guy ignored Ryan's question, his dark eyes sliding over me. He'd been chewing on the end of a pen, and he took it out, pointing at me. "You're skipping with a chick? Am I in an alternate universe? Did we switch roles?" He looked at Ryan. "Are you the badass rebel and I'm the basketball star?"

"Fuck off, Kirk." But Ryan seemed to lose his heat. He started grinning and rolled his eyes. "You're a pain in my ass."

Kirk cocked his head to the side, popping that pen back in his mouth. "Tell me something different. You've been a pain in my ass since we were kids."

Ryan laughed, and as Kirk held up a fist, Ryan met it with his free one.

They gave each other a sideways hug, and then Kirk nodded at me again. "Who's the chick? I thought I was the only bad influence on you."

Ryan lifted our linked hands, nodding toward me. "Mackenzie."

I waited for more of an explanation. Apparently, so did Kirk. We both looked at Ryan, but his mouth was set in a firm line. That was all he had to say.

Good.

I hid a grin. There she was—my twin speaking in my head like she was with me.

Kirk nodded slowly. "Nice." He held his hand up, his grin becoming wicked. "Nice to meet you, Mackenzie. I'm Ryan's real best friend. The others are just posers."

"Nice try." Ryan rolled his eyes again, knocking Kirk's hand down. "What are you doing here for real? You're coming back?"

The rebel-smooth-Casanova look faded. "Yeah. My folks are divorcing. I'm surprised Nan didn't tell you. I'm back with my dad."

"Emily?"

"My little sister stayed with Mom. They're down in Los Angeles."

Ryan winced. "I'm sorry, man."

"Yeah, well . . ." Kirk's eyes found mine again. A mischievous spark lit there. "Looks like you've been busy."

"It isn't like that," Ryan replied. His words seemed defensive, but his tone wasn't. He spoke as if they were discussing the weather. "We're taking off for the day."

Kirk nodded. "Don't worry. I'll watch over the posers."

"Be nice to Tom!" Ryan yelled as his friend headed inside.

A hand in the air was Kirk's response.

Ryan sighed, still watching his buddy.

"I'll be fine."

He looked at me, frowning slightly. "Hmm?"

I waved in the direction Kirk had gone. "If you want to go talk to him more, I can head out on my own."

"I gave you a ride here."

I shrugged. "I can call a car. That's no problem."

He shook his head. "No way. Kirk's crazy. I'm not this golden boy who doesn't do anything wrong. You're my *excuse* to skip today. I'm actually using *you*."

"Are you sure?"

He still seemed worried about his friend, but he nodded with a soft smile. Letting go of my hand, he threw his arm around my shoulders and pulled me into his side. "Let's go before the bell rings and the guys run out here."

We didn't quite make it.

The bell rang as we were getting into Ryan's truck. Students were heading out for lunch as we left the parking lot.

"So." Ryan glanced over. "Where we headed?"

I couldn't figure this guy out.

He'd wanted to skip school. I really *was* his excuse, but then his friend had shown up. The other guys he hung out with seemed like normal, loyal friends. Kirk seemed more dangerous.

Willow would've been all about Ryan until she learned that, until she got a glimpse that he wasn't the pretty boy/good guy she'd made him out to be.

Looking at Ryan, another small thrill coursed through me.

Maybe he *was* the guy I would've gone after in the first place. Willow could step aside.

"I don't care," I told him. "Anywhere is good."

CHAPTER FIFTEEN

We went to my house.

It wasn't original, but it made sense. My parents were both in the city at their jobs. They'd be gone till seven or even eight in the evening, and there was no Robbie during the week anymore.

Ryan didn't have the same emptiness at his place with his mom in and out, Peach coming home after school, and the staff.

So my house it was.

Going into the kitchen, I dropped my bag onto the counter and picked up a delivery menu. "We could order food since it's technically lunchtime."

Ryan smirked, jumping up to sit on the counter next to my bag. His feet almost touched the floor. "Whatever you want. You guys have food here?"

I opened the fridge.

Lettuce. Milk. Cheese. Two cartons of yogurt and some apples. The freezer wasn't any better: some diet ice cream bars for Mom.

I closed both doors and picked up the menu again. "Ordering it is."

He nodded. "Sounds good to me. Order whatever. I'll pay."

I grinned over the top of the menu, reaching for the landline phone. "Are we on a skip date?"

"We're on a skip day, and you can pay next time if you want."

I laughed, the sound a little hollow. "Deal."

After ordering pizza, we grabbed some drinks and headed into the theater room. I kept the door open and my phone close by so I could hear when the food arrived.

Ryan followed me in, lying on one of the couches and resting his arm up over the back. He kicked his legs up on the chair in front of him. I started to perch next to him, but he grunted and reached for me, hauling me almost onto his lap.

"What are you doing?" he grumbled. "After last night, you're shy?"

I felt the back of my neck heating up and looked at my hands in my lap. "Yeah, actually."

"What?" He pulled back so he could better see my face. "Really?"

I looked up. "I don't really know what I'm doing day to day," I admitted. "Hell, even hour to hour."

I kept to myself how I could almost see Willow sitting on the far end of the couch. She was everywhere.

"I'm going a little nuts."

He shrugged, taking the remote from me. His hand brushed against mine, leaving a tingle in its wake.

"I think if you weren't, something would be wrong."

I leaned my head back, watching him as he turned on the large screen and began scrolling through the channels.

"You think?"

His eyes found mine again, holding them a moment before softening. "Yeah. My friend died, and I wanted to rail at everyone. They acted like I was supposed to be over it and done by the time school started again. I got a four-day weekend to mourn. My parents didn't understand why I wasn't so interested in doing things afterward."

"What do you mean?" I sat up next to him, but he grabbed my legs and pulled them onto his lap. His thumb rubbed the inside of my calf.

He leaned back, turning toward the screen again, but he wasn't watching it. A mask settled over his face, one I was starting to recognize—it fell into place any time he talked to someone who wasn't one of his friends or me. Even his sister got the mask.

"I don't know." His chest rose silently and then fell again. "He died during the winter, at the end of our holiday break, so football was done by then. But I probably would've quit that. I played basketball, kinda had to. The whole town would have erupted if I hadn't, but I quit everything else. Baseball. Anything extra I was supposed to do. My parents were having a crisis. They didn't know what was going on with me. I stopped giving a shit about anything they did." He laughed quietly. "I smoked a lot of pot that year with Kirk. Drank a lot too."

"How old were you?"

"It was two years ago."

My chest ached. I looked over, and Willow seemed to have moved closer to us, but she was fading. I almost couldn't see her. I tuned her out and tuned into Ryan.

"I'm sorry."

His hand began to move again, caressing my leg, moving a little farther down the inside and back up.

My throat felt like it was closing in. "You and Kirk partied together that year?" I rasped.

"No. Well, yes, but that isn't why we became friends. Derek was Kirk's cousin. He was as messed up as I was. He says I was worse. I say he was worse, but yeah, we did a lot of stupid shit together that year."

"And he's been gone?"

"Yeah. He moved to L.A. last winter. His mom got transferred or something, but I guess he's back."

"You didn't know?"

He didn't answer. A few beats passed before he looked at me again, his eyes haunted. "He called the last couple weeks, but I didn't call back. I was distracted."

Me. I happened.

"Maybe he can come over later?"

Ryan laughed quietly, moving to face me more fully. Letting go of my hand, he slid his hands up the outside of my legs, grabbed my waist, and pulled me onto his lap.

I gasped and then moaned as his hands slid around to my ass. His mouth hovered over mine, his eyes darting from my lips to my eyes as he murmured, "I don't think so."

He dipped down, and I closed my eyes, already lifting to meet him halfway.

His lips touched mine at the same time the doorbell rang.

"Fuck." He pulled back, panting a little.

He deposited me gently onto the couch and then headed for the door.

I heard it open, and a second later, "Thanks."

The door slammed shut, and Ryan hurried back downstairs. He strode into the room, deposited the pizza on one of the other chairs, and lifted me once again. He sat and pulled me to straddle him. I smiled, feeling lazy and sensual as I looped my arms around his neck. My hands slid into his hair, grabbing fistfuls as I bent down to him. He tugged me the last inch separating us.

A thrill burned in me as I felt him plastered against every part of me.

God.

We'd kissed for the first time Saturday night. That was two days ago. He'd come over, and we'd fooled around more on Sunday and again that night, but those times were nothing compared to how this made me feel.

I was breathless as his mouth opened over mine, as I felt his tongue slide inside. His hand went to my waist and slid underneath my shirt. He paused there, waiting for me to let him know what was okay and what was not. It'd been the same way Sunday night. He'd asked before touching me then, and he was asking again. And like that night, I answered by touching him the way I wanted to be touched. My hand went under his shirt and slid up his torso, over his stomach muscles and chest as I pushed his shirt the rest of the way.

I began inching up my own shirt.

He pulled back. "Are you sure?"

I nodded, my mouth finding his again. I couldn't stop touching him, kissing him, tasting him. My shirt went up, and his hands were on my bare stomach, smoothing to my back, then down to my ass as he anchored me more firmly against him. I couldn't get enough.

I wanted more of him, more of this.

I wanted anything that helped me forget I was starting to feel like a ghost.

We kept kissing long past when the pizza had gone cold.

The sound of the garage woke me up.

The room was dark. The big screen was off, and an arm curled around me.

Ryan had fallen asleep behind me. We were tangled up together on the couch in the theater room.

I bolted upright. "Shit!" I shook Ryan's shoulder, but his eyes had opened as soon as I moved.

"Wha—"

We both heard the garage door going back down.

He repeated my sentiment, "Shit."

Groaning, he swung around from behind me, pulling his shirt on. I grabbed for my shirt and then looked down. Yes, my pants were fine. I glanced at his; they weren't. He was searching around, his hand raking through his hair.

I pointed. "Crotch."

"Huh?" He looked down, another curse leaving him. He quickly buttoned his jeans.

We hadn't had sex, but we went a little further than last night. Grinding 101. I'd definitely felt him against me, and I'd definitely strained to get closer to him, which was a reality that was hitting me like a sledgehammer, I was glad that was all we'd done.

"What if the school called them already?"

He grabbed for his phone, scrolling through his messages. "Tell them the truth. You thought you could handle it, and then you couldn't. You lost your sister, Mac. Your parents should be sympathetic to that."

He was right. I felt a little better, the old Mackenzie's guilt lessening over skipping half a day.

They would come inside. I could hear my parents talking to each other.

They would call my name.

When I didn't answer, they would go in search of me.

I wouldn't be in my room, so they'd call again.

They would come down because this was the obvious place I'd be. If I wasn't in my room or in the living room, then check the theater room.

So, I waited, my heart pounding against my chest, listening . . .

The fridge opened. I heard glasses clinking. My dad walked to his office.

The microwave started in the kitchen.

Plates clanked as someone pulled them out of the cabinet.

And then . . . nothing.

They never called for me. They never went up to my room to see if I was in there. My mom went down the hallway to their bedroom. The microwave beeped and then the oven. My dad walked from his office back to the kitchen.

"Food's done," he called.

My mom's soft tread came back to the kitchen.

Chairs were pulled out, moving against the floor.

I heard utensils hitting the plates, scraping.

I couldn't move.

Ryan's phone was flashing as texts came in, but he silenced it. Wait—I grabbed for my phone. I'd put it on silent too. There'd be a text from my parents, something to check in with me. They would've asked where I was, how school was, told me they were eating without me. They probably thought I was with friends. But when I looked?

The screen was blank. No calls. No texts. Nothing.

My parents weren't going to look for me.

Ryan scooted over and showed me his phone. He typed out: **Want to sneak over to my place? Rose made spaghetti.**

Did I?

A numb cold settled in. I saw the pizza we'd ordered and had never eaten. It was still on the chair, but I had no appetite. I ran through the scenarios in my head: go upstairs and pretend my parents hadn't forgotten me or go to Ryan's place. Peach would be there, but so would other people.

I nodded, suddenly desperate to be anywhere else.

CHAPTER
SIXTEEN

We didn't have to sneak.

As we were going up the stairs, my parents finished eating. I heard them put their dishes in the sink, and as we came to the top of the stairs, they moved past us. My dad went into his office. My mom went to their bedroom. I saw each of their backs disappear into the different rooms, and then Ryan and I headed out the door.

I locked it behind me.

Holding my phone as we drove, I was sure it'd buzz any second. My parents would remember me. They'd want to know where I was.

It hadn't moved by the time Ryan parked in his driveway, and with a sigh, I slipped it into my book bag.

Ryan eyed me as he rounded the front, waiting for me. "I'll give the guys a call and find out if we already have homework for tomorrow."

I nodded. There was a storm battling the icy cold numbness inside me, and I would've jumped at anything to quiet my mind. "That sounds like a good idea."

But turns out, he didn't have to do that.

When Ryan opened the door, yelling, techno music, and laughter assaulted us.

A blur streaked from the living room, past the entryway, and into the kitchen, then backtracked.

Peach gaped at us and hollered, "RYAN'S HOME!"

Footsteps stampeded toward us, coming from all angles. I stepped back instinctively. It was jarring going from my empty and almost haunted house to this. Ryan's was full of life.

Erin and two other girls ran from the direction Peach had come. Tom and Nick came down the stairs. Cora and Kirk busted up from the basement. As they skidded to a stop, most were red in the face and more than a little sweaty.

"What the fuck?" Ryan dropped his bag with a thud to the floor.

Kirk grinned at us, lopsided. He rested a hand against the wall next to him, his chin lifting in a cocky posture. "Your parents are at some banquet event overnight in the city—"

"And Rose cooked a bunch of food for us and then left. It's all in the fridge," Peach cut in, her chest heaving.

Ryan looked from her to Kirk. "So you thought you'd have a party here?"

Kirk lifted a shoulder. "Seemed the best option, especially since your ass skipped out today." There was an added heat to his words, and everyone's eyes moved to me.

You're going to take that? I could hear Willow hiss.

No, I answered in my head. *No, I'm not.*

I looked right at him. "You didn't seem to have any problem when you ran into us leaving."

"That was before I realized he'd be gone all day." He switched to Ryan. "Seriously, man—"

I interrupted, "Why the change of heart?" I flicked a look at the girls, who were following the back and forth like a volleyball game. "Have you been listening to my *fans*?"

Erin's eyebrows shot up. Her friends gasped, giving her nervous looks.

Peach got redder in the face.

Ryan looked from me to Kirk, his mouth curving down in a frown.

"According to them, you've been all over my man since you arrived on the scene. You're like a leech, taking him away from his friends, and I think it's bullshit." He raked me over, sneering. "I thought Ryan was taking you for a literal ride over the lunch period. Then I hear it's been like that all summer long."

This asshole.

I growled, jerking forward a step. "Are you kidding me?"

A twinge of wariness stirred in his eyes. The sneer dropped, but his glare was still there.

"Let's run down the timeline. My family moves to Portside in June. I see Ryan at our parents' company picnic June twenty-ninth. I didn't even talk to him. Eight hours later, my sister kills herself."

The glare faded.

"Four hours later, I'm at the Jensens' house. Fast forward another month, I go to the movies with Ryan and his friends. Fast forward almost *another* month, I saw him this past weekend and yeah, we skipped today. Want to know why?"

I didn't know when I'd advanced on him, but I didn't think anyone could hold me back. I was seeing red. "Because I couldn't fucking deal with not having my twin *motherfucking* sister with me today."

I felt Ryan behind me. His hand on my back acted like a coolant. I felt some calm seep in, but I could still feel everyone in that room—their attention, their derision, their judgment.

Willow would've creamed them in minutes.

Feeling a bit more in control, I said, "You lost a cousin. I lost my other half. Save your judgment for the bitches who got in your head today."

Silence.

If you're going to get away with clocking one of those bitches, I'd do it now.

Willow was in my ear again. I could imagine her snide looks at Erin. I suppressed a laugh, knowing I couldn't do either, but she *so* would have.

Ryan's hand found mine. Softly, as if he were crooning to a cornered wild animal, he said, "Come on. Let's go upstairs."

Another surge of rage was coming, so I let him pull me upstairs. Nick and Tom moved aside. Ryan said something to them, but it was so low I couldn't make it out. He led me upstairs to his room, and once inside, I waved him away. "Go. I know you want to talk to them. I'll be fine."

He hesitated at his door. "You sure?"

I nodded, not looking at him. "Yeah. I have to chill out. I know."

"Kirk isn't usually that wrong on things. He'll correct himself."

I wasn't holding my breath.

I was embarrassed.

Those girls wanted a reaction, and they got one. I'd lost it in front of them. They got the win. They'd used Ryan's best friend to get it out of me.

Point one for the rich bitches.

I sat at Ryan's desk, grinning slightly at Willow's words. She would've been impressed with them too.

You were cool as tight back there. Proud of you, little sis.

Cool as tight? I had no idea what that meant, but it was something my twin would've said, in a moment when she was "cool as tight" too.

There you go, thinking you're funny. And look at you, getting it on with Ryan like you're rabbits. Watch the sexual activity, twin sister. You don't want to pop out little babies for Mom and Dad to ignore too.

I was full-on smiling. *Fuck you, you dead bitch.*

She would've laughed, and I swear, I almost heard it.

God.

Her presence was so strong.

Head's up. Your Willow-replacement's little sis is approaching. In three, two . . .

"Mackenzie?" Peach knocked on the door.

I froze for a second and then looked around. Was Willow actually there?

No.

I was going insane. That seemed more logical.

Ryan's sister poked her head in. Seeing me, she pushed farther inside, shutting the door behind her with a gentle *click*. Her back kept to the door, and she looked down at her linked hands in front of her. "Um . . ."

She was there for something. I waited for whatever it was.

"I'm sorry."

She stopped after that, and I frowned. "For what?"

"For?" Her chest lifted. She took a deep breath and looked up. Shame hung heavy, like bags under her eyes. "I didn't really think about what you went through." She held her hands up. "Are going through, and I'm sorry."

Okay. She apologized. I had no clue why. "I don't understand you. What'd I ever do to you?"

Her face closed in on itself as if she were in pain. "You're going to think I'm an idiot."

I already did, so I kept quiet.

She sighed. "I was jealous of you, and worried because of you."

"Huh?"

"It's so completely stupid. I—Ryan doesn't like anyone."

I snorted. "Besides Tom, Nick, Cora, and Kirk?"

"Yeah, but they've only recently come back in the picture, and he doesn't talk to anyone in the family. I'm his sister, and after Derek died, Ryan only hung out with Kirk. Then Kirk left, and . . ." She didn't finish.

"What are you talking about?"

"Derek died during Ryan's sophomore year. Except for ball, he stopped doing everything for an entire year, and then Kirk left, and it was—he was like you until a few months before you moved here. When that happened with your sister, and you came here, I hated you. I saw how you attached yourself to him, but Ryan wasn't pushing you away. He pushed everyone away until you showed up." She faltered, glancing down for a moment. "I didn't want to lose my brother again."

"You thought I would do that?"

She jerked her head up. "I was scared he'd slip back into whatever had him before."

It made more sense. Ryan's response to me, why maybe I was pulled to him, even her attitude.

"I'm sorry for that."

"No." She shook her head, smoothing back some of her hair. "I'm sorry."

111

I saw the tears that lined her eyes.

She wiped them away. "Anyway, I wanted to say that."

She slipped out again before I could respond.

I sat there, feeling . . . nothing. Again. Or maybe still?

Another quick knock, and Kirk's head came around the door this time.

I read the apology on his face before he started to speak, and I held up a hand. "Please. Don't."

"What?"

"You're here to apologize?"

His head lowered. He grabbed the back of his neck, kneading it. "Uh. Yeah. I am."

I shook my head. "I honestly don't need it. I didn't go off on you and then come sit up here, expecting you to come to me with your tail between your legs."

"Well." He looked down, the beginning of a playful grin tugging at his mouth. "It's there." He moved his hips from side to side. "I can let my hair grow longer, if you want, so there'd be a real tail."

"No." I laughed a little at that. "Ryan's letting everyone have it down there?"

His hips stopped moving, and he nodded. "Yeah. I feel like a dumbass. Erin never told me any of that stuff. She just said that Ryan had changed since you came into the picture. I'm protective of him, and it isn't just because of my cousin. If you hadn't noticed, Ryan's loved. By *a lot* of people."

I was getting that.

I shook my head. "It's fine. Don't jump down my throat again, okay?" I laughed. "I think I've reached my quota of confrontations. There've been more the past few months than ever in all my life."

"Yeah?"

"Yeah."

I could imagine Willow standing next to me, her arms crossed over her chest as she rolled her eyes. *Yeah, because that was my job. You're stepping into my shoes, sis.*

Kirk rubbed his hand over his face. "Look. I might be overstepping, but I get what you're going through. I thought I was going crazy. After Derek died, I saw my cousin everywhere—or, I thought I did."

I didn't know what to say. "Did he go away?" I finally asked.

He didn't reply at first. A second passed, and a hollow look entered his eyes. He was staring at me, but he wasn't seeing me.

"Not really, no," he replied softly.

Great. I should just go ahead and reserve my room in the mental hospital.

"But I don't want him to." He nodded to me. "You won't either, if it's the same for you."

I sighed. "I'm sorry for going off on you."

"I'm sorry for being the asshole you had to go off on. And for the record, I deserved it. You don't have to apologize for anything."

Willow grunted next to me. *Damn straight.*

Kirk motioned for the door, grabbing the doorknob again. "Ryan sent me up here to grovel and see if you wanted the spaghetti he promised. He's heating some downstairs. Guess pizza got shot down."

I thought of the forgotten one at my house. I hadn't been hungry then, but my stomach rumbled. Spaghetti sounded good.

I motioned for the door. "Lead the way."

He paused before opening the door. "We're good, right? I can tell him we're good? He won't kick my ass then."

"He said that?"

"His exact words were, 'Get up there, apologize, and mean it, asswipe, or I'll kick your ass.'"

That made me smile.

CHAPTER SEVENTEEN

Ryan glanced my way when I returned with Kirk, a question in his eyes as to whether I was okay. I nodded and moved to sit in a chair behind the table. I was the new girl to this group. I'd fought for my place twice—and I would continue if needed—but as I observed everyone, I saw there was no more resistance. The only one unhappy with me was Erin, but everyone ignored her, including her friends. They seemed more eager to flirt with the guys, Kirk most of all.

When the food was heated, everyone got up and filled a plate before returning to the table. Someone pulled out drinks and passed them.

Ryan made sure everyone had food before grabbing his own plate.

He headed for the empty chair by Kirk, but before he could sit, the guys all moved down a spot, emptying the chair to my left. So Ryan took that one. Cora sat to my right, and no one paused their conversation as all of this happened.

I got it then.

All the resistance against me from the girls, from Peach, from Kirk—it was because they depended on Ryan. No one started eating until Ryan sat. And no one said a word about it. It was an unspoken rule. Once he touched his fork, so did everyone else.

Whether he knew it or not, Ryan was the core of this group. He was the glue.

A different emotion filled me. Warmth. It combatted that cold and almost-dead sensation, making me feel something I wasn't sure I wanted to feel.

"You okay?" Ryan asked quietly.

I nodded. "Yeah. I'm okay."

I felt proud of him, but I didn't know why. He wasn't my boyfriend. Yet, I'd laid claim to him somehow, and he'd reciprocated. I knew he'd had a choice, but in some ways, he hadn't—I'd crawled into his bed that night and woven a spell over him, never letting him go. The sane part of my mind knew that wasn't the case. He would've kicked me out, rejected me if he didn't want anything to do with me, and he hadn't.

I'd thought he was a nice guy who fell for the damsel in distress. He'd wanted to save me, but that wasn't the case.

He did what he wanted. He was turned off for a year. He smoked pot. He drank. He stopped caring about sports. He rebelled from his life and what was expected of him—in that way, we weren't the same.

No one had expectations of me.

Robbie does, I heard Willow remind me.

I sucked in some air, feeling moisture pooling at my eyes. *Robbie.* I hadn't texted him all day.

He's fine—stupidly happy at that school, but he's worried about you. Send him a text. Let him know you're fine, and then call him later.

I almost rolled my eyes, like I was going to take advice from a voice in my head. But I stood from the table. "I'm going to call Robbie."

Ryan nodded. "Okay."

I didn't go far, just sat on the front step and pulled my phone from my pocket.

Texting Robbie, I waited for a response. There was none. I didn't know his room number, so I called the school's main number.

"This is Haerimitch Academy. How may we help you?"

It didn't take long to be transferred to Robbie's room, and a second later, I heard his voice.

"Hello?"

"I'm a horrible sister."

He laughed. I could hear him brightening up. "Hey, terrible sister. I'm your terrible brother here."

I snorted. "Why are you terrible? I'm the one who didn't call to check in last night."

"I'm terrible because I didn't call to check in with you today."

"You didn't have to."

"But I didn't think about it."

"Let's cancel each other out so neither of us is terrible."

He sounded happy, and I relaxed a little. Maybe the voice in my head was all-knowing somehow?

He's happy to be away from the memories. Willow was sitting next to me.

Yeah, maybe. I spoke to her, but it wasn't aloud. I kept that last safeguard from slipping further toward my insane side. I wasn't talking to her as if she were a real person. She was a voice in my head.

Willow laughed. *You're such a dope. I'm not made up. You're too chickenshit to admit it.*

I ignored that, clearing my throat into the phone. "Tell me everything. I want to feel like I was there."

Robbie laughed. He sounded like a kid there, like a young genius, eager to be challenged for once.

Good.

Maybe my parents got one thing right after all.

As long as Robbie was okay, I'd be okay.

I listened to him for the next hour, hearing about his roommate, his classes, his teachers. They were talking about testing him for college courses already, and I wasn't surprised. My brother was damn brilliant.

He's going to be fine there. He's more worried about you. I ignored Willow again, but I could feel her smile as she added, *Don't give him reason, sis. He'll blossom there.*

As he should. Finally.

Toward the end of the call, he said, "Keep calling, Mac."

He used her nickname too. My cheeks were starting to hurt from the smiling and the beaming and the whole trying-not-to-cry thing. Damn. That was work.

My throat was hoarse because of all the happiness. "I will."

"You tell me how you are next time. Deal?"

"Deal." I stuffed it down. He didn't need to hear me being emotional. "When?"

"Um . . ." He was quiet a second. "Maybe Thursday? I talked to Mom and Dad. I'm going to stay here this weekend."

"What?" I went rigid.

"There are a lot of others who stay, and they have weekend programs." He sounded so sorry.

He'll come home when he wants to. Trust the little Einstein. He knows what he's doing. Don't make him take on your shit. He's eleven, not seventy.

I ignored her again, but Willow had a point.

"That sounds awesome. Maybe I should try to get in," I teased. "Think they have a placement for older students? You could be my mentor."

Robbie started giggling. Once he started, he couldn't stop. "That's silly, Mac."

There. There was my little brother.

"Okay." I felt like I could hang up. He *was* okay. "I'll call on Thursday."

"No. Let me call you. Some of us are going to create a video game, so I'll call you when I get finished."

My little brother: future creator, inventor, and computer hacker. I was so proud.

"Love you," I told him.

He said the same, and after ending the call, I sat for a minute.

I had to get up. Someone would come looking for me, probably Ryan. The guy was taking me on as if he were my mentor instead of Robbie. He didn't need to. I wasn't like him. He had slipped away, and Peach feared she'd lose him again.

It made sense, but I wasn't going to do that.

Right?

Or maybe I should pull away? Try giving him space, make him seek me out. Then it wouldn't be me affecting him. It'd be him, his decision. I could do that, except . . . I couldn't. Even thinking about it had a hard weight slamming into my chest.

I wouldn't be able to do it.

Somehow, some way, Ryan had become necessary to me. He shielded me, protected me. My head was above water with him. Without him, I would sink.

I would drown alone.

I heard the door opening and wasn't surprised when he sat next to me. His arm brushed against mine.

"You sleeping here tonight?" he asked.

Did I have any other choice?

Water pressed down on me. I felt the air slipping from my lungs. I almost felt myself thrashing, trying to get to the surface.

"I'll hide in your closet till your mom goes to bed."

His grin turned rakish, and mine matched.

He nodded. "Deal."

COUNSELING SESSION THREE

"You didn't leave during our last session. I think you're making great strides, and thank you again for coming back. I know you've been missing the other appointments, but I feel I need to remind you that the school and your parents both agreed these sessions are a necessity for you. It's been a few months since your sister died. I was hoping today you could talk to me about her?"

A heavy silence. "No."

She sighed. "I don't know your sister. I can't comprehend what it's like to lose a twin or to be the one who finds her. Please, Mackenzie. I really would like to know more about your sister. Tell me about her."

Another heavy silence. "Her name was Willow, and she left me."

CHAPTER EIGHTEEN

One month later

We were at a dance.

Black, silver, and pink balloons hung from the walls and pooled all over the floor. There was a pink banner at the back of the gymnasium—we were at our old school.

A sad song was playing, and our friends were dancing, their arms wrapped around each other. It was Homecoming.

Willow stood on the stage, her Junior Queen crown on her head and her pink dress shimmering. She looked like part of the it, as if they'd specifically designed the theme around what she was wearing.

If I hadn't known better, I would've believed that wholeheartedly.

Willow and I both had light brown hair and sometimes golden blonde hair. It ranged in shades—it all depended on the season or whether Willow had been to the hair stylist lately. She'd spent more time in the sun over the summer, and her hair was almost a normal blonde. It hung in curls down past her shoulders, extensions adding another six inches, and it looked good. She was like some sort of Greek goddess, owning the attention of everyone around her.

No, it was the way she wore it, the way she stood—as if she owned the entire gym. That was what drew everyone's eyes.

Only a few might've realized it, but we were all living in Willow's world.

She turned to look at me, her eyes haunted. "Don't ask me."

I stepped up next to her and looked down; I was wearing the same dress. I hated pink. I felt the crown on my head. I hated crowns. And I looked over my shoulder—my hair had grown and was a lighter shade than normal.

I was her.

I looked over the gym again. We were no longer at our old school. I didn't recognize this one. It was new to me, like the question burning in my throat.

"Don't. Please." She began to whimper.

I looked at her. I mirrored her body posture—chin raised, shoulders back.

"Why did you do it?" I asked.

Black tears rolled down her face, her makeup smudging. "I can't answer that."

I tried a different question, the one I almost hated her for. "Why did you leave me?"

I bolted upright in bed screaming.

A hand clamped over my mouth and pulled me back down. Arms wrapped around me, and Ryan pushed me into the bed. He braced himself over me, and I could barely make out his eyes in the dark.

"Ssshh!" he whispered.

Fuck.

Reality flooded back. I was in Ryan's room, Ryan's bed, and this was my fourth week of sneaking over.

A door flew open down the hallway.

"Shit!" Ryan jumped over me, running to his door.

Feet pounded down the hallway.

"What are you doing?"

"Hide!" he whispered. Then he was out the door and running to meet his parents.

"Ryan!" his dad bellowed. "That sounded like your room."

"It was Peach!" Ryan yelled back.

"It was Peach?" Their mom's voice hitched up in worry. "That didn't sound like one of her screams."

Three sets of feet ran down the hallway and then another door opened and a light went on.

He'd said to hide, but I had to be quiet. Stealth. They couldn't find me or this was over. Panic began clogging my throat. I pushed past it and started to slide from the bed.

"Peach? Honey?"

"Uh . . .what?" Peach's voice was groggy.

"You screamed," Ryan said.

"I did?"

"Honey, did you have a nightmare?"

"Uh . . . maybe? I must've."

"Oh, honey."

Their mother turned nurturing, and someone's footsteps crossed the floor as another two sounded closer in the hallway, as if they were leaving the room.

"You acted quick," Ryan's dad said.

I almost squeaked. It sounded like he was walking Ryan back to his room.

Moving like a ninja, I lowered myself to the ground and rolled under the bed. This had been my move to hide from Willow if she decided she wanted to talk late at night.

Two shadows stood at the door.

"How are you doing? I know you and that Malcolm girl have become close."

"What?" Ryan's voice matched the slight hysteria I felt.

Shit, shit, shit. If they found out about me, if they told my parents, if this, if that—so many ifs ran in my mind. But they couldn't. None of that could happen because then my parents would start watching me again. I wouldn't be able to sneak out, and Ryan wouldn't be able to sneak in, which was our pattern. We traded off unless we knew one of us absolutely couldn't get away.

"I talk to Phillip every now and then at work. He's struggling. I'd assume they all are. How's the girl?"

"Uh, she's dealing. I think."

"Peach said you were close. Rose said she's been over a bunch."

"Oh! Yeah. I mean, yeah. She's dealing. I mean, that's all I can say."

His dad sighed. "I suppose. Phillip said the littlest is at the gifted academy. He seems to be liking it a lot. They go down there four times a week to see him."

They do? That was news to me.

"What about her?" Ryan asked. "Are they checking in with her enough?"

I almost cursed. What was he doing?

"I suppose. It was her twin. I'd imagine they worry about her the most." A second later, he added, "Why? Are they not?"

"No. I don't know."

"You're friends, aren't you? You're acting weird, Ryan. What's going on with you?"

"No. I know. I mean, I'm not. Yeah, we're friends. She's in our group with all of us."

"She and Cora are friends then?"

"Uh." Ryan sounded so stiff, like he had a stick up his ass. "They're both the girls in our group. It'd be weird if they weren't."

"You're still being weird."

"It's in the middle of the night. What do you expect? Peach woke us up with a blood-curdling scream."

"Yeah." His dad sighed. "You're right. All right. Listen, go to bed. Maybe I'll ask Phillip if they want to come over for dinner sometime. Would you like that? Have your friend over for a meal with the 'rents?"

"Sure. Yeah. Sounds good."

Again, I wanted to smack him. He could've discouraged that in two seconds.

"Okay, son." A thump on his back. "Try to get some sleep. I love you, Ry."

"Love you, Dad."

One shadow entered the room, the door clicked shut, and soft footfalls moved back down the hallway. I waited for Ryan to come back to the bed, but he didn't move.

"Mackenzie?" he whispered, half-hissing. "You here?"

I could stay under the bed. He'd assume I slipped out, went home, and I could haunt him the way Willow continued to haunt me. But that wasn't nice, and he wasn't the person I wanted to get back at.

I crawled back out from under his bed. "You were having a nice chat with your pops there." I stood, sliding back into the bed.

He came over and reached for the covers. "What could I do? If I acted weird, he might've thought something was off."

"He *did* think you were acting weird."

He shrugged. "Normal is easier said than done. I kept thinking, *Whoa shit! I got a hot chick in my room somewhere, and they can't find out, and whoa shit, whoa shit, whoa shit!*"

I laughed, lying back down in his bed. "I got it. I'd be weird too."

He gazed down at me. "You aren't normally pissy with me. You mad about something else?" Waiting a beat, he added, "He brought up your family."

My throat burned, his words echoing in my head. "I didn't know they'd been going to see Robbie four times a week."

"They didn't tell you?"

I shook my head.

"Your brother didn't say anything?"

Another head shake.

I was barely home, and if I was, it wasn't for long or I wasn't alone. I had no clue they were driving to see Robbie. A part of me was glad, thankful they checked in on him, but another part of me ached with jealousy.

I was there. I was in their house, and I struggled every day to say something.

My parents weren't evil. They didn't mean to forget about me because they didn't love me, but I fully believed they didn't want to see me.

They saw her when they saw me.

So, I stayed away. Hell, I didn't even enjoy looking in the mirror myself.

My eyes were hers. My hair. My body. I'd lost weight, losing the healthy weight I held with those Cheetos. The more I dreamed about her, the more she talked to me, the more she haunted me—I was becoming Willow.

If I took her place, would they mourn Mackenzie? Maybe that would be easier for them.

"If they do the dinner, we can have everyone crash it."

I laughed lightly, my body curving toward Ryan's. "They'd love that, actually."

"Your parents?"

"No, the guys." The guys included me and Cora.

After the night of apologies a month or so ago, I'd gone to school the next day, and they'd all walked next to me like I was one of them. That was how it had become. I considered Tom, Nick, Kirk, and Cora friends as well.

A hand touched my cheek, and I started as Ryan brushed away one of my tears.

God. I brushed at it, and then the rest. My whole face was like a waterfall.

I groaned, turning and pressing my face into his pillow.

"Hey." His voice was so soothing, so kind, it almost broke me again. He straightened some of my hair and then smoothed his hand down my back. He shifted, lying on his side. He continued rubbing my back, and his voice came from above my head. "You never actually talk about her, you know?"

I shook my head, rotating from side to side.

I couldn't talk about her. I just couldn't.

"What was your sister like?"

He cared and thought he was doing the right thing. At least, that was what I told myself.

It *so* wasn't the right thing though.

I turned, not caring about anything except avoiding talking about her, and grabbed him. I pulled him down on top of me, finding his mouth with mine.

I was desperate for it.

I was desperate for hi—no. I had to be honest, at least with myself. I was using him. There. I admitted it. I did care for Ryan, and maybe there were real emotions underneath all the craziness inside me, but I wasn't in touch with them right at the moment.

He could chase her away; he was the only thing that worked.

"Ryan," I breathed, opening my mouth under his, coaxing.

"Mac?"

God.

I normally loved hearing her nickname from him, but not tonight.

I sat up, still kissing him, and feeling something rising in me—something reckless, something wild, something intoxicating—I took my shirt off. I didn't sleep with a bra on, so as soon as my shirt was off, his hand was on my breast.

Yes.

That helped.

She was fading. I could feel her go.

"Are you—"

I shook my head, my mouth finding his again. I didn't care if I was coming across frenzied and desperate. It was how I felt, but the throbbing for him had started too. I . . . I stopped thinking. That was the only way she'd completely leave, and tonight, I didn't care how far we had to go for that to happen.

I wanted him, and that ache grew more and more fervent.

I gasped.

"Shit, Mackenzie," he growled, pushing me back down and looming over me. He was panting, but he fitted himself between my legs.

I could feel him through his boxer briefs, through my pajama shorts. I reached down, grabbed his hips, and jerked him close.

Right there.

I felt him where I needed him, and I began grinding against him. He moved with me, his hands growing more sure, more demanding, more rough. My frenzied need stirred the same emotion in him, and he was crushing me, getting as close as he could.

I could feel him press into me.

Move his briefs aside, my shorts aside, and we'd be one.

My mind had stopped working.

I no longer knew why he wasn't in me already.

My mouth opened beneath his, and reaching down, I touched him.

He cursed, shoving against my hand. He broke his mouth from mine. "You sure?" he rasped next to my ear and then lifted to peer at me through the darkness.

I nodded.

I had a small window of sanity, but I was ready. We were going there anyway. Willow was making me crazy, but yes. I was sure.

"I'm on the pill."

He reached up, brushed some of my hair away from my forehead. "You are?"

Another searing pain in my chest. "Willow had sex last year with Duke. We both went on the pill once our mom found out."

Good old Wills. My mouth turned down, and his thumb fell to my lip, rubbing it out.

"I have condoms," he whispered. "We'll be safe."

I nodded.

Take a goddamn breath, Mac. Fuck's sakes. Think about this. This is major. S-E-X, the big sex here. He's the guy you want?

I almost cried out, hearing her concern, and why the *fuck* was my mind working again? My mind wasn't supposed to be on her, but I listened to her question and focused on him.

I focused on Ryan.

I was a virgin. Was he the guy? And suddenly, I felt Willow leaving again. She was fading and taking all the pain, all the anger with her until it was only me lying in his arms.

The answer bloomed in my chest, and I nodded.

I was ready. I did want this, and with no one else except him.

"Yes," I almost whispered the word.

I wanted nothing more, and it wasn't tainted by the pain of my sister. It was pure, rooted in the feelings I did have for Ryan.

"Please."

His eyes darkened, and that was all he needed. He bent down, his mouth finding mine again.

Yes.

CHAPTER NINETEEN

I had sex.

I did it. That particular first in my life was done, and I was happy about who it was with. Under the seven layers of my emotional shit, there were real feelings for Ryan. I mean, I knew myself. I wasn't so damaged by WWD (what Willow did) that I was completely screwed up and would lose my virginity to some asshole.

Ryan was the right guy. I didn't know what was in the future—I could barely function with the today—but there it was.

Done.

I was no longer a virgin, and I was supposed to be different. Right?

I was supposed to look different?

No?

Gazing at myself in the mirror after showering, and knowing Ryan was waiting in bed for some post-coital cuddles, I searched those two eyes where a soul is supposed to be.

I saw nothing. For real.

There was the usual iris, eyeball, and such. Eyelashes. The literal round hole, but that wasn't me.

I winced and averted my eyes.

Fuck. I didn't even want to look myself in the eyes. Me. *I* didn't want to see what everyone else must be seeing.

There was nothing there. Emptiness. Dead. Dull.

I was gone.

There was nothing lively in there. No happiness, elation, a big fat nada.

I'd lost my virginity, and I was half-considering going in there and doing it again just so I could feel something.

Morbid much?

Oh, lovely. Time for my usual haunting.

Hey, Wills.

She leaned against the sink and crossed her arms. *You know, Mac, if you're actually crazy, you wouldn't be thinking of me only when you can handle it. I'd be popping in all the time and really haunting you. I'd be telling you to kill someone or something. Isn't that what voices do? Tell you to do bad shit?*

I wouldn't know. I'm not schizo. I'm mourning.

Willow snorted. *You're a head case, that's for sure. And yeah, maybe you're mourning, but honestly, aren't you prolonging the inevitable?*

I shut her out.

I felt what she was going to say, and I stopped her, literally imagining her out of my head, out of the bathroom, out of the house, and far, far away. I could almost feel her flying backward.

Then I opened my eyes.

Still here, dumbass.

She hadn't moved an inch.

Bitch.

She laughed. *Finally. Some sass. You're so fucking depressing. What happened to you? I mean, I know.* She indicated herself, her hands moving up and down her body. *But you know what I mean. You should've had your shit together a long time ago, but you're sucking at it. Come on, Soccer Superstar.*

I wasn't the soccer superstar.

Yes, you were. You were the superstar in everything. You just didn't know.

I was lazy, and I ate junk food, and I—

You were normal, but you were the best on your soccer team.

But—

You were normal, Mac. Her voice was so soft. *And that was a good thing. You got to be the normal one of us, even if you really weren't. You were what we needed. You were our anchor, still are.*

"You're the strong one, Kenz." I heard Robbie's voice, and I could see him all over again, looking at me from the doorway to Ryan's room that day. I'd flipped the cover back and let my little brother hide in there with me.

If only we hadn't ever left that shelter.

I expected a smart comment from Willow, but none came. Then I looked, and I almost gasped. Tears glistened in her eyes, and her hands were balled as if she were trying not to cry.

I'm so sorry, Mac.

What? A searing and burning sensation began to build in my chest. I started for her, my hand reaching out.

If I could take it back . . .

And poof. She was gone.

"No!"

She was right there. She was real. I could see her, speak to her, and she was gone.

Footsteps pounded on the floor behind me. The bathroom door flung open, and Ryan's eyes were wild.

"Mackenzie? What?" He saw I was staring at nothing and turned in a circle, looking around the bathroom. "Mackenzie? What . . ."

The same words, but such a different meaning.

No. Nope. I wasn't—I couldn't say it aloud.

She wasn't real.

She wasn't there.

She *was* gone.

"She was supposed to be here for this." The words wrung from me.

He turned around and sighed. "Oh, Mac."

Tears rolled down my face. I felt them falling, but I couldn't move, and I couldn't stop them.

"Mackenzie." He said it quietly, tenderly, and he pulled me into his arms. "I'm so sorry."

He cradled the back of my head and held me.

CHAPTER TWENTY

"I know what you and Ryan did last night."

I jerked back, my hand hitting the locker and slamming it shut. I turned to face Peach, who seemed pissed. Her eyes were angry, her mouth a firm line. Her arms crossed over her chest.

She didn't seem it. She *was* angry.

And she was tapping her foot.

I eyed that foot. Who tapped their foot like that? Seriously?

"Say that again."

She couldn't be talking about what I thought she was talking about because then . . . ew. How the hell would she know that?

Her arms uncrossed, and her hands formed fists, pressing into her legs. "You screamed last night. I was dreaming about taking a puppy to a fair. Ryan put it on me, but it was you. I know what you two are doing. He's either sneaking over to your place or you're at ours. It was you who screamed last night."

Prove it.

I sooo wanted to say Willow's words to her, but the truth was, Peach could. Easily.

Open the fucking bedroom door at three in the morning, and the proof is there. So I kept my mouth shut.

Ugh!

I ignored Willow. I was still mad at her for disappearing last night.

Fuck you.

I ignored that too.

"What do you want?" I asked Peach.

Fine. She wanted to play ball with me? Well, there were consequences. I was going to call her on it.

She frowned, her head lowering an inch as she moved back a step. "What do you mean?"

"What do you want? If I screamed, what are you going to do about it?"

"Nothing." Her frown deepened.

"Then why'd you come over all heated like this?"

She shrugged, crossing her arms again. "I don't know. I wanted you and Ryan to know that I know. And why'd you scream?"

It wasn't something nightmare-worthy, at least not to others.

"I dreamed my sister and I were at Homecoming."

"Oh." She tilted her head. "That sounds kinda nice."

I snorted. "I knew you'd think that."

"It wasn't?"

I gave her a dark look. "It was my sister. Me. Homecoming. I'll never be able to go to another dance with her. You do the math." I turned toward my locker again.

I left out the part where I was becoming Willow. The creep meter was off the charts there.

"I'm sorry, Mackenzie."

Her quiet voice drew my eyes up to her again.

"I'm sorry your puppy dream got interrupted," I offered.

A giggle left her and then another. She shook her head. "Sorry. Just . . .puppy dream. Sounds funny when you say that."

I grunted. "I'd take a puppy dream over the weird shit in my head any day."

She sobered. "Yeah. I'm sure you would." A new softness emanated from her, and she murmured, "I'm really sorry about your sister."

I couldn't remember if she'd told me before, but the ring of sincerity told me she meant it this time.

Feeling choked up again, I nodded.

The warning bell rang.

I was standing in the hallway, getting all emotional with Ryan's sister four minutes before the next class.

Fuck this.

"I'll see you later," I told her.

I didn't wait for her response. Everyone else had started for their classes, and I merged with the stream to veer toward my classroom.

Ryan and I had sex.

Yes, I was on repeat, but I was giving myself a break. I had to process things while I was refusing to process something else, and that something enjoyed haunting me.

Aaand back to processing what I could: I was no longer a virgin.

It hurt at first, but then it felt good. Then it felt really good.

I was there for Willow after she had done the deed. I sat on her bed and listened to every detail.

I hadn't been crying last night because I couldn't share that experience with her. I cried because I wouldn't have.

Willow was supposed to know. She would've cried, begged me for the 411, and I wouldn't have said a thing because Ryan would've been important to me. Willow would've been jealous. She would've wanted him for herself, but I had him, and I got him because I crawled into his bed that night.

Willow was supposed to know . . .

Get over yourself. I'm so here, but you won't admit it. Right, Mac? When did you start talking to yourself? Yes. Yes. You're crazy. You're so nuts, they'll ship you to a hospital so you don't do what I did. That's your real worry, isn't it?

"Enough!" I roared, and like that, I was staring at my classroom, and Willow was gone.

Every person in the room—including the teacher—was looking at me.

I was smack dab in front of the door as the last bell rang.

Mr. Breckley cleared his throat. "I quite agree. Enough. It's time for some learning." He ignored the light smattering of laughter and motioned to me. "Now, if you'll close the door, Miss Malcolm, we'll get to today's lesson."

My neck felt warm.

I kicked the doorstopper out and went to my seat, ignoring the questioning looks from Tom, Nick, and Cora.

CHAPTER TWENTY-ONE

"Hey."

Ryan's greeting shouldn't have stood out with all the noise in the hallway, but it was as if I'd become attuned to his voice, his body, him. The rest of school, all of it melted into the background, and I turned, knowing he'd be standing there, watching me with the quiet concern maybe he shouldn't have had. The tension eased from my body.

This was wrong.

I shouldn't be depending on him this much, but I moved toward him. My body was already betraying me.

"Your sister knows." I meant to say more, explain, but the need to get Willow from my mind made me forget.

I stepped toward him, and he mirrored me. It was as if we moved as one unit. My back went against the lockers, and he stood in front of me, his hand resting against the locker beside me. I couldn't stop myself. I leaned into his hand and reached for the loop on his jeans. He reacted to my touch, sucking in his breath, and I saw him go rigid, but I didn't pull him against me. I held on to that loop. It was an attachment to him.

"What?" His eyebrows went up.

"About me sneaking over," I clarified. "That I screamed last night, not her."

"Oh." His shoulders slumped. "Not about the other thing, right?"

"No. Not that."

"Fuck, Mac." He gave me a crooked grin. "You gave me a slight heart attack."

I smiled. "Yeah. Not that."

"We didn't talk after . . .well, after us and after your bathroom thing," he said.

Right.

I glanced down, feeling all sorts of awkward again.

He'd held me until we had both fallen asleep. His first alarm woke me, and I told him I could hurry to my house alone. I'd started bringing clothes to his place and vice versa, but it was never the same as getting ready at your own house. I needed some space this morning, and when he'd picked me up an hour later, I'd been the Avoidance Girl.

Avoid the sex talk. Avoid the bathroom meltdown. Avoid. Avoid. Avoid.

I felt the walls closing in on me, and I knew I couldn't keep avoiding forever, but I was going to do my best. Call me the Superstar of Avoidance. I'd wear that pin proudly, if I got around to it.

I shook my head, a small signal that I still didn't want to talk about it, and my finger moved against his stomach.

His eyes warmed, and an invisible rope tightened between us, pulling us toward each other. He leaned closer, and I felt myself moving away from the locker door.

The next bell was going to ring. We'd have to go into our class, but I didn't want to pull back. I didn't want to be with other people. I wanted to stay here, stay with him, or go somewhere else and just be alone with Ryan.

I wanted to skip.

I hadn't skipped since that first day, and a part of me didn't want to do it again. If I did, I didn't know whether I could stop myself later. Already I could barely manage the temptation to disappear with only him. I could shut everyone else out, shut out the world, and yes, shut out Willow. She was the main one I wanted to shut out.

Love you too, asshole.

That was all I needed.

"Let's get out of here."

"Yeah?"

I nodded, scanning up and down the hallway. The others were starting to head to class. If we were going to go—I saw Kirk and Nick headed our way. Their eyes were right on us like we were targets and they'd locked in.

"Never mind."

Ryan looked around and cursed under his breath before he moved, half blocking me from their gazes. "Hey, guys."

Nick's eyes narrowed suspiciously, but he hung back as Kirk stopped in front of us.

"Let's skip," he said.

Ryan and I both straightened in surprise.

"What?" Ryan asked.

It was only then that I noticed how Kirk's eyes were blazing. A scowl was firmly in place, and everything about him radiated anger. He shoved his hands into the pockets of his black bomber jacket, pulling it tight around his form.

"I gotta bounce from here. Let's skip." He looked around at all of us. "You game?"

Nick wasn't saying anything, but Ryan looked at me.

"I'm in," I said.

Ryan studied me a moment.

"Are you going?" I asked Nick.

Kirk shifted, throwing his arm around Nick's shoulders. "Hell yes, he is." He thumped him on the arm twice. "He's coming."

"Yeah. Sure."

His tone didn't suggest he was eager.

Then Ryan pulled me away from my locker, opened it, and put away his books. Grabbing my hand, he shut the door and nodded. "Lead the way, Kirkus. You got point on this one."

"Sweet. Let's go."

A few others saw us go, but Kirk ducked out through a side door, and we jogged across the lawn, heading for the parking lot. Nick and Kirk went for his truck, but Ryan grabbed my arm and pulled me a different way.

"We'll follow in mine," he called.

Nick looked like he was going to say something, but Kirk raised his arm. He didn't look back, and if anything, his pace picked up. After a couple of beats, Nick turned and hurried after him.

Ryan and I wove through a few rows of vehicles, closing on where he'd parked. Without speaking to each other, we broke apart, going to our doors. I waited until he unlocked the truck, and then I was in and grabbing the seatbelt.

He climbed in, and a moment later we were easing out of the slot, waiting for Kirk's truck, which didn't take long. A black SUV sped past us, only pausing for a second at the exit before it took off.

Ryan wasn't as fast, but he caught up after a block.

"Where are we going?"

"I don't know; Kirk will choose a place."

I remembered the almost-crazed look in his eyes. "Did something happen? Do you know?"

"Who knows. Kirk gets like this. He needs space or has to get his mind off something."

"What do you guys do when that happens?"

Ryan shrugged, flicking on his turn signal and pausing at an intersection. "Honestly, this isn't that normal. I mean, it is for Kirk and me, but since he's come back, he's been with the others more than he was before. It used to be him and me."

I read between the lines there. "And you're with me most of the time now."

"Yeah." He started through the intersection, glancing at me as we moved in behind Kirk's SUV.

"You okay?" he asked moments later when we pulled into a driveway.

We parked behind Kirk's truck, but I didn't see anyone still inside.

"Where are we?"

"Kirk's place."

"Won't his parents—"

Ryan laughed. "His dad works in the city like yours, and the staff won't say a thing. Kirk skipping *is* normal."

Great. Another abnormality that was becoming normal. I was on the fast track to becoming a juvenile delinquent.

"Okay."

Ryan laughed a little and then sighed. "We didn't talk about last night."

He'd brought this up earlier. I wanted to evade it then, and I still wanted to.

Normal life, normal Mackenzie would've been freaking. I would've called or texted Willow from the bathroom. I would've lain awake the rest of the night, wondering if I'd done everything right. If I should've showered or was I clean enough? How was I supposed to lay with him? Any move he made, I would've analyzed. Or, who knew? Maybe I was channeling Willow again, because that was what she would've been doing.

Willow told me all about her first time. She freaked out, but she never showed it. Not in front of her boyfriend, not in front of the guy she'd been dating at that time, not even in front of her friends. I saw the freak-outs. They were behind closed doors. Always behind closed doors.

Goddamn. Duke's abs were like a seven-layer cake I could lick all day, but he was as dumb as the barbells he used in the gym.

I almost sighed and thought to her, *Thank you, Wills, for reminding me.*

Happy to help. You're going on this whole memory-lane journey. I want to clean it up, make sure you're using my language and not yours.

Yes. Thank you. I was not serious.

Willow snorted.

"Mac?"

A rush of heat swept through me. Ryan had been staring at me the whole time I talked to Willow in my head.

"Sorry. What?"

"You okay?"

I was going insane. "Totally fine. Let's go." Opening my door and jumping out, I took in Kirk's house.

The driveway curved up and around a hill and there was a Spanish-style fence outlining a large yard. The house looked Spanish, too, and it had with brightly colored tiles and a veranda in front. Large, neatly trimmed bushes ran up and down the length of the yard.

Kirk's house was huge, but I wasn't surprised. They had a cleaning lady and a butler, and as Ryan predicted, neither seemed surprised nor disapproving as we all traipsed in.

"Thanks, Mitchell." Kirk clapped the butler on the shoulder.

His dark blue suit didn't seem to move under the touch, and he barely blinked an eye. He had one of those faces that might've been warm and friendly if he smiled. He didn't. His face seemed encased in plastic, like if he smiled it would break the whole thing. I placed him around sixty, with silvery graying hair, perfectly combed in place.

"Will your guests be staying for dinner?" he asked.

Ryan opened his mouth, but Kirk said, "Yes, and we'd like to have a full-course meal from Joann's delivered."

That got a reaction.

Mitchell blinked a few times. The muscle near his mouth twitched and then . . . nothing. The mask was back in place, like he'd magically gotten a dose of Botox.

"Very well." He disappeared down a hallway.

I watched him go. I saw his shoes touch the tiled floor, but heard not a sound. How was that even possible? Willow could take haunting lessons from him.

She snorted. *The stiff has nothing on me.*

Kirk led the way to the back. He hit a button and two walls on the end slid open, revealing the pool. Parts of the backyard were outside, but parts were indoors with glass walls separating them. There were benches made out of blue and white tiles, but there were also couches and lounge chairs with cushions on them. Two different grills sat on opposite ends of the deck, and the whole thing was covered in cobblestones.

The backyard was massive.

Kirk went to a refrigerator and hollered over his shoulder, "Who wants a beer?"

Nick moved past me, grunting. "If we're going to skip, let's do it the proper way."

Kirk threw him an almost evil grin, and I was surprised to see Nick's eyes darken, matching it.

Putting the beer away, Kirk pulled out a tequila bottle instead. Grabbing five shot glasses, he held it in the air. "Tequila it is."

Ryan groaned. "This is not a good idea."

"Come on, lover boy." Kirk's eyes narrowed, passing to me before moving back to his best friend. "What? You think you're the only one who can be the bad boy? Move aside, buddy. I was your partner in crime before. I'm claiming my place again."

Ryan laughed. He was close enough that I could feel the tension ease from his body. "Fair enough." He moved ahead, his arm brushing mine. "All right. Let's do this the proper way, hmmm?"

Nick frowned. "What's the proper way to take a tequila shot?"

Kirk and Ryan shared a grin as Kirk bent, bringing out salt and limes from the fridge.

Ryan narrated as Kirk poured tequila into all five glasses. "Salt that hand."

Kirk salted.

"Lick it."

Kirk licked.

"Down the shot."

Kirk drank it in one gulp.

"And suck on the lime."

Kirk sucked.

"Holy shit!" Kirk spat out the lime, wincing and shaking his head. "Now that's the right way to do a shot." He pushed all the ingredients toward Nick. "You're next."

Nick eyed everything warily. "We're going to be hurting by tonight, aren't we?"

Ryan laughed. "Did you really see any other ending for one of Kirk's skip days?"

Nick groaned as he reached for the salt. "You're right. God. This is going to hurt." He poured it over his hand and eyed Ryan at the same time. "You aren't on the football team, but I am. I was supposed to have practice today."

"Convert. Join the basketball team with me."

Kirk started laughing.

Nick grumbled before licking his hand. "I'm on that too." He made a face as he grabbed the shot, downed in, and planted a lime in his mouth. "Goddamn! That burns."

He moved back, still grimacing, and then it was Ryan's turn.

There were no words or pauses. He took the shot like a pro and had no reaction afterward. It was as if he drank water. I couldn't decide if that was alarming or if it turned me on. Either way, it was my turn.

Three sets of male eyes settled on me.

This was what I wanted: another way to escape my life.

I reached for the salt, and the world melted away.

This scene should've made me nervous, right? Drinking tequila in the middle of the day with three guys I barely knew? This never would've happened a year ago. I would've been in school, talking with friends, and griping about soccer practice.

But that was then, and things had changed.

I wanted to do this.

I felt Willow at my side. *Come on, Mac. This is stupid. Getting drunk? Really? You already had sex. I mean, how many more cliché ways can you rebel against—*

I blocked her out, pouring the salt. I licked it and then took the shot. Ryan held out a lime, but I ignored it. I reached for him instead and fused my mouth to his.

Yes! There was the burn I wanted, and after a thorough kiss, I reached for the salt again.

I heard the guys saying something, and I felt Ryan's surprise, but he was behind me. His hand fell to my waist and tightened there. I could sense him thinking of saying something to stop me, but I shook my head, and his grip softened.

I took a second shot, ignoring the lime once again and fully turning into Ryan's arms.

He was waiting for me this time, and as his mouth opened over mine, I was aware of him pulling me away from the others. He kept kissing me, licking, tasting, teasing until suddenly the sounds of the water, of Kirk and Nick, all fell away. Darkness surrounded us. We were in a building, and when Ryan reached for the light switch, I stopped him.

"No." I grabbed him, pulling him back, and he pressed me into a wall.

His mouth became more urgent, more demanding.

My body grew heated, and as my head fell back, gasping for breath, I knew this was what I had hoped to be doing today instead of sitting in class.

I wanted to get lost with the feel of him, and I wanted more tequila.

I didn't want Kirk and Nick there. I wanted to be alone with Ryan, and as his mouth fell to my throat, I could tell he felt the same way. His hips pressed into mine, and I could feel him wanting me.

With a growl, his hands caught my hips, and he ground into me.

CHAPTER TWENTY-TWO

A knock came on the door. "Horny lovebirds!"

Kirk stood outside the door, and he gave two more knocks before Ryan pulled away.

Growling, he jerked the door open an inch. "What?"

A smug snicker came from the other side. "You two can get it on later. Today's my day."

Ryan wasn't amused. "Your skip days are usually about getting high, drunk, and/or laid."

"Not today."

I caught a quick flicker of a grin on Ryan's face before he masked it and moved farther away from me. His hand still rested on my waist, but once my hot flashes had subsided, I enjoyed watching this exchange play out on Ryan's face.

He loved Kirk. That was obvious, but he was wary of him. Still, he was becoming more open to whatever Kirk was going to say. His hand had relaxed on my waist, and since we were at his friend's house, I thought maybe the right thing was to cool our lust jets a bit. But once we were alone again? Hell yes, I'd be jumping Ryan.

And you still think you aren't trying to be me?

I stiffened, hearing Willow's mocking tone. I ignored her.

I'm you, Mac. You can't ignore me, and you know it. That's like you ignoring yourself.

I gritted my teeth and caught Ryan glancing at me.

I can ignore myself all I want, I shot back and shoved toward the door—and out of Ryan's hold.

"Wha—" Ryan watched me stalk past Kirk, who shifted quickly out of the way.

I went back to the tequila bottle, saw a shot already poured, and downed it. Salt be damned. I still didn't need the lime either.

And goddamn—that burned. I felt it this time, and that meant I needed another one. I was reaching for my fourth shot when I felt another presence beside me.

Goddamn Willow. She was never going to leave me alone.

"So, not to be blunt in an offensive way, but . . ."

Not Willow.

I looked up. Nick was staring at the shot in my hands like he could see a worm in it.

His eyes flicked up to mine. "But your damage is your sister, right?"

It took a second for his question to penetrate. The booze was starting to fog everything. I blinked at him. "What?"

"I mean . . ." He coughed, turning around to rest against the table. He gestured over his shoulder to Ryan and Kirk, still talking outside the pool shed. "Kirk's damage is his parents' divorce, and his dad is hardly ever around. Ryan's damage is losing his best friend close to two years ago, and yours is your sister, right?"

My hand felt like punching him.

I scowled. "Yeah. That. No big deal." My tone was biting.

He paused, and then a crooked grin formed. "Oh. Sorry." He straightened from the table, his hand running through his hair. "I'm not trying to be a jerk—"

"Too late."

He didn't blink. "I wanted to ask because I didn't want to assume anything. My sister says I do both. I'm a jerk, and I assume too much."

"I might love your sister."

He laughed, easing back to rest against the table again. "I know we've all been hanging out for a while, but since you and Ryan are obviously more than fooling around, I figured I should try to get to know you a bit. You know, one on one."

I took the shot, dropped the glass on the table, and moved away from him. Without breaking stride, I said, "That's weird."

Four shots. Dear Tequila Lord, please work more. I don't want to feel *anything* anymore.

He followed me toward the pool. "My sister says I'm that too."

Nick mostly stuck to conversation with Kirk and Ryan. If he wasn't talking to them, chances were high he was ragging on Tom. He rarely talked to me, and I could see why. I was on edge, and I knew he had a mean streak in him, so I was thinking this combination wasn't a smart one.

I called to Kirk, "You have bathing suits around here?"

Kirk pointed inside the pool shed. "In here. Marie keeps everything washed, so if it's on the floor, just leave it. It hasn't been cleaned yet." He hit Ryan's shoulder and jerked his head backward. "Come on. Let's take another shot."

He stepped aside as I came over to them. His words were for Ryan, but he was watching me. "I don't want to lose you in there with your girlfriend again. Who knows when the two of you will come back out."

I stopped right between the two. I could feel Ryan behind me, and I knew he was going to touch me. And in three, two, one, his hand came to rest on the small of my back.

I suppressed one of the good shivers and forced myself not to lean back against him. It would've been so easy.

Instead, I fixed Kirk with a glare. "Tsk, tsk. You're coming across as jealous."

Kirk's smug grin vanished. His eyes widened, and he straightened. "That isn't what I meant."

"Still." God forbid we didn't play by Kirk's rules for how he wanted the skip day to happen. I winced inwardly at the amount of anger I felt.

I didn't like being chastised by Kirk, but I also didn't like the way I was acting.

I could feel Ryan's gaze on me as I shut the door with him outside. He was saying something to Kirk, and I recognized reproach in his tone. I leaned back and let out a deep breath.

Good God, what was I doing?

Skipping. Taking four shots of tequila. Making out with Ryan and smarting back at his best friend? Being snide to his other friend?

Reaching behind me, I locked the door and slid down, my head hanging between my legs. One moment. I needed one goddamn moment for everything to settle.

Willow sat next to me. *It's only going to get worse, twin sister.* Go away.

I have nothing better to do. I check in with Robbie, and he's sad, but he's at least grieving me in the right way.

Was I going to indulge in this? Yes. Apparently, I was. *What are you talking about?*

He cries, but then he goes and plays with his friends. When he feels the grief, he stops and feels it. He doesn't deny it like you do.

I couldn't. She didn't understand. If I let it come—I shook my head and pushed myself back to my feet. I couldn't have this conversation, real or not. If I let any of it in, I'd be crushed. It was a mountain of raw, blistering pain, and I wouldn't come out intact.

She didn't know. She didn't understand. No one did.

Swimsuit, Mackenzie, I told myself. *Find one and stop thinking. It's fucking simple.*

I felt Willow's presence as I found a suit and put it on. She was always there, but I was getting better at pretending she wasn't. And feeling the tequila really begin to kick in, I knew she'd be gone real soon.

Completely gone.

Grabbing a towel, I threw open the door. *You can stay in here.*

After that, I walked right to the pool and dove in. Once I was in there, I didn't stop. I couldn't. The tequila was fast starting to dull my senses, but it'd wear off. I had to keep going. I started doing laps. I'd tire myself out.

And it worked. I don't know how long I went, but I just kept going until the others jumped in with me.

I felt the splashing before a pair of arms slid around my stomach, and then I was airborne.

147

Shrieking, I saw Ryan grinning at me a second before I crashed into the water again. I rose back to the surface in time to see Kirk lunge at Ryan, and then the wrestling was on. Nick cannonballed over them, letting out a yell as he joined the fray. The three dunked each other a few more times until Ryan noticed me watching. He grabbed my ankle, yanking me to him. I felt the slide of his body against mine before he threw me in the air once again.

After that, it was war.

Kirk, Nick, Ryan, and I spent the next hour trying to dunk each other. I was mostly the loser, but every once in a while, I pulled out a surprise and got one of them.

I'd gone from feeling crazy, to wanting to jump Ryan, to almost fighting with Kirk and Nick, to crying, to laughing and playing in the pool.

As skip days go, it was one of the better ones.

After another hour, I pulled myself out. My body was tired, my mind lethargic, and the booze still securing me in a warm fog. That was all I cared about. I padded barefoot to one of the lounge chairs. Two towels were on the end of the chair and I settled back, pulling both on top of me like blankets. I settled in, curling as much into a ball as I could, and watched the guys roughhouse.

At some point a shadow blocked the sun. It was enough to wake me, and I opened my eyes to find Cora frowning down at me.

"You were sleeping?"

I sat up, rubbing a hand over my face. There was a small pounding behind my temples—goddamn tequila. I looked over, but the guys weren't in the pool anymore. They'd moved to the couches, tossing a basketball back and forth.

"Yeah. I guess." I skimmed over her, noting her backpack still on and her shirt untucked from her jeans. "What time is it?"

"Almost four."

"You came over right after school?"

She nodded, studying the guys before letting out a sigh and dropping her backpack to the ground. She sat on the lounge chair beside me but didn't move to lie down. She stayed on the edge, turned toward me, and kept her eyes on the guys.

I saw the worry lines around her mouth and sat farther up, pulling the towels with me to keep warm. I was a little chilled.

"What's wrong?" I asked. "They in trouble for skipping?"

Her narrowed eyes met mine briefly. "I doubt it. Kirk never gets in trouble for skipping. He never did. Nick's mom will probably get a call, but she doesn't really care. If he says it's because one of the guys had a hard day, she'll be okay with that. And Ryan . . ." Her bottom lip stuck out farther, and she trailed off.

Aha. I got it. She was worried about Ryan.

"I thought you were okay with me and Ryan?"

Her eyes jerked back to mine, widening slightly. "What?"

"You're concerned about him."

"No." She tugged at her shirtsleeve and then smoothed the ends of her shirt over her pants. "I mean, he skipped the first day because of you, and now he skipped because of Kirk. He went downhill the other year because of him."

"His friend died."

"I know, but . . ." She stopped talking, her teeth sinking into her bottom lip.

She didn't get it. It didn't make sense to her how grief could be overwhelming. It made more sense to blame Kirk's influence than Ryan losing a friend.

Fuck. What did she think my problem was?

"It must be nice," I murmured, resting my head back against the chair.

Her eyes flickered. "What?"

"Not to have lost anyone."

Her head lowered. "My hamster died when I was twelve."

Pets could be family members too, but I didn't assume hers was. She didn't sound too broken up over it.

Real and genuine jealousy slammed through me. It hit my chest, my heart, my stomach, every single cell in my body—all the way from my toes to my hair. I wanted her life. I wanted it so badly I was almost crying.

I would've given up Ryan to have what she had.

"Everyone knows the four of you cut today."

I was still envisioning life without that pain, so it took a second for those words to register.

It was my turn to frown. "So?"

"So." She reached up to tighten her ponytail. "Everyone knows you guys skipped."

I wasn't following her. "Is that a problem? Or what? I'm not getting what you're saying."

"No." She went back to chewing her bottom lip before shrugging. "Stephanie Witts knows. All the girls, and guys. They wanted me to call them when I found out where everyone was."

Oh. Shit.

"Tell me you didn't call. Right?" I leaned forward, pulling my legs in and tucking the towels under my arms. "You didn't call those girls."

She didn't answer, and I could see she was chewing the inside of her cheek.

Fuck! She did. I groaned, letting my head fall forward to smack my palm. "How long until they all descend?"

She jerked up a shoulder, sitting silent.

"Hey!" I waved my hand in the air. She was staring at the guys and barely answering me. "When did you call them?"

"Oh." She glanced at her phone. "Like ten minutes ago."

More voices came from around the side of the house. Tom rounded the corner of the house first and the rest of the guys followed. I saw Peach and Erin with them. There were more shadows behind her, and as Tom reached over a fence and opened the door, they filtered in. Erin's friends had come with her.

The line didn't end.

I recognized some guys from my grade coming in.

Cora muttered almost to herself, "Those are the basketball players. The football team isn't here. They had practice." She watched as Nick pounded a few of the guys on the arm. "Nick's going to get in trouble for missing today."

More people came in, flooding the entire backyard.

I stopped watching, but I heard what she said.

His coach would get upset, but not his parents.

Erin called Cora's name, and I jumped up from the lounge chair.

"Where are you going?" she asked.

I didn't answer. As Erin headed over, I zipped back into the pool shed and locked the door behind me.

I couldn't do this. Not all these people.

My insides felt pulled apart and put together wrong. Nothing felt right anymore. I couldn't sit on a lounge chair with Cora, hearing whatever Erin had to say—whether she was going to take digs at me or kiss my ass. She'd resorted to the latter over the last few weeks, and I didn't get it. Whether she wanted to be friends or not, it wasn't happening.

My only real friend was Ryan.

And that's the problem.

God, not now! I snapped at my ghost.

Willow rolled her eyes. *You haven't made it right with Zoe and Gianna at home, and you aren't making friends here. I get that Cora's a little weird, but Mac, you're fast becoming weirder. You're almost a leech on Ryan.*

Shut up. I paused a beat. *And Zoe and Gianna, that's on them. They wanted me gone, not the other way around.*

She snorted. *So yell at them. Curse them out. Get mad. Don't just disappear. I mean, I know.* She changed the subject. *I get it, Mac. A part of you wants to go grab your boy and pull him away from his friends, but you can't. Let the guy have a fun day for once. Don't make yourself his problem. If you're together or not, it isn't going to last if you keep going on like this.*

I said shut up.

This is tough love. I get that you're falling apart because of me, but don't mess up the one thing you've gotten right. Give him some space.

She was right, but I didn't want to be lectured anymore. Surging to my feet, I changed back into my clothes and grabbed my bag. I had no clue where Kirk's house was, but I figured I was safe. Everyone was talking or laughing when I slipped out of the pool shed. Some were in the pool, but I didn't see Ryan anywhere.

Guessing he was inside, I moved around the backyard and left through the same gate everyone else had come in through.

I'm not running away, I told myself firmly. But I was lying.

I was totally running away.

Not wanting to be a clinger, as Willow claimed I was becoming, I sent Ryan a text.

Me: **I'm heading home. I forgot I was supposed to go see Robbie with my folks. I'll give you a call when I get back.**

My phone vibrated almost right away.

Ryan: **Are you sure? How are you getting home?**

I was walking, but I pulled up the car service app. After ordering one to pick me up, I relayed that to Ryan.

It took a moment before my phone buzzed back.

Ryan: **Okay. Call me later then.**

I thumbed back, right as the car pulled up next to me.

Me: **Totally. Have fun!**

Then I climbed in, and the car took me away.

CHAPTER TWENTY-THREE

I expected the house to be empty when I got home.
It wasn't.

I walked inside, dropped my bag onto the counter, and looked up to see my mom at the kitchen table, her laptop in front of her. A coffee mug sat to her right and there was a bowl of fruit to her left. She wore her headphones, and she bit her lip before she looked up.

Seeing me, her eyes widened, and we stared at each other.

"What are you doing here?" I asked.

She took off her headphones. "What are *you* doing here?"

I frowned. "It's after school."

"Yeah, but you never come home anymore."

I pointed to her computer. "You're working?"

She turned to look down at her laptop as if she'd forgotten it was there. "Oh. Oh yes. I decided to take a day at home." She stood, her chair sliding back, and she paused there. It was as if she wasn't sure why she'd stood. "Do you want something to eat? An after-school snack?"

I didn't want to, but I felt myself grinning. It was like I was in third grade again. "What? You're going to cut up apples for me?"

"No. I would . . ." She stopped and continued to frown at me.

I heard her in the mornings, moving around, getting ready for work. My parents used to check in every night, and I stayed in my room until that was done, but they'd stopped last week. I stared at my mother, trying to remember the last time I'd seen her, the last time I had really talked to her.

I couldn't remember.

But I did see how she flinched when she met my eyes, how she looked back down, how her hands gripped the table, and how she swayed in place as if she were about to collapse.

A silent storm built inside me. I felt a scream in the back of my throat, and as I stared at her—not moving, not looking away—I could feel that scream ripping at my insides.

I was wailing. I was crying. I was pleading for her to look at me again—because what mother doesn't want to see her child's face? But no sound came out.

I stood there for another minute. She didn't look up. It was a reverse staring contest. I was demanding her attention in a passive and peaceful way, and she wasn't budging.

"I'm still your fucking child."

Her head snapped back. She was already pale, but her lips seemed to turn blue, and she swallowed.

"I know." It came out as a whisper.

I moved forward a step and then stopped. She wasn't saying anything else.

She should've been saying something else.

I waited, my heart pounding, and I heard her sniffle.

Her hand brushed over her cheek, and I saw her tears. She was crying so soundlessly, I wouldn't have known it if she hadn't moved.

She looked away before she began to speak. "I lost a child, and I have continued to fuck up being the right parent ever since. I work too hard every day to keep my mind straight. I don't sleep at night because I know you aren't in bed, but I'm so scared to make demands of you. I know you can make demands on me in return. Your father and I barely talk, except when we go see Robbie, and we haven't once told you about those visits." She heaved a deep and shuddering breath. "You don't sleep at home, but then some nights you are here, and I have no idea how I'm supposed to feel about anything anymore."

I couldn't—what did she say? "You know where I am at night?"

She laughed bitterly. "I've not been the best mother, but I'm still a mom. You're goddamn right I have a tracker on your phone." She stared at me hard. "Are you having sex with him?"

My mind raced, but my stampeding pulse stopped completely. I felt it fall with a thud to my stomach.

"You know?"

Her lips barely lifted in a smile. It was more of a grimace. "Of course. I've known, and so do they, Ryan's parents."

"I . . ." I had no words.

"Nan called the other day, said you'd screamed in the middle of the night. Ryan put it off on their daughter, but they guessed it was you later on. She didn't know if I knew or not."

I felt lightheaded. "How long have you known?"

She took a breath and sat back down. "The first night you didn't come home. You were with him?"

"You knew then?"

"We didn't. We guessed."

"Oh."

I reached for the chair in front of me and pulled it out. My butt hit it with a hard *thud*.

My mother laughed again, the sound hollow. "It started that first night, didn't it? Nan told us how Ryan helped you sleep, and then it continued."

God.

I gulped.

My throat hurt so much.

Her voice grew thick. "We have never stopped watching out for you, loving you, or thinking of you. But we've been selfish, selfish people lately."

She still wasn't looking at me. Her eyes remained fixed on her computer.

"I'm supposed to be at the office today, and your father and I were going to go see Robbie, but I couldn't bring myself to go in. I got ready. I sat in the car, and when your father began to back out, I told him to stop."

Tears traced down the sides of her face.

"I've been working all day here."

"What about Robbie?" I winced. My voice sounded gruff and hoarse.

"Maybe I'll go tomorrow." Her eyes found mine, and they seemed clearer for a moment. It was like seeing the moonlight on a clouded night—one second it was there, and the next second, the clouds closed over it. "Would you like to come?"

A lump the size of the Titanic settled in the back of my throat.

I started to nod, and then I couldn't stop myself. I kept nodding and nodding. "Yes. I'd like that."

She stared at my bag on the floor. "Do you have homework to do?"

"I skipped today."

Her eyes flicked back to mine, and she swallowed. "Really?" She coughed once and frowned. "What did you do today?"

"We went to Ryan's friend's house."

Her head shook once. It was swift, an abrupt movement. "Was there drinking?"

"Yes."

We'd had almost no communication for weeks, and it was as if the dam had opened, and I wanted to tell her everything. I wanted to get in trouble. I wanted . . . I wanted to be normal again.

"Sex?"

Okay. That wasn't one of the things I wanted to share. "No."

"No as in ever, or no as in today?"

Her eyes were beady and staring hard.

Damn. She had me.

"No as in today."

Her eyes closed, and her chest lifted in a silent breath. "Okay. That answers the question you avoided. You and Ryan have had sex?"

My tongue felt heavy. "Yes."

"When?"

"Last night."

She looked up, her eyes wet. "Was last night the first?"

I nodded as my throat closed.

"Ever?" That word was hoarse.

I nodded.

"So you're no longer a virgin?"

156

I felt my tears then. They rolled down my cheeks and somehow, I felt a piece of me fit back in the right place.

"Yes."

Her shoulders began to shake. She lifted balled-up fists to her mouth and hunched over, shoving her chair back. Her head rested on the table as she cried.

I couldn't hear a sound. Still.

CHAPTER TWENTY-FOUR

"*She knows everything?*" Ryan asked.

I lay on my bed later that night, my phone to my ear. "They've known about it the whole time."

"Shit."

"Yeah." I rolled to my back.

I could hear music blaring in his background and assumed he was still at Kirk's. He'd texted a few times since I'd gone, so after the meltdown with my mom, I called him. He needed to be warned about what was coming. I'd also had to fess up about not going to see Robbie.

"You lied?" he'd asked, his voice sounding off.

"I didn't want to be a clinger and make you hate me for being all fucked up in the head."

He laughed. "I've never told you, but I think the reason I let you stay in my bed that first night was because of how fucked you are in the head."

I sat up. "No way."

"The more fucked up they are, the more I like them."

I rolled my eyes, hearing the teasing in his voice. "You're messing with me."

He laughed again, a short bark. "Yeah, I am. You aren't that messed up, and if I'd met you without everything that happened, I still would've wanted you. I can tell you that much. You don't have to worry about me."

You hear that, Willow?

I imagined her response: *Bite me.*

But we moved our conversation on to the fact that I was going to see Robbie tomorrow.

"Are you going during school or after school?"

I frowned. "I imagine after school? My mom wasn't too thrilled to hear that I'd skipped today."

The two pieces that had molded together earlier seemed to reach out and fit with another. That was three pieces of me put back together right. I could feel an almost calm emanating from them.

I could only smile, knowing I looked like an idiot, if anyone were to see me. They would've assumed I was glowing because I was on the phone with Ryan, but nope—just me, my messed-up self, and three little pieces.

It would've made sense only to Willow.

Hearing the shout of voices from his end, I asked, "You're still at Kirk's?"

"Yeah." He sighed and then barked at them, "Leave me alone! I'm on the phone!"

Something slammed, and the sound was suddenly muffled. He came back to the phone, clearer. "Everyone's drunk. Kirk's shut himself in a room with two chicks. Cora is crying, and she won't tell me why." He sounded so tired. "I made Peach go home, but I'm pretty sure she hates me now."

He was being a good brother. "Come over here."

He didn't reply at first. "Are you sure?" he finally asked. "I mean, with your mom knowing . . ."

"I'll sneak you in." I suddenly wanted to see him so badly. "Can you drive?"

"Yeah. I only drank when you were here, and it was those two shots of tequila. I've been holding the same beer bottle since then so everyone stays off my back."

My heart sped up.

He was coming over.

"Okay. Park around the corner. I don't know if my mom is back to being a mom or if she was on a break from her mourning this afternoon, so it's better to be safe than sorry."

He chuckled, sounding tired. "Okay. I'm sneaking out of here. Be there in a bit."

After we hung up, I went to my door and opened it an inch. I listened, but there were no sounds coming from anywhere in the house. I knew my mom was home. And it was around eleven, so if my dad wasn't home, he'd be coming soon.

Tiptoeing down the hallway, I felt wrong—like I was breaking and entering on my own property, but I wanted to know. If my mom was up and about, that'd make things difficult for sneaking Ryan in.

The main living room was empty.

So was the study.

Her office.

The kitchen.

No longer caring about sound, I ran upstairs. My heart pounded again.

It was still somewhat early for us. Usually, my mom would be in her office or in the living room, but I never checked their bedroom.

It should've been the first place I looked, and once there, I flung open the door.

I expected . . . something. Snoring, the blankets bunched up where my mom should've been.

But there was nothing. Absolutely nada.

No one in her bedroom, her bed, her bathroom, her closet. I even looked under the goddamn bed, because you never knew. I was hoping.

I raced down to the basement. Nothing.

I still turned on every light in every room, even in the freaking closets.

The same. Nothing.

The back patio. Some nights she would sit out there with her laptop and a glass of wine, and I held my breath as I climbed the stairs. But to no avail. Even before I opened the back door, I knew no one was out there.

I felt the dread stirring in my gut.

I had one last place to look, and going to the garage, I stood a moment in the doorway before I comprehended what I was seeing.

There were no cars.

My dad had the main one, but . . . our Tahoe was gone, too—the vehicle my mom used if she had to go somewhere on her own.

They were both gone.

She had left me.

After the whole no-more-virginity talk and everything . . . well, there hadn't been a talk. She'd sat and cried until I got uncomfortable and started to slip away. She asked if I wanted something to eat. I told her no and changed my mind later.

I went back down to the kitchen, but she wasn't there. I'd heated up some food—who knows how long it had been in there—but nothing else looked good to me.

It made me wonder if she been gone this whole time. Had she already gone then?

I was walking back to my room to get my phone when I saw the answering machine blinking. I usually ignored the messages. They were always for my parents, but what did I have to lose? Maybe she'd called and left me a message?

Hitting the button, I heard, "You have one new message, sent from Charlotte Malcolm."

I moved closer.

"Hey, honey. Your cell isn't working for me, for some reason. I went to the store to get some food. We only have old pizza in the fridge, but your father called. Something came up. I'm heading into the city tonight. Be a good teenage daughter. No sex. I'm sure Ryan will sneak over, and that's fine as long as you guys sleep. Only sleep. You got that, right? And go to school tomorrow. I'll leave work early to pick you up before going to Robbie's. I love you, and—" The message clicked off.

I hit the next button, skipping to the message after hers, but it was someone for my dad.

I don't know how long I stood there.

She hadn't left me. She'd called. She remembered me.

She was gone for the night because things came up. That made sense.

The three little pieces, which had started to splinter apart again, started to settle back into place. They were still intact.

I took a calming breath.

My hands were sweating. I rubbed them down my lounge pants.

They still cared.

She still cared.

A soft knock came from the door, and I looked through the window.

Ryan had arrived.

CHAPTER
TWENTY-FIVE

I was barely sleeping when I heard a soft thud.

Sitting up, I felt Ryan's arm tighten around my waist, and I paused. His breathing was still even. I hadn't woken him. Gingerly slipping out from underneath his arm, I crept out of bed.

There were two nightlights set up in the hallway, one at each end, so I could walk toward my parents' bedroom without needing to turn a light on.

Shivers moved down my spine as I padded away from my room.

Thud!

"Shit."

I paused. That was my father. Frowning, I moved closer. Their door wasn't closed. It was open two inches. One of the lamps was on, and as I peered inside, my dad walked past me, heading for the bathroom.

The bed was made. No one was sleeping. Instead, piles of clothes were all over it with a bunch of boxes set around the room. Some were open, and some were already closed. They had been moved closer to the door, as if ready for pick-up.

My dad came back out of their bathroom, his arms full of toiletries. He dumped them into one of the boxes and tossed some of his shirts on top before closing it.

"What are you doing?" I moved inside, opening the door wider.

My dad cursed, whirling around. He ran a hand over his face. "Holy shit, Mackenzie. Warn a dad next time, would you?"

I ignored him, focused on the boxes. "What are you doing?" Were we moving?

I knew we weren't.

That wouldn't have made sense.

"Oh, honey." A whole new voice came from him—the one I'd heard when he told me we were moving to Portside.

I started shaking my head.

"Where's Mom?" I asked.

"She's . . ." He took a breath, looking around, and his hand went to his hair. "I can see how this looks, but—"

"It isn't that? You aren't moving out?"

My eyes met his, and I knew it was happening.

I could feel Willow behind me, but she was quiet. For once.

"No." His shoulders slumped suddenly. His hand fell to his side. A look of sadness flashed in his eyes.

I didn't feel sorry for him.

A foreboding dread sat at the bottom of my sternum. It wouldn't move so I could breathe easier. It was blocking everything, and I felt like I was going to throw up.

"What are you doing? No bullshit, Dad."

He gazed around the room once more and gave me the strangest look, like he was seeing into me.

"I'm moving out."

I didn't know if I should be relieved or sad. I was neither. I just was. I nodded, looking away.

This made sense.

Grief tore families apart. Didn't a brochure tell me that one time?

I hugged myself, half turning away. "Are you leaving Mom or are you leaving us?"

He didn't respond at first, and I knew the answer.

I wanted to turn completely away, give him my back, but I couldn't bring myself to do it. I could feel his gaze.

"I'm moving closer to Robbie."

So he was just leaving Mom and me.

I knew Robbie was at a school and that he seemed to be enjoying it. I knew it was probably good for him not to be living in this dead house, but that was all wrong too. He should be at home. My mom should be there too. My dad shouldn't be leaving.

I shouldn't be left alone.

"Mac?"

And the award for best timing ever went to Ryan.

The floor creaked from down the hallway.

"Who is that?" my dad demanded gruffly. "Is that a boy?"

I wanted to roll my eyes. I refrained. Barely. "You're leaving us. What do you care?"

His mouth closed with a snap, and his Adam's apple bobbed. I could see him thinking about it, and that was when I noticed the graying hair at his temples. There was more around his ears. The bags under his eyes were epic, and I could've sworn his wrinkles had doubled since this summer.

My dad wasn't an old man, but he was close to resembling one.

"Mac?" Ryan's whisper was a lot louder. He was right outside the door.

"Who are you?" my dad demanded.

Ryan opened the door and looked at him but had no other reaction. He knew what he was walking into.

"Ryan Jensen, sir. You work with my father." His shoulders were firm, and he didn't slouch as he spoke. He wasn't going anywhere.

That was when I knew for sure. He had come for me, no matter what happened after this.

"Oh." My dad lost all of his fight. "That's right. Your father talked to me, mentioned you and my daughter were friends." He looked between the two of us, lingering on my tank top and shorts before going to the lounge pants Ryan wore. He had pulled on a T-shirt.

My dad rubbed at one of his eyebrows. "You're sleeping here, Ryan?"

"Yes, sir."

"He's sleeping with you, Mackenzie?"

I nodded. "You know he is."

"No. No, I didn't." His tone was quiet. "Your mother's been in touch with Nan. I'm assuming that's what you're talking about? Your mother knows?"

I nodded again. Why did it feel like I couldn't swallow anymore?

Silence filled the room, and Ryan moved closer to me. "Are you okay?"

My dad started laughing and turned toward one of his boxes.

I shook my head, my gaze holding Ryan's, but I said, "My dad is moving closer to Robbie."

Ryan didn't respond. He wasn't there for the details. He was still waiting for my cue, if I needed him to stay or if he could go.

I hadn't made up my mind, so I didn't answer.

My dad resumed packing, his shoulders tight, and he flung a hand up, knocking his tie over his shoulder.

He was still dressed for the office. I hadn't registered that before. It seemed pertinent for some reason.

"It's almost three in the morning," I murmured, half-asking myself. "Why haven't you changed clothes?"

Had he gone somewhere after work? Was he going in to work early?

Willow snorted behind me. *I doubt he's even going to work, sis. You aren't paying attention. Smell, Mac.*

Smell what?

Him. You aren't wearing vanilla perfume, and I don't think your honey is either.

I felt choked, like someone had reached around and tightened their hold on my throat. She was right.

There was a distinct smell, but it wasn't vanilla. It was lavender. He smelled like flowers.

I turned to Ryan.

My mom wore a citrus perfume. She hated lavender.

"Mom said you wanted to meet up in the city. Was she wearing perfume when you saw her?" Somehow, I doubted that was hers. My mind was putting two and two together faster than my emotions could, and I felt myself weaving on my feet.

Ryan moved closer, resting his hand behind my hip. His touch steadied me enough to keep me from falling.

"You're seeing someone else."

My dad whirled back to us. The blood drained from his face, and then his eyes found Ryan's hand.

"Get your hand off her."

I ignored him and surged forward. "Who is it? Who are you leaving us for?"

"Honey." He flinched as if I'd slapped him across the face.

"Does Mom know?"

His shoulders slouched, and his head hung down. He balled up the shirt in his hand, holding it against his chest. "She knows."

He couldn't look at me.

He wasn't just leaving us; he was going to someone else.

A new family.

Willow and I thought the same thing at the same time.

My stomach twisted, and I could feel the bile rising

"Who?"

"You won't know her, honey."

He was speaking in whispers. I wasn't. My voice grew firmer with each question I asked.

"Who?" I might not know her, but maybe Ryan did. "Is it someone you work with?"

It had to be.

He'd only worked since Willow. And he went to see Robbie, but that was with my mom. Right? They went together?

"Mackenzie, we can talk about this late—"

"WHO?"

I didn't need Ryan to help hold me up. Rage was doing fine all on its own.

"Mackenzie, honey . . ."

My nostrils flared. "I said who. I want to know who!"

His mouth clamped shut. His hands went to his hips, the shirt too, and he regarded me. It was as if the air had turned solid between us, and my question was like trying to cut through it with my bare hands.

So be it. I wasn't afraid of blood. Anymore.

I took a step closer. "Who, Dad?"

"This isn't the time to talk about this."

"You tell me or I will make your goddamn life hell."

Our eyes locked, and he seemed to be weighing whether I meant my threat. I did. I *so* did.

He let out a sigh. "Her name is Mallory Lockhart. And yes, she works with me."

I didn't look back, but I sensed Ryan's surprise.

"You're moving in with her?"

"I . . . yes. At least for a while. Your mother and I talked about everything earlier tonight."

I couldn't fathom any of this. My mind went blank, and I pushed forward. I needed to get as much information as I could.

"Where's Mom right now?"

"She's at a hotel near Robbie."

That was three hours away. I wouldn't be going anywhere except to school tomorrow.

"And that was a lie? You saying you were going to move closer to him?"

"No. Well, yes. Mallory's home is closer to the city and closer to Robbie." He coughed. "I don't think your mother is going to be home tomorrow. Are you, I mean . . ."

I looked up. He was watching Ryan with a hard expression. "What?"

"You'll be okay to fend for yourself? At least for a few days?"

I laughed then.

I knew everything I needed to know.

No Robbie tomorrow.

No Mom tomorrow.

No Dad until who knew when.

I didn't answer my dad. I turned, my hands brushing against Ryan's as I did. It was as if I were watching us from outside my body. It was the three of us again.

I left.

Ryan went behind me.

And Willow brought up the rear.

COUNSELING SESSION FOUR

"You told me a bit about Willow last time. How about you today?"

Naomi's smile was nice and bright, and I wanted to scratch it off her face. She folded her arms over her lap and gestured toward me, her smile trying to make me feel like we were friends.

"Your mother called. She said you're seeing a boy. What's his name?"

A heavy silence. I was becoming so used to them; they were my real friends in this room. I smiled and leaned forward. "We fucked."

That nice smile-that-was-not-really-my-friend vanished. "What?"

CHAPTER TWENTY-SIX

Mallory Lockhart was thirty-seven. Her relationship was complicated, and she was an ads manager at West Coarse Technology. She had brown hair, a heart-shaped face, hazel eyes set a little too close together behind wire-rimmed glasses, perfectly trimmed and arched eyebrows, and a petite and compact body.

Her bachelor's degree was from West Scottridge University.

She'd shared five puppy memes over the last day, three sarcastic quote memes over the last week, and she had more than two thousand social media friends.

She'd recently gotten a golden retriever named Bugsy, and she was "excited to have her new pup for a new chapter in her life."

I leaned forward to see the timestamp on that last post. It was four days ago, posted at 7:03 in the evening. I scrolled through the comments.

"Love you!! So proud of you."

"Big hugs, babe xoxo"

"Can't wait to meet Bugsy!"

"Adorable! Yay!" (insert a gif of a puppy tearing up a pillow and then falling backward off of a couch.)

Heart emoticon heart emoticon heart emoticon heart emoticon

"Wonderful to hear. So happy for you."

I stopped reading them. Apparently, all her friends were ecstatic for her. I wanted to piss on each one of them.

Fuck them. Fuck her. Fuck my dad. Fuck them all.

That "new chapter" wasn't just about a dog. I bet they didn't know that. Maybe I should educate each one.

"Are you still cyberstalking her?" Cora asked as she dropped into the seat next to me in our school library.

Still. I almost laughed at that, but rage had been a firm friend since last night.

I hadn't slept after Ryan and I went back to my room. He had, but I couldn't. I went right to the computer and got all the information on my dad's mistress. I knew her mailing address and her birthday. I had figured out her family members. I knew where she had gone to high school and college. And Google had helped me guess at her annual income.

But none of that told me why.

Why my dad? Did she pursue him? Did he seek her out? How did they meet in the first place? A joint project? Did she work with him on projects? Had they started flirting at the water fountain? Coffee hut, maybe?

I hated her.

I didn't know her, but I hated her.

I looked over at Cora. I'd given Ryan the task of questioning his parents about Mallory Homewrecker Lockhart, but I needed someone as crazy as I was with the stalking skills.

"I want to drive to her house and slice her tires," I told her. "No, no, I want to drive to her house, ring the doorbell, and make her as uncomfortable as she's made my family hell." Which would be a lot.

I didn't need Willow to call me out. I was projecting everything onto this mistress, and I knew it.

I didn't care.

My dad was grieving. He was supposed to go to my mom for that.

Pot meet kettle.

Okay. I heard Willow there. Our family sucked all around at comforting each other, except that my mom had actually decided to be a mother. She went above and beyond. I got a text saying the visit to Robbie had been postponed and she knew I'd talked to my father. She promised to speak to me later because she knew I would have questions. And if all that wasn't enough, she'd called Ryan's mom.

I was supposed to stay at the Jensens' for the rest of the week and weekend, but not in Ryan's bed. I was to go home after school, pack a bag, and Ryan would drive me to his house.

I rolled my eyes when I read that last text. Such a silly (or delusional) mother, acting like I was in third grade and she'd arranged a weeklong sleepover. I'd go over to Ryan's, but probably not in time for after-school snacks. I'd go when I wanted to go. Sometimes she forgot I'd actually turned eighteen.

I rolled my eyes and clicked on the mad icon under one of Mallory's posts.

Cora leaned forward and laughed under her breath. "You're in your sister's Facebook account. That's creepy and hilarious at the same time."

I felt Willow's pride and shrugged. "She'd think it was awesome."

Cora looked at me, her gaze lingering, but I ignored it. I kept scrolling through more of Mallory's posts to put the mad icon on all of them.

"She'll know it's you. You know that, right?"

She would, and I grinned. "She can prove it."

Cora shifted back. "Dude. You look evil right now."

If she only knew what went on in your head.

I ignored Willow and clicked the mad icon under another post.

"That's a Pinterest meme on DIY Halloween decorations."

I kept scrolling. "My dad hates Halloween. She should know that."

Cora laughed again, but the sound was becoming less amused and more cautious.

I couldn't be bothered with any of it. I was a madwoman on a mission. If my mom wasn't going to rage about this whole situation, I was. Willow would've been going nuts. She would've screamed, demanding answers. She would've been on the phone, calling the mistress and our mom at the same time.

She would've burned our house down—figuratively . . . I think?

I waited to see if Willow had anything to say, but she was quiet. Come to think of it, she'd been quiet more and more lately.

I'm taking on her personality.

That was why. Willow was living through me, so she didn't need to—and the bell rang.

Thank the gods. That stopped me from having a whole conversation in my head about why my dead sister wasn't talking to me anymore . . . in my head.

Cora grabbed her bag and stood. She hugged it against her chest as I clicked out of everything on my computer. "Everyone is going to Patty's for lunch. Are you going too?"

I grabbed my bag and began walking out of the library. "Who's everyone?" I asked as we got to the door.

She ducked out behind me. "The guys. Ryan, I think. Erin. Her group." She shrugged. "I don't know. The popular people."

Ah. Popularity.

The stuff normal teenagers cared about.

I glanced over at her, but she wasn't looking at me. "I'm not popular."

"Yeah, you are."

"No." I shook my head. "I'm not."

"Yes, you are. Trust me. You are, even if you don't know it. You're with Ryan, and the other girls are scared of you."

They should be. There were two of me, and one of us could haunt their asses. I snickered at that but didn't reply. I wasn't popular, and I didn't care. I hadn't cared in Arizona, and that hadn't changed. Ryan was the only benefit of moving.

I stopped in the middle of the hallway. Some students protested behind us. I ignored them.

Cora had taken a step forward, but she stopped and looked back.

"Is that why you wanted to be with him?" I asked.

Her eyes enlarged, and her mouth made a popping sound. "Uh, what?" She adjusted the bag in front of her, hugging it tighter.

"You want to be popular?" I shook my head. "But aren't you? You're friends with those guys. Shouldn't that make you popular too?"

A strangled squeak left her throat. "This is so embarrassing."

"Why?"

People were trying to press around us. One guy cursed at us, then saw me and coughed to cover it up. "Sorry. Hey, Mackenzie." He was gone before I could say anything, but I could see the back of his neck turning red.

"See? DJ Reynolds has no idea who I am. That would not have happened with me." She pointed in the direction he went.

"No, I'm not. I'm . . ." *Damaged. Broken. Half-dead. Having sex*—make that I *had* sex. Once. I was sexually experienced, kind of. "This is not normal me. Trust me. Normal me is not popular. Normal me . . ." I hesitated, but normal me was like Cora. Somewhat.

Everyone likes you, Mac. Get over yourself. You never have to try for anything.

Willow had said to me the day we found out we were moving. I flinched when I remembered.

She had been so wrong. She was the one everyone liked. Even my two best friends had dropped me because they missed her so much. Didn't she get that? Had she really not gotten that? She was the star.

I looked away. "Normal me was invisible. Trust me."

I was wrong. I hadn't been like Cora. She cared the way Willow cared, but Willow had succeeded. She'd thrived with the social hierarchy stuff.

I needed to stop thinking about Willow.

I felt her snort and thought to her, *Sorry, but you make me slightly deranged.*

Only slightly?

Cora and I needed to get moving. The next bell would ring soon, and I clamped on to her arm. She was watching me with her head tilted to the side, but I wanted to make sure she heard me.

"I lost my sister. My brother moved to a different school, and I found out last night that my dad is leaving our family. If I could switch places with you, I would. I'm not saying you don't have problems or struggles. Everyone does, but I'm saying rethink what you want. If you want to be popular so much, forget it. It isn't worth it."

She looked down, but I heard her say, "It isn't worth it to you."

"It isn't worth it to anyone."

That would be utopia. If everyone was kind, if everyone was worthy. If there were no hatred, pain, or suffering. If people couldn't see someone's skin color, quality of their clothes, where they lived. If nothing mattered except the heart and mind.

I wanted to live in a world like that. I could almost taste it, I wanted it so bad.

I gentled my tone, "If I'm popular, then trust me. I'm miserable. You aren't. I've seen you with the guys."

The second bell rang.

I was late, but as I turned down the empty hallway, which was thankfully empty, I looked back. Cora hadn't moved, her back toward me.

Hope fluttered in my chest. It was small, but it was there.

A fourth piece inside me found the other three. They fit the right way.

CHAPTER TWENTY-SEVEN

Cora acted differently the rest of the day. I don't know why it made me feel good, but it did. We went to lunch with everyone else, taking seats in the booth next to the guys. When Erin and her friends came over, Cora didn't react like she normally did. She didn't get all nervous. She didn't start fidgeting. She didn't jump when Erin said hello.

She was cool. There was a confidence radiating from her, and I knew the guys took note. Erin too, with a slight frown as she went back to her table of friends. The guys kept sneaking looks at Cora on the way back, and for the rest of the day.

I wasn't sure if Ryan noticed anything. He was more perceptive than people realized. He just hid it better.

Kirk nudged my shoulder in our seventh period.

"What?"

He pointed his pencil at Cora, who was filling out the worksheet we'd all gotten. "What's going on with her?"

As if hearing him—and she might've—she straightened, holding her head high. If she'd been wearing a crown, it would have remained firmly in place, not like the other times when she'd duck her head or hunch her shoulders.

I almost smiled with pride, but I shrugged instead. "I don't know. She looks sexier than normal, doesn't she?"

Ryan glanced at me, a strange look on his face.

But Kirk was studying Cora, and he nodded. "Yeah. She does." A mystified expression flitted over his face. He nodded again. "Yeah."

He grabbed his worksheet and bag and left our table. Sliding into the seat next to Cora, he nudged her arm.

I felt Ryan's gaze on me, but I bent over to finish my worksheet.

His foot went to the book rest underneath my seat, and he pulled my chair toward his. He drew me close enough that our legs pressed against each other's. "What happened there?"

I shrugged. "Beats me." But I was grinning. I almost felt silly. Something felt right. For once.

Ryan didn't push it. I knew he'd ask later, and I'd tell him. Cora was his friend. He'd be happy.

After a few more minutes, I stopped trying to fill out my worksheet. My concentration was useless, so I sat back and studied the way Cora and Kirk were half-flirting/half-studying each other. They both knew something new was happening, but neither fully understood what it was.

Ryan gave me the answers for the few problems I didn't have done, and after class, I hurried to catch up with Cora.

I bumped into her arm, grinning.

She looked over and ducked her head, but I saw her smile.

"So." I jerked a thumb toward Kirk, who was headed toward his locker. "What was that about?"

"You know." She weaved over, deliberately bumping back into me. "I took your advice to heart."

"That you aren't miserable?"

She laughed, shaking her head. "No. Well, yes." We veered toward her locker.

I went with her and Ryan passed us, moving toward his. But he looked back with the same questioning expression on his face.

Later, I mouthed, and he nodded, stopping at Kirk's locker first.

"Do you like Kirk?"

She'd never talked about him, just about Ryan.

"I don't know." She opened her locker and began to put her books into her bag. "Maybe. I mean . . ." She paused, looking at him as he joked with Ryan. "After Ryan, he's the hottest guy in school."

She stared at him, really stared at him, and let out a sigh. "What am I doing? He made out with the Bellini twins last night. He'd never be interested in me."

I frowned as I really looked at Cora.

She was a little smaller than me. Her brown hair was pulled back into a messy bun with some fraying ends framing her face. Aqua eyes. A fair complexion under a smattering of freckles. She wasn't beautiful in the heavy-makeup kind of way. She was pretty in a natural way.

She was kind, shy, and loyal. I never heard her say anything negative about her friends. The only person she'd been negative about was Erin, but that made sense. She was terrified of the girl.

There was no reason Kirk wouldn't want to be with her.

"He'd be nuts not to want you," I told her.

She fixed me with a dark look. "Come on."

"I'm serious. I mean, I'm taking inventory. If he doesn't want to date you, the only reason would be because he wants to keep fooling around with people who aren't girlfriend material. Sorry, Cora, but you're dating material. And he was interested. He asked me what was different with you today."

"What'd you say?" She was so still.

I leaned against her neighbor's locker. "I told him I didn't know, but you seemed sexier to me. He agreed."

Her mouth almost fell open and color splashed across her cheeks. "He did?"

"Yeah. He did."

She ducked her head again, sneaking a look at him.

Ryan and Kirk were both watching us.

Kirk was staring at Cora like he'd never seen her before. Ryan watched me with the same expression. It took me a second to place it, because it was different. His eyes were locked on me, his mystified expression from before mixing with a look of approval. Then it hit me, and I almost fell back against the locker behind me.

I was the old me.

This was something I would've done.

I would've helped a friend who needed a pep talk. There might've been a guy I helped steer in the right direction, and I would've been at that friend's locker talking to her about the guy. This was the real me. It felt good. I mean, it felt weird, but it felt right.

Ryan was seeing this side of me for the first time.

I pulled my gaze away and glanced down.

Willow was with me. I felt her, and I waited, expecting her to say something. She didn't. She remained quiet, and I couldn't help myself.

Really? I shot at her. *You don't say anything this time?* And like she was really standing there, I heard a huff right before she turned and walked away.

She left me. I was struck speechless a second.

"You okay?"

Cora had shut her locker and had her bag over one shoulder. She was waiting for my response.

"Oh yeah." I stood straight. "I'm good."

My ghost of a sister left me, and I didn't want her to go.

I'd gotten used to her haunting me.

CHAPTER TWENTY-EIGHT

"What was up with you and Cora today?"

I knew this question was coming, and I looked over to Ryan in the driver's seat. He'd asked me where we were heading after school, and he hadn't flinched one bit when I said, "My dad's mistress's house." He hadn't questioned how I knew her address.

I rested my head back against the headrest and smiled. I hadn't needed a PowerPoint presentation to get him to be a stalker with me.

But I did need to answer his question. I gazed at him as we drove down the highway, the wind whipping his hair back.

How could I explain that I'd only said a few words to Cora, but it seemed to have helped? Or how much that meant to me for some stupid reason?

How could I tell him Willow had left me today, and I ached at her absence?

How could I—*Dude, stop. Talk to him.*

I almost grinned, hearing my sister's voice again. It settled me. "I don't really know," I said aloud.

Ryan frowned as he rolled up his window. The wind noise faded, and it seemed intimate in his truck. "What'd you say?"

I cleared my throat, sitting straighter in my seat. "I don't really know. That's what I said."

"What does that mean?"

I shook my head a little. "She was telling me that I'm popular, and I told her to go jump off a cliff." *Same sentiment. Different words.* I shrugged. "I'm miserable—" Ryan turned to look at me for a second. "Being popular isn't worth it."

He was still frowning, but he nodded as he went back to watching the road. Flicking on the turn signal, he merged into the passing lane, and we moved smoothly, seamlessly around a white car.

"Kirk thinks she's hot," he said. "Was that your doing?"

I turned to sit almost sideways, as much as my seatbelt allowed. "Cora used to like you until I came along. Is there a part of you that wishes she still did?"

I stared at him hard.

He threw me an annoyed look. "That's what you got out of that?"

"You're annoyed with me."

"Annoyed?" He flashed me a cocky grin. "No, never annoyed. I've started to be able to read you and figure out where you're going, but this thing with Cora threw me. That's all. I'm not worried about Cora or Kirk. If Cora's new confidence is attractive to him, I hope she keeps it up, and I hope he doesn't hurt her. I'm more worried about you."

"Why? I'm fine."

I was. Totally sane.

I was fine that my mom wasn't home again. I was fine that I wasn't driving to see Robbie today. I was fine that I'd lost another member of my family.

Yes. It was all copacetic with me.

There were no slightly psychotic tendencies at all.

My nails sank into my arm. I didn't pull them out, even when I felt a trickle of blood. It felt good, refreshing.

Thirty minutes later, we turned off the interstate and Ryan glanced down. "Holy shit! Mac!" He reached for my arm, and I pulled my nails away. Five indented pockets had formed, and blood flowed from all of them.

He cursed under his breath and hit the turn signal, veering into a gas station parking lot. "What the fuck just happened?" Slamming to a stop in front of the building, he threw open his door. "Get out. We're getting that fixed."

He held my arm, locking the door with his free hand and pocketing the keys. With a firm hold, he led me inside and asked for the first aid kit. The gas attendant eyed me warily but handed over the kit and said the bathroom was in the back.

We started down an aisle, and he barked at us, "I meant outside."

Ryan glared at him. "Thanks. Your sensitivity is commendable."

The attendant shrugged and grabbed some smokes for another customer.

Ryan's back hit the door hard, and he continued to pull me with him, glaring over my head.

There was a metal picnic table around the corner near the hose. Ryan went there instead, patting the top. "Hop up."

He placed the kit beside me, and as I sat, that numb feeling came back. It was like a blanket encasing me, shielding me from the real pain going on. The nail cuts weren't even a blip on my radar.

One of the four pieces loosened. It was going to fall away.

I frowned. "I was getting better."

Ryan was hunched over, cleaning out my cuts. He paused, straightening to meet my gaze. "What?"

"I was getting better." My head felt so heavy suddenly.

I was sleepy. I bent forward, my forehead resting on Ryan's shoulder.

"She went away today, and there were four pieces," I mumbled against his shirt. "They all fit. I was getting better."

Ryan went rigid and slowly, agonizingly slowly, reached up to cradle the back of my head. "Who went away?"

"Willow."

But that wasn't completely right. She'd spoken to me, hadn't she? That had been her in the car. Right?

He was like a statue. "Willow's been with you?" His voice sounded rough.

I nodded, straightening. It hurt to look at him. The sun behind him was so bright that it made me tear up. "She left me earlier, but she talked to me in the car."

"She talked to you?"

"Once."

That had been her? The question was still bugging me.

"She's been talking to you?"

His hand moved to my neck. He traced some of my hair, smoothing it over my shoulder. Bending forward so only a few inches separated us, his eyes found mine.

I looked away. I couldn't look him in the eyes. I didn't know why, but I had messed up.

I wasn't able to think clearly. What did I say wrong?

Willow, what did I do?

I felt a tear slide down my face. "She won't answer me."

"Willow won't?"

Willow . . .

I shook my head. "She's gone."

I wanted her back. My heart clenched. I wanted her back. I wanted to talk to her again, feel her again.

More tears slid down my face. "Ryan, where did she go?"

He stared at me, his pupils dilated.

Willow. I wasn't supposed to talk about her. But she was gone again.

I crumpled inside. I felt myself curling into a ball, and Ryan cradled me to his shoulder once again.

I cried while my arm bled.

CHAPTER TWENTY-NINE

The sanity ship sailed. I'd officially snapped.

I was talking to dead people, seeing dead people—and I wasn't psychic.

Ryan drove me to Mallory the Homewrecker's house. He'd cleaned up my arm after I got myself back together, but I kept using my arm to clean my tears. So the bandage was soggy, and blackened from my makeup.

Going up to the door, Ryan knocked. His other hand laced through mine.

I considered lifting my bag and saying, "Trick or treat," but the door opened, and nothing came out of me.

The woman gasped, seeing me.

"Is Mr. Malcolm here?" Ryan asked.

Her hands shot up to cover her mouth. She matched her pictures on Facebook, but she was even prettier in person.

I hated her.

My hostility helped push away some of my craziness, and I was able to stop some of the tears—some of them. I was still sniffling like a crack head.

She eyed me for a moment and leaned forward. Comprehension flared, and she stepped backward. "Phillip!" she yelled over her shoulder before turning back to me. "You're Mackenzie."

I didn't answer. I summoned all my energy into a glare. I wanted to give her the full force of Willow and me. It was only right, since she was missing out on the more wrathful one of us.

She sucked in her breath, her mouth twitching down.

Footsteps came from behind her, and she moved back. My dad filled the doorway, frowning at her and then us. "Wha— Mackenzie?"

His gaze switched to Ryan, whose hand tightened around mine. "Can we, uh . . . can we come in?"

I don't know why Ryan brought me there—if it was closer than a mental hospital, if he didn't want to deal with me, if he wanted to pawn me off on my dad. It could've been any of those reasons. When I'd realized where he was taking me, I had tried to pull my hand from his in the truck.

"No, Ryan. Take me where I need to be to get the right help. Going to see her won't do it. I was wrong."

He hadn't let me go, and he'd pulled our hands from the console between us into his lap. "We're going to see him." His voice was gentle but firm, and his eyes were tender as he looked at me. "And that is where you'll get help. Trust me."

His gaze almost sent me off on another crying escapade, not that I had really stopped. But as he kept holding my hand, a fifth piece had melded with the others. I didn't know why, or how, but it had happened. I was coming together even as I was falling apart.

Go figure that one out.

"Yes. Come in, come in." My dad ushered us in, his hand falling to my shoulder. I heard him murmur to Mallory, "Can we use the screened-in porch?"

"Yes. Sure, sure. Anything you need."

"I'm sorry."

I stiffened and whipped around. "Yes." My tone was scathing. "Please, Dad. Keep apologizing. Tell your whore you're sorry we showed up here because I'm losing it over my dead sister. So goddamn sorry to inconvenience you."

"Wha—"

She turned to my dad, but he coughed, interrupting her. "We'll be outside if you need me."

"Phillip."

His hand tightened on my shoulder, but Ryan tugged me out from beneath my dad's hold and led me toward the back patio.

He opened the glass door and shut it behind us, leaving my dad behind.

I took the seat farthest away, and Ryan sat beside me.

He didn't reach for my hand again, and I didn't know if I wanted him to. He watched my dad and Mallory talk just on the other side of the door.

His hand went to her arm, but she pulled away. She looked out at us with angry eyes as she said something else to my dad. His shoulders drooped, and she crossed her arms over her chest, disappearing down a set of stairs.

"I might be crazy, but I don't think your dad is with her like that."

I grunted. "Trust me. No one will be calling *you* crazy."

He grinned at me, leaning back in his chair. "You know what I mean."

"Still no. You're amazing. Not crazy."

Raking a hand over his head, my dad regarded us through the glass doors. I noticed his clothes. Sweatpants and a thermal long-sleeved shirt—he paused just outside the door to slip his feet into a pair of black slippers.

A low growl started in my throat.

"Where's your robe, cigar, and newspaper?" I asked as he opened the door. "You look more at home than you ever did at the new-new house."

He stiffened and then stepped out and shut the door behind him. I looked for the bags under his eyes that I saw last night, but they were gone. The bastard looked almost refreshed.

"You're angry." He sat across from Ryan.

I snorted. "What gave it away?"

Fuck him.

He got the new job.

He wanted to take it.

He made the decision to move.

He was the one who brought us to this town.

I leaned forward and hissed, "You promised us a better life."

He looked at the floor.

Ryan coughed, sitting forward too. "Uh, Mr. Malcolm?"

He was a lot nicer than I was.

My dad looked up, and I saw the anguish on his face. It was real and genuine. He mirrored everything I was feeling inside. Torn and twisted.

The bags under his eyes might've disappeared, but a grayish tint had settled under his skin, making him look almost half-dead.

He tried for a kind smile. "Yes, Ryan?" The smile faded fast. It'd been only a small blip.

"I don't know my place here, but I feel like I should speak up about something."

This was it. My heart started to press into my chest. He was going to tell him about Willow. I was slipping to the mental side.

Ryan folded his hands together on the table, and looked at them. "I've been spending a lot of time with your daughter— enough to know I shouldn't have been."

What?

He looked up then, staring right at my dad and not looking away. "I'm aware of the hell your whole family has been put through, but if you were still doing your job, your daughter wouldn't have been in my bed half those nights she was."

Good Lord. What in all the Willows was he doing?

My dad's face went flat. "You think so, huh?"

"I know so, sir."

"You think you know how I should've been parenting more than I do?"

Ryan didn't flinch, grimace, cringe, or look away. His tone was soft but strong. "When it comes to Mac, yes."

My dad was the one who twitched. My nickname acted like a repellant. I could almost see my dad shriveling, and I knew he was going to make an excuse, stand, and ask us to leave.

It was coming . . .

He sighed, leaning back in his chair. "Maybe you're right."

Uh, what?

I sat straighter in my seat. I hadn't heard that right. I should've been halfway to the door by that point.

"I *have* been messing up this whole time, and it takes a seventeen-year-old to set me straight." He laughed, the sound bitter and weak.

"I'm eighteen." Ryan grinned, shaking his head. "Not that it matters."

"Oh. Well." My dad tried to grin back, humoring him. "That one year makes me less pathetic, I'd say."

I didn't know if I should laugh, make an inappropriate joke, or what? Dissolve into tears again? What would Willow do?

I'd attack, sweet cheeks. I could hear her again, and I relaxed.

"Willow talks to me," I announced.

They both looked at me.

I kept on, needing to do this. "She's around me all the time. I have conversations with her. I dream of her. And I hated it at first. I didn't want to think of her, feel her, hear her, but she wouldn't go away. She haunted me, until today." My voice broke and I let my eyes drop. "She went away today, and I fell apart." *Keep going.* "I hate her, and I love her, and I need her. But Dad . . ." A break. My throat ceased to work, just for a moment. "You're the one alive. I need you more, and you left." I wasn't talking about just the night he moved out. "You stopped checking on me. You stopped knowing where I was." I faltered again.

I heard sniffling and my dad clearing his throat over and over again.

"Mackenzie."

His chair scraped against the floor. I couldn't look up. I didn't have the heart, and then I felt his arms around me. He knelt beside me, holding my head to his chest, and he took a deep breath.

"Mackenzie, I am so sorry." His arms tightened around me.

I could've fallen apart then. I could've stopped, contented myself with the confessions I'd given, but that wasn't all the truth inside me.

"I couldn't bear to see myself, so how could I make you look at me?" I whispered.

I missed her.

I wanted her.

I didn't want my dad's arms around me.

I wanted *hers* around me.

"I don't want her to be a ghost, Dad."

"I know." He patted my head and pushed back some of my hair like my mom used to, like Willow did at times. "I know. Trust me." His voice grew thick and hoarse. "I miss your sister so much that I can't bear it some days."

It was right to be crying to my dad. But he wasn't the one I needed. I thought it was him. I thought it was my mom. It wasn't Robbie either.

There was one person I needed to hold me, and she couldn't.

I pulled away from my dad, and he framed my face with his hands. "I'm sorry, honey. I'm so sorry." His hands fell from my face to my shoulders, and he pulled me back to his chest, wrapping his arms tight around me.

I looked at Ryan from within my dad's hold, and he must've seen something in my eyes because he leaned forward in his seat again. "Uh, Mr. Malcolm?"

My dad eased back. "Yeah?"

Ryan watched me, and I nodded to him, smoothing out my shirt. There were stains everywhere.

"What's really going on with you and . . ." He gestured inside. "Oh."

My dad looked at me, and I tried to smile. "I'm fine."

He still paused.

"Really," I added.

"Okay." He sat in the chair closest to me and ran a hand over his face. "I'm not cheating on your mother. Mallory is a work colleague, and I came here because we have a project that needs to be finished as soon as possible. We've been working at it all day and had to call in more people to help. We have to work around the clock, and—" He looked up and found the clock on the wall. "We might get interrupted shortly. More of our colleagues are supposed to be coming here. They're coming straight from the office."

"You told me you were leaving us. You said you were leaving us for her."

"I did, but I'm not." He didn't seem flustered by the accusation in my voice. "I mean, I said I was moving closer to Robbie, and that's the truth. Your mother is with Robbie today, and I'll be going tomorrow. Coming here wasn't planned until my boss called me last night while I was on the highway. I thought I was cleared for the day off. That didn't happen."

I shook my head. "Why did you tell me you were leaving us for another woman?"

"Because it made sense. That's what you thought, so I just let you." He took a breath, started to say something, and took a second breath. "I was working yesterday with Mallory, but that's all it was. Work. And your mother and I *are* separating, but I'm not leaving her for anyone. I'm here for work, only for work. And I *am* moving closer to Robbie, at least until your mother and I work things through."

I could feel Willow railing inside me, but I had enough clarity to know it wasn't really her. It was me. It was the part of me that was still connected to her.

"None of this makes sense," I snarled. "You aren't making sense. You or Mom." I leaned forward. "I get it. I'm not talking, but neither are you. Why is no one talking?"

I was yelling.

"Fucking start talking! Talk TO MOM! TALK TO ME! TALK TO—I DON'T CARE! TALK TO A FUCKING COUNSELOR!"

No one told me to lower my voice. No one hushed me.

And if they had, I would've turned on them.

This was my anger. It was deep and unhealthy, and I had it in excess.

Calm down, Mackenzie, I told myself.

A beat of silence passed on that porch.

We heard the doorbell ring. Mallory came up the stairs, glancing to us before moving toward the door.

More people were arriving. They flowed in, wearing work suits and business skirts. My dad hadn't lied. They looked like they'd come straight from the office.

He hadn't lied.

He hadn't lied.

Shoving my chair back, I pulled my feet up and hugged my knees to my chest. I rested my head against them and breathed.

He hadn't lied.

When I didn't say anything more, Ryan said, "Maybe we should go?"

I nodded, moving my head against the tops of my legs.

"Are you going to be okay, Mac?"

God. He used her nickname—but that wasn't fair. Everyone in my family had called me that. It'd become *her* nickname for me since—I felt the anger and hysteria rising up.

"You want to go?" Ryan leaned closer to me.

I lifted my head, feeling raw and stripped bare. I nodded again. "Yes."

Ryan took my hand and led me back through the house. My dad followed us, saying something to Mallory as he passed. All of their people had gone downstairs where she'd been earlier.

"I'll be right there," he told her. "Give me a moment with my daughter."

He stepped outside to the front steps with us, closing the door firmly behind him. "They ordered food from the office, so we might get interrupted again." His eyes fell to me.

It was hard not to see my dad's suffering. He looked closer to sixty than forty.

"If you need me, I'm here," he said. "I will drop everything and come to get you. I mean it."

I'd needed him when Willow died. I'd needed him all the months in between, and I would need him until I was an adult. But how could I say that when he was choosing work today? Could I even say that?

Yes, you can.

Fuck it. "I need you at home, with Mom, with Robbie. I need my family back together."

He winced, but he didn't look away.

I waited, staring at him.

Then he nodded. "Okay. I'll call your mother. We'll make it happen."

I looked down and saw how white Ryan's hand was. I'd been squeezing too tightly. Relaxing my hold, I gave him an apologetic look. He shook his head. He didn't care.

"You're okay to head back to the house?"

I turned back to my dad, and I felt that fifth piece.

"Yeah. I'm okay." And like that, a sixth tagged along.

We were starting to go when my dad asked one last question, "Did you troll Mallory's Facebook account?"

CHAPTER THIRTY

Ryan drove us back to my house.

It was dark, but I knew my mom would still come back tonight. Ryan asked if I wanted company till then, and I told him no. It felt right—the most it had in so long—for me to go inside, do my homework, and hope to get in trouble for still being up whenever my mom came home.

I kissed him and said, "I'll be okay." And I meant it. I gave him a smile before heading inside.

The house was cold when I got in, so I kicked up the heat and ordered a pizza. After that, I did what I would've done last year.

I did my homework at the kitchen table, paid for the pizza when it came, and I had half of it eaten by the time the garage door started to open. I was getting up, intending to pour a glass of wine to further mess with my mom, but as I reached for the bottle, I heard his voice.

My heart stopped.

"Mackenzie!"

I whipped around, my feet moving before I realized it.

I was halfway to the garage when the door flung open. Robbie threw himself at me.

I caught him and held him up. It'd only been a month and a half, but I swore he'd gotten bigger.

"Robbie!"

"Heya, sis," he mumbled into my neck, his arms wrapped tight. One last squeeze, and then he pulled back.

I didn't want to let him go, but I had to. I kept my hands on his arms and set him to stand on his own feet. "You look so big. You're tall too."

He was an inch shorter than I was. I looked at our mom. "Is that normal? How tall is he now?"

She laughed, coming inside with a pizza box and two other bags hanging from her arms. "Well, he shot up half an inch, but I don't think he's the one who changed."

I frowned at her, eyes lingering on the pizza box.

"You lost weight!" Robbie nearly shouted. "I got taller, but you got smaller." He could wrap his fingers around my arm, or the bottom of my arm. My bicep still had some muscle to it.

I shrugged, grinning stupidly. "That's probably going to change." I pointed to the pizza I'd ordered.

Our mom started laughing. "I got confused for a second." She held up the one she was carrying. "Robbie insisted on stopping and getting you food. He was worried." She gazed at him, her eyes softening. Everything about her softened. "I told you, you didn't have to worry."

He smiled. "I'll always worry." Then he tightened his hold around me again, hugging me. "I've missed you, Mac."

I hugged him back, closing my eyes. "Me too."

If I could've held him all night, I would've. It was as if he wasn't just my brother anymore, but half me, half my son, half my responsibility. Or that might've been Willow's influence. She was gone, and I didn't want to lose anyone else, ever again.

"Okay." Mom clapped her hands, pushing her sleeve back to peer at her watch. "It's close to midnight. Robbie, you don't have school tomorrow, but you need to go to bed. And Mackenzie . . ."

I waited for her order, my arm resting around Robbie's shoulder.

She paused, staring at us and rubbing away a tear. "We have lots to talk about, but you do have school, and you aren't allowed any more skip days. Off to bed, and no boys sneaking in. Got it?"

She was pretending to be the stern parent. Robbie and I both saw right through the act, though.

We nodded, and Robbie went first, hugging her before running upstairs.

"Take your bag!" she called after him.

His footsteps pounded back down the stairs. He grabbed a bag and gave us a huge smile. His cheeks were flushed. "I forgot." Then he was off again, pounding the stairs as if he had never been gone in the first place.

I felt her hands first, a soft touch as she pulled me in for a hug. "Are you okay, honey?"

I didn't know for sure, but I felt a seventh piece attach to the others. Fitting right.

I hugged her back and whispered, "Please bring Dad home too."

"Oh, Mackenzie."

I wasn't the only one who'd lost weight. Her almost-frail form shook in my arms. She smoothed a hand down my back, brushing some of my hair.

"I will. I will." She coughed and leaned back, holding me like I'd held Robbie moments before. Her eyes traced all over my face. "Please be okay. Please."

My throat swelled, and I blinked a bit at that. Shocked.

I nodded. "I'm trying."

"Okay." She tugged me back for another hug. "And I mean it; no Ryan tonight."

I nodded again, and with a soft smile and flutter in my stomach, I went upstairs after my brother.

I was getting ready for bed, or at least curling into bed with my Kindle, when there was a soft tapping sound.

I almost went to the window, thinking it was Ryan, but my door creaked open.

Robbie poked his head around the corner, his hand still hanging onto the doorknob. "Hi."

He might've been eleven, but he was three in my mind. He was still my little brother.

Feeling everything melting inside, I patted the bed next to me. "Come on."

A big, wide smile appeared, and he hurled himself onto my bed. Scooting under the covers, he laid his head on my second pillow and gave me his toothy smile.

This guy—he owned me. I balled up a fist and pretended to punch him in the stomach. "How's it knocking, little brother?" Instead of hitting him, I began tickling.

He laughed, shrieked, and twisted around, but he looked over his shoulder when I stopped. I started tickling his side, and cue the shrieks and laughter again.

"Hey! What are you two doing?"

Robbie was breathless, panting as we heard Mom yelling from downstairs.

I chuckled and then yelled back, "Robbie won't get out of my bed! Mom, come make him."

His mouth dropped and he sat upright. "She's tickling me, MOM! It isn't true!"

We could hear her laugh, and I closed my eyes for a moment. This was what I had needed all summer long.

My mom was laughing.

Robbie was laughing.

I was smiling.

And Dad was coming home.

We're going to be okay, Wills.

She didn't answer, but I knew she wouldn't, and I didn't need her response. I already knew she was happy for us.

The tickling continued until Robbie yawned, and I started to feel bad that he was still awake. It was long past his bedtime. Hell, they came home after his bedtime. After a minute he curled up with my blanket. Without asking, I brought up one of his favorite books and began reading to him.

Five minutes later, he was sleeping soundly.

He had the entire blanket wrapped around him. I didn't have it in me to wake him or carry him to his own bed.

Sneaking around my room, I checked my phone. There were a couple of texts from Ryan:

Ryan: **How's it going?**

Thirty minutes later.

Ryan: **Finished my homework. Want to talk for a bit?**

An hour after that.

Ryan: **I'm hoping everything's good on your end. I'm heading for bed.**

And ten minutes ago.

Ryan: **I think I'm in love with you.**

Ten seconds ago.

Ryan: **Goodnight.**

I almost dropped my phone, but with my heart pounding its way to my eardrums, I texted back.

Me: **Goodnight. I think I—**

"Robbie's sleeping?"
I jumped. The phone flew in the air. Stifling a curse, I caught it, and my hand hit the send button.
Oh no!
Shit, shit, shit.
My mom stood in the doorway, frowning as she watched me.
"I—hold on." I glanced over, but Robbie was still sleeping. I moved closer to the door. She moved back, and I followed her out. She closed the door with a soft click, and I checked my phone as she did.
Oh my God.

Oh my God.

That text had gone through. I hadn't answered, and—I couldn't think.

"What's wrong?" Mom looked from me to the phone.

"Nothing." I held it behind my back. "I didn't have the heart to take Robbie to his room, and I've missed him. A lot."

She nodded, resting against the wall. Her arms crossed over her chest, and a tear slipped down her face. "We worried whether seeing you was good for him or not." She gazed at my door. "I think we did more harm than anything. I'm sorry we kept you guys apart."

They'd done this on purpose? I had wondered that, but to hear it confirmed . . .

"I thought he wanted to stay there?" I was gutted and reeling. How could they do that?

"He wanted to stay, but he wanted to see you too. I don't think he wanted to come back here."

It was a new house. Willow didn't have a room there, but her things were still with us. My mom had hung her pictures on the walls. As if feeling her presence coming from them, we both looked over.

Willow smiled back at us from her junior-year school picture. She'd straightened and brightened her hair so it was almost platinum blonde. She had it pulled over one shoulder, her head tilted to the side as she flirted with the camera. A coy smile on her face, she looked on the verge of bursting out laughing.

"Oh, honey." My mom reached out, wiping a tear from my face.

She was still crying, and I realized I couldn't be angry with them. We all tried to cope in our own way, whether wrong or right, healthy or unhealthy.

"I'm going to go back in to sleep."

She nodded, pressing a kiss to my forehead. She rested her cheek there. "Be safe and be smart. Okay, Mac?"

I nodded, looking up at her. "Don't take him away again. I mean it, Mom."

She pulled back. She started to nod, but then she did a double take. Mine was not an idle threat. She'd find out what would happen if she did.

I moved back into my room and texted Ryan back.

Me: I want to say things to you, but not till tomorrow. Let's talk in the morning?

Then I checked to make sure my alarm was set, put my phone on silent, and grabbed a second blanket. Curling up next to my brother, I closed my eyes.

Ryan said he loved me . . .

CHAPTER THIRTY-ONE

Ryan was waiting for me in the front of the school the next morning.

He had texted earlier to see if I needed a ride, but I'd said no.

"Okay, honey." My mom put the car in park. Her eyes looked past me to where Ryan was waiting, and she sighed. "That's Ryan?"

"Yeah."

"He's handsome, isn't he?"

"Mom!" The back of my neck got hot.

She grinned, ducking her head. "What? I have eyes. I'm not blind." She bit her lip and narrowed her eyes. "Have you guys been sexually active since that first time?"

Yep. My neck was definitely burning up. "You're killing me here."

She rolled her eyes, tsking me under her breath. "You're so dramatic." Her grin softened. "Keep it up. I know Willow would be ecstatic for you."

"Mom." I looked down at my lap, tugging at my backpack's strap.

Why'd she have to bring Willow up? All it brought was different feelings, the twisty and angsty ones.

"But I mean it, no more sex."

She was trying to be stern, and she was serious about the sex, but I could tell part of her was trying to move on. There was no real oomph behind her words. I'd still been awake when my dad got home last night, and I heard them talking for hours after that. When Robbie had started tossing back and forth, I'd shut my bedroom door and turned on my fan to drown out the last murmurings. I was able to sleep after that, and I was pretty sure my mom had been sporting a little glow this morning at breakfast.

There was a bit of a spark in her, but she couldn't entirely mask the big hole that was still there. I saw it, because I felt it too. We all did. Robbie had it in his eyes.

"Mackenzie."

She'd been waiting for a reply from me.

I blinked a couple times. "What?"

"Tell me you aren't going to have sex again."

"Ever?" I reached for the door handle.

"Ever."

I began to edge out of the vehicle. "Come on, Mom. You know I can't promise that."

She frowned. "Mackenzie! Don't you shut that door before—"

I shut it, bent, and waved at her with a bright smile plastered on my face. "Love you, Mom. Be safe. Have fun with Robbie."

"Mackenzie!" she shouted again, but I was hurrying across the sidewalk and lawn toward Ryan.

He grinned as I joined him to walk toward the doors. A bunch of students were lingering out front. Most seemed to be talking, but a few were riding skateboards up and down the main sidewalk in front of the school.

I didn't usually enter the school this way. The parking lot was in the back, so I knew that side would be three times as busy, but this still seemed too busy for the conversation I knew Ryan was waiting to have.

This conversation was the real reason I'd stayed awake as long as I did.

Ryan stopped to lean against the building and nodded at my mom as she pulled away from the curb. "Your mom isn't working?"

"Robbie's home, so she took time off. She asked this morning if she could drive me in."

He nodded. "You need a ride home then?" He shifted, turning to face me and resting his shoulder against the school's brick exterior.

This felt weird, and I frowned.

"What?" He straightened, but the movement drew him even closer.

My backpack hung behind me, and I fiddled with the strap like I had been in the car. I fingered the shredded ends and, without thinking about it, began shredding more of it.

"I got your text last night."

He grunted. "Which one? I sent you four."

"All of them."

He was silent a moment. "I see."

No. No, he didn't. He was guarded, and I could only guess as to the reason, but I knew he had no clue what was going on with me.

I took a breath because I needed some extra air. "You don't know. You don't see everything. I got your text, and I . . ." How could I explain this? I didn't even know if there were words. I had to try. "I'm reserving the right to respond."

His eyebrows went up. "Say what?"

I flushed, feeling the heat scorch my cheeks. "You told me the L word, and I was ecstatic to read that, but it wasn't fair. I'm . . . I'm behind you."

His hand rested on the wall, and he moved forward, leaning over me, and I moved so my back was against the brick. I gulped, my throat and mouth suddenly dry. His hazel eyes locked on mine, starting to smolder.

God.

I'd forgotten how tall he was.

"Have you gotten taller?" I asked breathlessly.

A smirk pulled at his lips, and he shifted again. His hips were almost touching mine, but he still braced himself with a hand above my head.

I was fast forgetting what I was going to say, and I wet my lips. "Ryan."

"Mmm?" His eyes were on my mouth.

I touched his chest but pushed him back an inch. "You're making me not be able to think."

His free hand went to my waist. "Is that a bad thing?" He didn't move back. I could feel his chest moving up and down with shallow breaths and his muscles shifting under my touch.

He was as affected as I was.

"You're reserving the right to respond to my text."

"Yes." I nodded again, trying to clear my head. I was remembering the first time he'd kissed me at the college party, when we'd kissed again in my theater room, and how he'd felt sliding inside me. "I'm a mess."

He chuckled, and good gracious, even *that* was a caress.

"Ryan," I murmured.

"Yes?" He dipped closer.

I closed my eyes because I could feel him, his breath on my face. I felt him straining under my hand, holding himself back, and I couldn't help myself. I moved my thumb side to side over his chest. It was a small touch, but it elicited a groan from him.

"You want to take this somewhere else?"

Yes! But I groaned. "I promised my mom I wouldn't skip."

"And that's important."

It was. Wait, he was agreeing with me?

I opened my eyes, and he was right there. If I tilted my head a fraction, he'd be kissing me.

What had I been saying before? It felt important, too important to go a day without saying.

I was a mess. Yes. That was it.

I began again, clearing my throat first. "Things are just getting to be a little normal at my house. I don't know if it's going to last or what's going to happen, but I've been a mess." I still was. The hole was still there. She was still gone. I kept going before a different ache had me sobbing in his arms. "I'm trying to tell you that—" I flattened myself back, giving me an inch, and I looked up to his eyes. "When I return your text, I don't want it to be because you said it. I want to feel it, and I want to mean it, and I want . . ."

Some of the smoldering dampened. "You don't feel it?"

I pressed my hand against his stomach. "It isn't that I don't feel it; it's that I have too much other stuff going on inside me. My parents are home today. Robbie is back today. Willow . . ."

My stomach knotted, but it was too important that he understood what I was saying for me to stop. "I've been trying to ignore that she was gone." I've been trying to ignore a lot of things. "I used you to do that. I skipped school to run away. I tried tequila." *Deep breath, Mackenzie.* My heart beat in a rapid staccato. My hand wrapped around his shirt and tugged. "There are layers of pain inside me. Pain that I can't put into words, and underneath it all is hell. It's raw and bloody. Agony. Suffering. Torture."

And denial. That lined the bottom of me. It was a dark, black hole.

His hand curved around my waist, but the touch took on a different feeling. It was more soothing than sensual.

"I can't text you that back because it isn't fair to you, or me. I want to say it when I'm feeling that and only that. Willow's gone, and I'll always feel as if half of me has been ripped away, but I know someday those wounds might heal over. I'm not saying I'll completely be right one day, but I'm saying that until most of those layers of pain have gone away, I can't say it back. There isn't enough room inside to say it back. Not yet."

I pulled him against me, feeling his surprise before he caught himself so he wasn't crushing me against the building. He put an inch of space between us, but that was too far in my mind. I wanted all of him against me, his whole body plastered against mine.

That soothed me, but I wanted more than soothing.

Ryan's hand cradled the back of my head. His thumb brushed over my cheek. "I know what you're saying, and I'm not mad."

"You aren't?"

He shook his head, his eyes firmly attached to my lips. "When I texted you that, I knew you couldn't say it back. That isn't why I sent it. I pressed send because it felt right to tell you. I wanted you to know, but I get it. I really do." He groaned again and dipped down. His lips finding mine for a brief second before he pulled away.

I went with him, arching on my toes, not wanting to break the kiss.

He rested his forehead to mine, his gaze boring into my eyes. "You say it when you can, and I'll still be here."

An eighth piece fit with the other seven.

Five hundred ninety two to go, but it was good. So much good.

I tugged him back to me.

CHAPTER THIRTY-TWO

Two months later

COUNSELING SESSION FIVE

I sat on Naomi's couch, and she took the seat across from me.

To say I'd been a participant—willing or otherwise—in the first four would've been an outright lie. I'd walked out of the first one. I'd refused to talk the second one. The third session lasted a few minutes longer as I recited obvious facts, like that Willow had died. And I'd dropped the bombshell about Ryan and me in the fourth one.

Naomi smiled at me. I saw the caution there and felt a little remorse.

She was in her mid-thirties with a medium complexion. Her black ringlets framed her face today as she'd let it hang loose. Some days they were slicked down with product, but today they were a little frizzy and free.

I liked how they looked. They seemed to match all the freckles on her face—almost like they didn't want to be tamed. They wanted to be themselves.

I could relate. Somewhat. Okay, not at all. The counseling sessions had been the only limitation put on me by my parents since WWD, except lately. They had given me too much freedom in the beginning, but after everything blew up, it was starting to be the other way around.

"How are things going at home?"

I'd been waiting for Naomi to speak, and I looked up. I was somewhat surprised. She usually came at me friendly, but with a determination to get me to talk. That wasn't what I heard today.

She sounded curious.

Some of the tension left me, and I found myself answering. "Better."

Her mouth dropped open, but she coughed and smoothed out her shirt, sitting more upright in her seat. "What do you mean by better?"

I told her.

I didn't see why I shouldn't start being honest, at least a little. I still didn't want to talk about Willow, but a conversation about my family was something else.

When I was done, I glanced at the clock. That had taken me twenty minutes. She'd sat in silence the entire time.

"In my work, I've learned that families either come together in times of severe grief, or they fall apart. The fact that your father was leaving doesn't strike me as uncommon. The fact that you stepped forward, you said something, and everyone listened to you is *not* common." She stared at me. "You changed the narrative. Do you realize what you did?"

I frowned. I didn't know what she was talking about, and I was starting to wish I hadn't said anything.

"You helped your family, Mackenzie."

"What?"

"You spoke up, and your parents listened to you. I've had other children in here because of grief. In some cases, they didn't speak up, or if they did, no one listened. I can only speculate as to the reasons your parents were going to separate, but you said your father moved back home?"

I nodded. "He's been home since the day I talked to him. My mom too."

"Is your little brother at his school again?"

"He's there during the week, but he comes home on the weekends."

We had movie dates every Saturday afternoon.

Her hands rested on her knee, one on top of the other, and she leaned even closer. "I don't know your sister. I never met her, but I can tell you this one thing: she would be proud of what you did."

The session turned awkward after that, at least for me.

Naomi said a bunch of nice things about me, and I tried to change the topic every time. A joke. A debate. I asked her ridiculous questions about why she didn't have more plants in her office. I even tried to piss her off. I told her if she didn't stop praising me, I'd feel like I was being propositioned and could report her. She only grinned and went right back to telling me all the good things I'd done since Willow died.

She was wrong.

Everyone was wrong. I knew my parents looked at me a little differently since the whole Mallory-stalking/yelling-at-my-dad event. It was like they were seeing someone new.

I didn't understand it, and I didn't like it.

And there was one other topic I didn't want to talk about, and so far, Naomi hadn't brought it up.

She did when I was leaving this time.

"Mackenzie."

I was at the door and I paused, looking back. "What?"

"We have to talk about your sister's suicide note before I'll sign off on these sessions."

Yeah. That.

CHAPTER THIRTY-THREE

"How was your session yesterday?"

I jumped, and my hand hit my locker as I whirled around, but I shouldn't have been surprised.

Ryan and I had talked a little last night on the phone, and I knew he would seek me out today. This was the new normal. Things were returning to a more regular schedule at home, which meant my mom stayed home twice a week. She reserved the right to drive me to school those mornings, and this was one of them.

Cursing, I waved my hand around.

"Shit." Ryan touched my arm and leaned forward to inspect my fingers. "I didn't mean to scare you."

I tried for a smile, but it felt like a twisted clown grimace. My fingers really hurt. "Oh. No problem. It was my bad. I was zoning out."

He ran his thumb over my knuckles. "You jammed two of your fingers. I can reset them, if you want. This happens all the time with basketball."

Oh God.

My knees wanted to crumble because it hurt so bad. I jerked my head in a nod, bracing my other hand against his shoulder. "Okay. Do it."

"Yeah?"

"Yea—"

He pulled, and I screamed.

"AH!" I did crumple this time. Grabbing his arm, I caught myself.

People were watching us, and I was being a bit overdramatic, but I was happy. I could be dramatic about this. *This* pain would go away.

"You okay?" He ran his finger over mine and murmured, "All better now?"

I tensed, waiting for the pain, but none came. I moved my fingers around, bending and wiggling them. "No. It's fixed. Thank you."

A cocky smirk came over him. "I found my calling. I'm going to be a doctor. I like fixing girls and having them swoon over me."

I hit his shoulder with my other hand. "So hilarious."

He chuckled, his eyes darkening.

I straightened, responding to him. That throbbing need began to build, and I leaned toward him.

"Yo."

Kirk, Nick, and Tom sauntered over to us.

Kirk held his fist up, and Ryan met it with his, turning to rest against the locker behind me. His hand moved to my waist as he nodded to the others. "What's up?"

"We're having a party after your first game, right?" Kirk was the spokesman. He glanced to Tom and Nick, who both nodded.

Ryan's hand flexed on my hip, but his tone remained casual. "Yeah, sure. Your place?"

"I can throw it. That's no problem." Kirk looked at me. "You coming, Mackenzie?"

I looked at Ryan before speaking. "I think so."

"I gotta ask because you've gone all goody-student lately. No skipping. No drinking. You haven't partaken in our parties, and we haven't had to interrupt you and Romeo here during any PDA. What happened?"

I'd started healing. "Things got better at home."

Things weren't a hundred percent. That wouldn't happen. But they were definitely over the fifty percent mark. One day, I figured I'd have to claw my way higher. It would suck. There were layers in me even I didn't want to share, but I'd have to deal if I wanted to get up there.

I was okay where I was for the moment.

I settled back, moving to lean fully against Ryan as he talked over my shoulder with his friends. His hand on my waist moved behind me, and I felt it slide under my shirt, rubbing up and down. It felt good, calming.

We stayed like that until the warning bell rang and everyone dispersed. It was nice to have just the guys at my locker. That wasn't a normal thing anymore—there were almost always girls around too. If it was Kirk standing with us, sometimes Cora would come over. Kirk would throw an arm around her shoulder and talk to Ryan while flirting with her. Sometimes, Erin approached, and if she came, her friends followed behind. Things were still tense between us, but she'd been giving me a stiff smile or hello lately, and sometimes I gave it back. She didn't deserve my friendliness, in my opinion, and it'd be a long day in hell before she and I became anything other than civil to each other.

After seventh period ended, Ryan caught up to me at my locker. "Are you sticking around during practice?"

I switched out my books, putting the ones I needed for homework into my bag. "Yeah. My mom and dad are going to a counseling session tonight."

"So we can hang out afterward?" He moved in as I closed my locker, tugging me close so I was almost resting against him. I felt him through my jeans. He was already hard, and I knew what else he was asking.

Feeling my body warm, I grinned at him. "Oh yes."

"Yeah?" His eyes were teasing, a twinkle in them. He tugged me closer, closer, closer until every inch of my body was plastered against every inch of his.

I could feel his breath against me, and I murmured back, "Hell yes."

I felt him smiling before he kissed me.

A loud slam sounded right next to us, and Ryan's head jerked up. His hands tightened on my waist as he growled, "What the fuck, man?"

The guy grinned at us as he bounced a basketball. He threw it at the locker on our other side, moving down the hallway. "Want to make sure you're coming to practice," he called over his shoulder.

"Now I might not."

The guy caught his basketball and stopped in his tracks. "You serious, man?" His fingers tapped on the ball.

I didn't know who the guy was, but it wasn't a stretch to guess he was a senior. No junior would've talked to Ryan like that.

"I'll come when I come." Ryan pushed away from my locker, standing in front of me. His shoulders were rigid, and he kept a tight grip on my hand.

Kirk and Nick materialized from behind us, moving in to flank Ryan.

Kirk's hands shoved into his pockets. "What's the deal, Wachowitz?"

"My deal is Jensen. He's more interested in getting laid than getting to practice."

A low growl came from Ryan, and he started forward.

Nick held his hand up, halting Ryan, but he was speaking to Wachowitz. "You might want to watch your words. Ryan hasn't missed one practice this week, and he's already captain. You know he has a say in who gets nominated."

"Team nominates the co-captain."

Nick's grin went wide, and his head cocked to the side. "But Ryan gets final say. If he doesn't like you, he isn't going to pick you."

Wachowitz's stance grew less intimidating. His head lowered, and he stuffed one of his hands into his pocket. "You serious?"

Ryan released my hand. He passed both his friends, moving purposefully. He went up to Wachowitz and shoved him against the locker. "I don't give a rat's ass if I'm captain or not. You come at me like that again, and I'll get your ass kicked off the team."

Kirk and Nick pushed forward, standing close behind Ryan.

Wachowitz swallowed, his Adam's apple bobbing up and down, and he moved his head in the same motion.

"Yeah, man. I apologize." He held his fist up, but Ryan ignored him.

Meeting my eyes, Ryan spoke to Wachowitz, "Do it again, and we'll have more than fucking words. Got it?"

Wachowitz's gaze jumped to mine, and he swallowed again. He didn't say anything else, only turned and disappeared down the hallway. He didn't bounce the basketball against any more lockers.

"Well, that was fun," Kirk said as Ryan came back.

Ryan was still holding my gaze. I had darkness in me, but so did he. There'd been a few glimpses over the last couple months, but this was the first time I'd really experienced it. It was a window into how he'd been before I showed up.

A shiver went down my spine as Ryan bent to kiss me.

"I'll see you later?" he said softly.

I nodded, feeling all sorts of flutters in my chest.

He stepped back and clapped Nick on the shoulder. "Let's go. Wachowitz is going to have a hard practice today."

Nick's grin was almost evil. "Hell yes, he is."

They took off, but Kirk lingered behind.

"Basketball isn't your thing?" I asked him.

He laughed, shaking his head. "Sports in general are not my thing. I love to watch, bet on the game, hit on chicks in the bleachers, but that's it. You?"

Me?

Come on, Soccer Superstar.

I heard Willow calling me that again and found myself saying, "Soccer, actually."

"Really? It's a spring sport here for us. You going to play?"

I heard myself saying, "Yeah. I think I am."

I wasn't sure who was shocked more, him or me. Then again, I hadn't thought about sports since June twenty-eighth.

CHAPTER
THIRTY-FOUR

Bouncing basketballs sounded like a thunderstorm—with whistles shrieking, tennis shoes squeaking against the gym floor, and a whole ton of yelling. The smell of sweat filled the room, but someone had propped open the double doors so fresh air circulated through, along with the sound of dance music being played somewhere down the hall.

I'd gone to the bathroom and saw some of the dance team practicing a routine near my locker.

There were a lot of students out and about in the school, but I was one of the only audience members for basketball practice. The coach came in, saw me, and started to protest. I saw how his shoulders tensed, and he scowled, but Ryan ran over, with Nick and another guy hot on his heels. They talked to their coach and after a bit, his shoulders relaxed and the scowl flattened to a firm line of disapproval. He said something to Ryan, who nodded and ran back to his place for drills.

I went back to my homework, not making a peep, and finally practice ended.

The guys stayed around for a scrimmage game, and I sat and marveled at how damn good Ryan was. He'd been the first to finish the drills. He'd given the calls.

I mean, I could be biased, but he seemed to be the best at shooting, and he worked the hardest.

Wachowitz, on the other hand, was dragging. He'd been lagging behind half the team since the middle of practice. He missed a pass, and after he missed another, one of his teammates yelled for him to tag out.

He did just that, and the game kept going.

"Can I sit?"

I turned, surprised that I hadn't noticed anyone coming up the bleachers, and saw Cora pointing to the seat beneath me.

I nodded. "Sure." I moved down a little, giving her some space.

She sat, straddling the bench so one foot was next to mine and the other was below her. She watched the court. "I always forget how good Ryan is until I see him."

"Really?"

She nodded, her gaze solemn.

We watched the game for a moment. Ryan's teammates cut across the gym, and he passed to one of them. The toss was so fast that the ball was in his teammate's hands before he blinked.

She sighed. "Just get ready. It's about to be insane, especially with you being Ryan's girlfriend."

"What do you mean?"

She looked to me, almost reluctantly pulling her gaze from the court. "Ryan's nice and humble, not arrogant. People forget how good he is until the season starts. But they remember real quick. Friday night, after our first game, it's going to be insane. Girls will be throwing themselves at him nonstop."

Lovely. Willow had slowly stopped talking to me over the last two months, but I might have to pull out some of my inner Willow for this. Bitches might have to go down.

And as soon as I thought that, I was tired.

I was tired of the fighting, tired of the cattiness, tired of the way some girls seemed to hate each other just because.

"Don't you get sick of it all?"

"What?" Cora frowned at me.

I glanced over and saw that she wasn't the only one who'd come into the gymnasium once practice ended. A whole bunch of others had congregated beside the bleachers. Erin, her friends, Peach, some of the popular senior girls. There were guys with them too—half were talking to the girls, and the others shouldered past the group to sit on the first row of the bleachers.

I gestured to the group forming. "What you were saying—all the girls, all the fighting."

She stared at them and raised a shoulder. "I don't know. I don't really get an option, you know?" She turned back. "I feel like I have to fight just to have my friends notice me."

"Not Kirk."

She threw me a look, half rolling her eyes. "He noticed me because you told me not to give a shit. I didn't, and he came right over, but it hasn't been like that since. I give a shit. I don't know how not to. I'm not at the top of the food chain. I mean, look at him." She gestured to Kirk, who had his arm around Erin. His face was bent toward her neck, like he was nuzzling her, and she laughed. "He flirts with everyone, makes out with everyone—"

"Not when you're around."

She gave me another one of those "are you serious" looks. "I'm around right now."

"Bet he hasn't seen you yet." I flashed her a grin and hollered, "Kirk! Up here."

"Mackenzie!" she hissed under her breath.

Too late.

Kirk lifted his head, saw us, and a broad smile lit up his face. His arm dropped from Erin's shoulders. She shot me a scathing look as Kirk left her side and came darting up the bleachers to where we sat.

He dropped down next to Cora, straddling the bench like she was. She could've leaned back into him, and he eyed her backside like that was what he wanted.

"I didn't see you guys up here," he drawled. "What are you doing?"

Cora stiffened, pointing to me. "She's waiting for Rya—"

"I'm talking to you. I know what Malcolm's doing here." His eyes were steady on her.

I saw her blush; it traveled up her neck to her cheeks.

"I'm talking to Mackenzie," she said quietly.

"Interested in going somewhere and talking to me?"

Cora's eyes were glued to mine, and they widened. I watched as she sucked in her breath.

"What?" It came out as a strangled squeak.

Kirk snorted, moving up behind her so there was no point in her not leaning against him. If she didn't want to be touching him, she would have to move forward. She didn't.

He ducked his head so his lips could find her shoulder. "You heard me."

Another strangled sound came from her. She still didn't look at him, but she wasn't moving.

Kirk's eyes flicked up to mine in confusion.

The buzzer sounded, ending the scrimmage game. I nodded to Ryan, who was walking over to his bench. "I'll be taking off with him in a minute," I told them. "Go. Hang out. Have fun."

Kirk's grin widened. "Yeah. What she said. Let's hang out and have fun."

Cora was so stiff that when she nodded, it came out looking like a robot. "Yeah. Okay. Let's hang out."

"Great." Kirk was up on his feet, pulling her with him. "Tell your boy I'll call him later," he told me. He tugged Cora behind him, though she couldn't seem to stop looking at me. Her mouth hung open.

I waved at her, and when Kirk turned around, I gave her two thumbs-up instead. *Have fun*, I mouthed.

She flipped me the bird, but she was grinning.

I chuckled to myself.

The bleachers moved underneath me, and I looked up again. Ryan was loping up the seats, but he stopped and turned in the direction Kirk and Cora had disappeared.

"Did I see what I think I saw?" he asked.

"You think he'll hurt her?"

He looked at me, his eyebrows shooting up. "They leaving to mess around or something?"

I frowned. Was he clueless? "They're holding hands."

"Kirk holds hands with every girl." He thought about that and growled, "Except you. He better never touch you."

That made me feel good. "If she likes him, you think that's a bad thing?"

He sat next to me, straddling so one knee was touching mine and his other knee was behind me. He was sweaty and smelly, but neither mattered. I felt myself calming, just having him this close, and I was startled to realize I hadn't even known I wasn't calm until he touched me.

I relaxed into him, and he pulled me close. "I don't know. Kirk always had a thing for Cora growing up."

"He did? When did that stop?"

He didn't answer right away, and I turned to look at him more fully. He was suppressing a grin.

"When she started liking me."

I swatted his knee. "And you pretended to play dumb, didn't you?"

He shrugged, pressing a kiss to my shoulder. "I never liked Cora like that, but she never said anything. I would have been an asshole if I'd told her straight up not to like me."

"There were little ways you could've set her straight."

"I did. I dated other girls. I emphasized that she and I were friends, but that's all over." He hugged me close. His chin rested on my shoulder, and I felt his voice through his chest to me as he spoke, "Who knows? Maybe that'll be a good thing. I think Kirk actually does like her."

I was starting not to care, being in his arms.

"Ryan!"

And I was back to caring.

I looked down. Erin was waving at us—at him—wildly enough that her shirt rode up, showing off her midriff. I felt a growl forming, and Ryan bit back a laugh.

He nipped my shoulder. "Easy now."

"Right." I locked eyes with him. "Imagine me saying that to you about Wachowitz two hours ago."

He winced. "Sorry." Lifting his head, he called out, "What, Erin?"

She stiffened. That hadn't been the inviting tone she wanted, but she pushed out her chest anyway. "A bunch of us are going for pizza. You want to come?"

I waited to be included in the invite, but it didn't happen.

A full growl erupted, and I surged to my feet. "You did not do that, did you?"

I wasn't waiting. I started down where she was, and Erin squeaked, backing up.

I didn't know what I was going to do, but I wasn't going to let the insult stand.

"Hey." One of her friends backed up in front of her like she was going to block me. She waved her hands in the air. "Come on, Mackenzie."

I ignored her. I ignored everyone watching us, and I really ignored how I knew I was overreacting. But this was a personal affront.

How could I *not* react?

I went right up to Erin, and I kept going until she was backed against the gym wall. I slammed my hands against the wall beside her, trapping her.

My eyes were dead. I couldn't see myself, but I knew they were. I was channeling all the anger, grief, and sadness inside me, everything I'd started to suppress. I let it all up to the surface and turned every ounce of it on her.

"What do you think you're doing?"

She gulped, not daring to look away. "I was going to ask you the same thing."

"You ask your ex out for pizza while he's sitting right next to his girlfriend? When I'm right in front of you. What'd you think I was going to do?"

I felt Willow snort beside me. *It's because you've been nice. She's forgetting the crazy in you.*

Fine. I'd let her see how crazy I was, and I pulled back the last remaining wall. I let her see the girl who cyberstalked her dad's mistress (well, who I thought was his mistress) and showed up at her house. I let her see the girl who'd been talking, seeing, feeling, smelling her dead sister, and I let her see the girl who had yet to talk about what it was like to find her sister in her own pile of blood. That girl had never been let out, yet.

I let her see the darkness in me.

Erin had almost shrunk in half, starting to ball up, but I wasn't letting her go.

This was an insane scene. I was causing it, and I knew people were recording it on their phones. They'd talk about what a lunatic I was, probably talk about how Ryan deserved better, but I didn't give a shit. I meant what I'd said to Cora—you couldn't care. Once you did, they had you.

Are you really fighting them? It wasn't only Willow's voice in my head. It was Robbie's. It was my dad's. It was my mom's. It was mine.

Maybe not. Maybe I was fighting myself.

Maybe I was fighting something else entirely.

"I don't know, okay?" Erin yelled, throwing her hands wide and shoving me back.

I gave a step, but I didn't flinch. I didn't even feel it. I knew it happened because I heard the crowd gasp behind me.

"I don't know. All right?" She was heaving, her hands in the air, and she stormed at me.

I didn't move.

Not one goddamn inch.

She could've hit me, but she backed up at the last second.

I smiled. "You're a fucking liar. You know exactly why you did that, and you're lying about it right now."

"What? Are you going to hit me?"

I contemplated her question, my head moving to the side. "No, but if you hit *me* again, yes."

She paled at my words. I didn't think she knew she'd hit me.

"What do you want, Mackenzie?" She shoved some of her hair from her face.

"I want you not to hit on my boyfriend in front of me, or at all. I want you to stop thinking I'll take it. It isn't even him. You come after anyone I care about, I'm going to say something." I narrowed my eyes, moving a step closer to her. "I'm going to fight you, whether it's physical or verbal or mental. I've been through hell, so I have no problem reaching up and pulling you down with me. If you're looking for a girl to bully or intimidate, it isn't me."

She should've known this, but apparently she really had forgotten. It'd been months since our last real exchange. Or maybe she forgot in the rush of basketball? Cora had warned me, and maybe I was setting the precedent. Go after Ryan and expect a fight. No. That wasn't me. Girls would hit on him. If he indulged, that was his decision. I'd walk then. I wouldn't fight that, but this was a different situation.

"Was it even about him?" I asked her.

"What?"

"Just now. Did you really want Ryan to go for pizza with you? Or was it about me?"

She rolled her eyes. "Of course, it was about you." Her eyes moved past me, and I saw the group of senior girls standing there. "They dared me to ask Ryan for pizza and not include you."

They were testing me.

I kept my eyes narrowed and took a step toward them. "You'll have to excuse me," I called. "I've been preoccupied since coming to Portside. I have no clue who the 'leader' is here."

The girls were shocked, their mouths hanging open, except for one.

She pushed forward and pushed her hair over her shoulder. "I guess that's me."

"You have a problem with me?"

"Yes."

"Why?"

"Because of Kirk."

I was dumbfounded. "What?"

She exchanged looks with her friends before turning back to me. "He was talking to us."

"His arm was around her." I gestured to Erin.

She huffed and then shrugged. "But I was the one he was talking to."

"You're pissed at me because I called him over."

No. As she was talking to me, she kept looking at Ryan. This fight wasn't about Kirk. This fight was about Ryan. Cora's warning might've been more realistic than I realized.

"You are what's wrong," I said.

"Say again?" I saw the storm building in her eyes.

"You're what's wrong. You're saying this is about Kirk, but I think you're full of bullshit. You're going at me, and you're sending Ryan looks this whole time. This is about him, and why? Your ego is bruised because he isn't with you? Is that the problem?"

She shook her head. "You are unreal. You have no clue who—"

I stepped right into her face. There was an inch between us, and she stopped talking. I waited, watching as she struggled against moving back, but she didn't. She knew how this game went.

I was in her space. I could feel Willow riling up next to me. She used to live for this stuff, and a bleak part of me thought to her, *You've been silent for almost two months, and now you're back?*

I'm here because you need me here.

"You think you're going to win?" snapped this girl, smirking. She'd been at the pool party at Ryan's house, and later at Kirk's after we skipped. "I have friends. We can make your life miserable—"

"Do it." I included her friends, sweeping a look over all of them. "Cyberbully me. Text me *whore*, *skank*, whatever other fucking stupid words you can find that are beneath you. Do it. Send it to me. Call my house. Whisper to my mom about how she should wish her second twin would kill herself too."

I felt their surprise at those words. But I'd said it before. I knew it was out. They knew about Willow.

"Send me the emails about how I should die. Slice my tires. Slice my mom's tires. Write *loser* on my locker. Do all of it. I will fucking eat everything up. I will record your calls. I will screenshot your tweets. I will save every fucking email and forward it to our principal. I will turn every goddamn thing you do to me back on you threefold. I will make it so you bury yourselves until you're the ones getting called to the principal's office, where you'll hope the *best* thing that happens is being expelled. Do it."

I hated them in that second.

I hated what they stood for.

I hated what they did.

But it wasn't really them I hated, not even a tiny bit.

Erin wouldn't step up to the plate. Cora backed down right away. Even Peach had expressed her sympathy, but these girls—they were worth the fight.

I wanted this fight. I could breathe it in. It could be my purpose for living. But none of them replied, and I glimpsed Ryan in the back corner. I locked eyes with him, and just like that, the rage drained from me.

It left me weak, and shame bloomed in my chest.

I felt tears coming to my eyes, and I turned away.

It wasn't them I wanted to fight.

CHAPTER
THIRTY-FIVE

"Mom?"

My phone began ringing not long after my standoff with whatever-her-name-was, so I didn't have much time to dwell on how embarrassed I should be. Grabbing it, I moved out to the hallway and huddled against a locker with my finger in my ear so I could hear her.

"Yeah! Hey, honey. How was your day at school?" She didn't wait for my answer. "Listen, something's come up. Nothing bad, but your father and I are staying in the city tonight. We'll go to work like normal tomorrow, and then pick Robbie up for the weekend. We'll be home tomorrow afternoon."

Oh.

I felt someone standing behind me, and I knew it was Ryan before I looked. I was attuned to his presence.

I turned to face him, still leaning against the locker, and put my other finger in my ear. "You aren't coming home at all tonight?"

His eyes lit up.

I rolled mine, knowing what he had on his mind.

"Yes. I mean, no, and Mackenzie, please be good. Please, please, please, no Ryan in your bed tonight."

Wait—what was she saying? I leaned forward. "But he can stay over?"

I heard a long sigh from her end. "I really wish you'd make some female friends, but yes. Ryan can stay over as long as he doesn't sleep with you and there's no sex. Got it?"

I gave him a thumbs-up. "Yes. We got it. No sex, and he won't sleep in my bed."

Ryan was grinning when I hung up. "We're sleeping in the basement then?"

"Hell yeah."

He tugged me in for a kiss.

I let myself get lost for a few seconds before pulling away. My anger was still raw from the gym confrontation, but his touch helped calm the edges. I didn't feel so much like a combustible balloon—one prick and I'd explode.

"Thanks."

"For what?"

For making me feel sane again. "For not looking at me like I have two heads." I started to pull away, not wanting to see his response, but he tugged me back.

A fierce look filled his eyes. "Hey," he said softly. "I get it. Okay? You've only had words with a few girls. Kirk and I trolled for actual fights some weekends. It was stupid, and bad—really bad."

A slice of fear went through me at the thought of Ryan in a fight. "Were you hurt?"

His grin turned lopsided. "That was kinda the point."

"Did your parents know?"

He nodded. "I couldn't hide the evidence, but I stopped. Peach looked traumatized every time she saw me afterward. I couldn't do it after a while."

I was shaken by the thought, but I remembered how it had felt to square off against the girls in the gym. Flames started flickering, warming me. It was almost addictive, and so simple. Hurt or be hurt. Those were the options, and both were an escape from what I didn't want to feel.

I shuddered, feeling it starting to burn again. "Let's go." *Before I go in search of another fight.*

I didn't feel Willow beside me, but I heard her. *And you always thought I was stupid for fighting. You get the appeal now? You can forget yourself . . .*

They were her parting words as I walked away.

We went through a drive-thru for a couple of burgers. Ryan pulled up to the window and started fishing for his wallet to pay, but an older guy replaced the food attendant at the window. He shook his head, holding out the bag of food. "Not for you. Your food is always free during basketball season."

Ryan grimaced. "No. Thank you, but I'd rather pay, sir."

"I won't hear of it." He held the bag out and shook it a little. "I know you're going to take us to the championships again. This is an easy payoff. Take the food, Jensen."

I could tell Ryan was reluctant, but he took the bag. "Thank you."

The man nodded before pulling his arm back inside and letting the window close behind him.

Ryan didn't move forward, not at first. His head bent forward, the bag in one hand and his money in his other. "Fuck it," he growled.

There was a donation box for a children's hospital past the window, and Ryan stuffed the entire wad of cash inside before heading out.

I didn't say anything, only took the food from him so he didn't keep squeezing the bag. I understood—Willow was the artistic star, and Robbie is a genius. I understood the special favors that came their way because they were that: special.

"I know it may seem stupid, but—"

I cut him off. "I get it. I've seen it happen time after time with Willow and Robbie."

People like people who are deemed gifted, which was a good thing, but there were consequences to that too.

"It's starting. I like getting free shit, but after a while, there are hooks inside you, and you never know when someone's going to pull one." He paused at a stoplight and looked over. "Does that make sense?"

"Yeah." I said it lightly, but I knew how he felt. I saw it tear Willow apart some days. "People give you things and are nice to you, and it's wonderful at first, but there can be strings attached."

"Exactly." He rubbed at his chest. "You start to owe so many people that you lose yourself. It's a weird feeling, and I feel like a dumbass bitching about it. There's a reason I'm getting the free shit. I shouldn't be complaining too much."

"No." I turned toward the window, lost in thought. "I get it. I do."

Was that what Willow had been feeling?

Did she feel pulled in too many directions? Did she feel like she owed too many people? Or did that add to the problem?

"You okay?" Ryan asked.

"What?"

We had started to drive again, but Ryan was skirting looks at me. "Did I lose you just now?"

"Sorry. I . . ."

I needed to talk about her. I knew I did, but the words weren't there. I could think them. I could feel them, but the idea of saying them aloud filled me with dread.

I shook my head, turning back to the window. "No. I was thinking about something else. I hear you, though. Too many people wanting something from you can make you lose yourself."

CHAPTER
THIRTY-SIX

Ryan and I pulled the queen-sized mattress from one of the guest rooms out to the theater room. We'd fallen asleep watching a movie, but the credits had already rolled through and the screen shut itself off, so I didn't know what woke me.

I didn't need to go to the bathroom.

There was no chill in the room, but I sat up, the sheet falling to my waist. The mattress was on the carpet so I crawled to the floor before standing. Ryan was still sleeping. He was turned toward me, his arms curled under his pillow, and I watched the way his shoulders and chest moved with each deep breath.

I didn't want to be one of those girls who devalued themselves, but I didn't get why he cared. I really didn't. I was a mess, and yes, he said he understood. He said he'd been there, but I had baggage up to my neck, and I'd only dealt with the tipping point of it. There was so much buried deep inside me, buried so far down that I was half wondering if Willow's ghost had woken me. That made sense.

Willow and I had shared a Jack-and-Jill bathroom at the old, new house, and there was one of those in this basement. The two guest rooms shared it, but no one had used either of the rooms so far. This was the first night we'd even touched the room, pulling the mattress from the frame.

Maybe that was what had woken me. Awareness had tugged at my subconscious all night. Maybe it had finally rose to the surface. I left the theater room and went to stand in the doorway.

I could smell her.

She'd liked vanilla-scented perfume, and she'd mixed it with a lotion called Pink Promises. It always reminded me of a vanilla rose. I could smell it. The early morning sun wasn't up yet, so I didn't know what time it was. My guess was around four or five, maybe even earlier. The moon was still out.

I shouldn't go into that bathroom. I knew I shouldn't, but my legs weren't listening to me.

I was pulled there.

My stomach churned in its place.

I could hear her laughing. It was a whisper on the wind—but there was no wind, and I knew there was no whisper. It was only an empty room and me.

There was light coming from inside the bathroom and spilling out into the guest room.

The laughter faded, and a song took its place. Willow's favorite song.

I shook my head. Recognizing the song, I knew it wasn't Willow's favorite. It had only recently come out, and I'd heard it for the first time this morning. "Barbies" by Pink.

I heard the rest of the song play out in my head.

"Ow!"

I almost fell. That was Willow's voice, but it wasn't in my head. It sounded real. It sounded from the bathroom.

My knees were shaking as I stepped inside.

Willow was bent over, shaving her leg, her hair pulled up into a messy bun. She wore a tight top over cut-off jean shorts, and the radio on the counter was blasting that song.

I rubbed my eyes.

I was seeing things. I had stepped into a full-on hallucination, and my next stop would be the hospital.

Pinch yourself. You'll wake up then.

But as I reached over and pinched myself, I felt the pang. I wasn't dreaming.

Willow danced in place, that razor sliding up her leg in rhythm with the bass.

"Willow?" My voice cracked.

She looked up, a bright smile on her face. "Took you long enough. Jeez. Do you know how many times I've shaved my legs, hoping to get you down here? Too many, my sister, too many." She touched her leg where there was no shaving cream and rubbed it. "Feel it. Totally smooth. I don't even need to shave, but what do you do, I guess."

"This isn't real."

She straightened, putting the razor in the sink and cleaning it off. "That's what you think. It feels real to me."

"You're a ghost then?"

She tilted her head to the side, her messy bun tipping too. "No, I don't think so. I don't feel like a ghost."

"But I can see you. I can hear you." I could talk to her. I could smell her. If I reached for her, would I be able to touch her too?

Could I hug her, one last time?

She finished rinsing her razor and put it in the drawer. "You've been talking to me for months, but you keep thinking I'm a voice in your head."

She was. Wasn't she?

I rubbed my forehead, starting to feel some pressure there. "You're saying this is real?"

She held her hands up in a helpless gesture. "I'm saying why do you have to classify it? Maybe you're supposed to see me tonight? Maybe you're supposed to hear me at times? Maybe you're supposed to let me help you when I can, and maybe this is all your baggage trying to wake you up. Who knows? Who cares? You shouldn't. You aren't getting more messed up by talking about me. Trust me. You'll only get more fucked up by *not* talking about me."

I couldn't handle this.

Grief rose in me, sharp and hungry as it threatened to eat me alive. I felt it taking over me, taking little bites.

What was happening to me?

But then Willow was in front of me. She had crossed the room. A light came from behind her, and I felt its warmth on me. Her vanilla-scented rose infused my nostrils, and she was so real. Tears slid down my face.

I wanted her to be real.

I wanted to see my sister one more time.

"Ssshh." She touched my cheek, and all the pain was gone.

It was swept away, replaced with a warmth like sun touching my skin.

"Willow," I choked out.

"I know. I know." She traced her hand down the side of my face, tucking some of my hair behind my ear. "I know, Mac. I really do, and I am here. I am real. I'll always be here."

I was still crying. "You aren't really here. I can't laugh with you, grow with you. I can't—I'm alone, and you know it."

I didn't know when I'd be able to touch her again.

"Why'd you go?"

I couldn't bring myself to say the actual word for what she did, but I could see it all again.

My face: dark eyes, golden blonde hair, heart-shaped chin

My body: slender arms, long legs, and a petite frame

My heart: beautiful, broken, bleeding

All of it on the bathroom floor in a bloodied pile.

I was down there. I lay beside her, my palm in her blood, and my face turned toward hers.

"Don't. Don't, Mac." She tried to soothe me, pull me back. Her hands kept tracing down my face, trying to shake my memories. "Don't go there. Don't remember me that way. I was sick. I was sad. I was hurting, and I didn't ask for help. I was sick, Mackenzie. I was sick. You can't understand because I never told you."

There were warnings. I knew there had been.

Her dried puke on the toilet.

Her exercising at midnight.

How she cried when she got an A- on a test. Her spending whole weekends in bed.

"You shut yourself off from us."

"Yes." She made sure I maintained eye contact with her. If I stared at her, I couldn't see her the way she'd been the last time I saw her. "I was sick, Mackenzie. That's the best I can tell you. It was horrible what I did. I can't go back. I can't make things right. I can't . . ." She broke off, and I saw her crying.

Could ghosts tear up? Could she do that, whatever she was?

She sniffled, shaking her head briskly to clear the tears. "I never talked. I never said what was going on with me, but you have to. You have to talk. You *have to* talk about me. You can't keep yourself bottled up and suppressed. Nothing good will happen then. I know you don't want to feel the grief. I know you don't want to let me go, but you have to. You will make yourself sick like I was. I don't want you here. You got it? I don't want you with me. Not you. This is mine to carry. Not yours. I want to watch you live a long life. I want to see you married. I want to see my little nephews and nieces. I want to see what my children would've looked like—"

I gripped her arms and squeezed.

"Please. Please, stop. I don't want this," I whimpered.

She wasn't letting me pull away. She wasn't letting me fall back. The more she said, the more my grief rose and bubbled inside me.

I didn't want to feel what she wanted me to. I wanted to stay like this, with her. She was happy. She was dancing. She was alive. I felt her sunshine against my face, and I only wanted that. I didn't want to think about her gone.

If I started, that darkness might open again. I shoved it down. I'd gotten better the last two months. Things were better.

"No," she snapped. Her eyes blazed with determination. "You aren't better. You're faking. I can't let you do that. Feel me. Mourn me. Say goodbye to me. Then . . ." She was fading.

The warmth chilled. The room's coldness returned.

The light was leaving. The shadows were returning.

I couldn't smell her perfume anymore.

The song fell away, leaving the ticking of a clock from the hallway.

"Willow," I cried out.

Her legs disappeared.

Her arms.

Her face—I clung to her eyes. I clung to the feel of her hands on my face, and then she said, "You have to tell them, Mac. You have to tell them."

Her hands were gone.

So were her eyes.

I was alone.

But I heard her last words, "Remember me, and cherish me. That's the last step, Mac. I love you . . ."

I collapsed, sobbing. My chest heaved. Salt filled my mouth, and not knowing what else to do, I crawled to where I remembered her lying as if we were back there, as if this was that same bathroom.

I lay there, my palm down, my face turned toward where she'd been.

And I stayed like that until I fell asleep.

Two more pieces fit. They fit right.

A bunch of things happened later that day.

I woke up before Ryan did, and I crawled back into the bed with him.

We went to school.

Robbie came home.

My mom and dad smiled at each other.

I didn't know if Willow was real in that bathroom, though, I did know I wasn't going to torture myself trying to explain it. I'd always thought I was going crazy, but when I woke that morning in Ryan's arms, I felt a little less crazy.

I felt a little bit better.

And I felt a little more whole.

CHAPTER
THIRTY-SEVEN

The stands were full. Almost literally.

People couldn't line up against the court's walls—it was a safety hazard—so at any given moment, ten people were huddled in the doorway. Their necks craned as they tried to watch the game. A few students hung out on the side of the bleachers, but every few minutes, someone acting all official would go and wave them away.

Basketball had been popular in Arizona, but not like this.

When I saw a woman wearing a basketball jersey with Jensen on the back, I assumed there was another Jensen on the team. She wasn't his mother, and he hadn't mentioned any other family coming to the game. But there wasn't. There was no other Jensen on the team, and when the players came out to start warming up, the second Ryan was visible, a roar took over the gym. Both sides of the bleachers.

It was insane.

Cora saw my look and started laughing. She patted my knee. "Yeah. Get ready. Ryan isn't like any other player on the team, on any team in the state." She leaned across me, pointing to a bunch of guys sitting in the back who were all wearing baseball caps pulled low and writing on clipboards. A few other guys, wearing Portside apparel, sat with them. "Those guys aren't college recruiters."

I nodded, remembering the ceremony. "He already committed."

"Those are professional guys."

I knew Ryan was good, but I hadn't thought he was *that* good. I sat up straighter, feeling proud of him, and as if he could feel me watching, he sank a three-pointer and glanced up to me.

My mouth watered for him; his hair was messily rumpled like I always loved. Some guys had shirts under their jerseys, but Ryan didn't. I could see the definition in his shoulders and upper arms. As he caught the ball and jumped for another shot, his shirt bounced up. A nice glimpse of his stomach showed me what I already knew. He was tightly muscled, and it hit me. All the warnings I'd gotten about him—how intense basketball season was, how much he was loved by his friends and family—hit me like cement bricks.

He wasn't just the top of the chain within his group of friends. He was literally the top over everyone. That time we went for food and got it free? That wasn't the only time. That'd been the first of many times.

I was starting to understand why.

Cora nudged me again, nodding below us on the bleachers. "Stephanie Witts is planning on making a pass at Ryan tonight. Just warning you."

That was the girl I'd had the confrontation with yesterday, and she was sitting with a bunch of her friends. Erin and Peach were at the end, but whispering on their own. Tom was in the row behind Peach, along with a few other guys I didn't recognize.

"Where are the other guys?"

As if hearing my question, Kirk and Nick showed up, walking in from the hallway. Two other guys were with them, but I only recognized Pete.

"That's Nick's cousin, right?" I asked Cora. "And why isn't Nick playing?"

"He got in trouble. I don't know why he's not on the bench with them. And yeah, that's his cousin."

She stood, waving with a smile stretching over her face. "Hey! Pete! Up here."

He looked around and saw us.

Kirk and the other two lingered behind, talking to Stephanie and her friends, while Pete came toward us. There was an opening by Peach, so he started his climb there, ruffling her hair in greeting and pausing to knock fists with Tom before coming the rest of the way.

"Hey, Cora." He grabbed her in a big hug before smiling politely at me. "Mackenzie, right?"

I nodded. "Peepee, right?"

He barked out a laugh. "Man. That's right." He sat right behind us, his knees behind Cora, and she leaned back, draping her arms over his legs. He was a human backrest. He jiggled her a bit. "Not that I'm not excited to see you, but please, please let me flirt with you. Kirk's already warned me off. I could die happy if I could shake him up a bit tonight."

Cora stilled at his words, watching me.

Pete just laughed again, moving his knees to jostle her. "Hmm? Cora?"

She was watching me.

I just shrugged. "I'm fine."

She nodded, only needing that before turning and punching Pete in the leg.

"Ow! What was that for?"

He was clueless. "You're an idiot sometimes," she told him.

"An idiot like my cousin and your new beau?" He tapped her shoulder, pointing to where we'd just been watching.

Kirk was watching us, a keen look on his face. He narrowed his eyes, focusing on Cora before turning to respond to something Stephanie said. She leaned forward, her hand touching his arm, before falling back as if she'd made a joke. Her friends began laughing. Nick swept an easy grin over Kirk's face before sensing his focus on us. He looked up then too, his eyes narrowing at Pete.

I glanced over, seeing that Pete had leaned forward to drape one of his arms around Cora's shoulders. He was wiggling his eyebrows in suggestion.

Cora shook her head. "You're going to get beat up." But she wasn't moving away from the touch either.

Kirk lifted a finger and waved it side to side.

His message was clear, but Pete only laughed harder. "The fucker can sweat a little." He pretended to rub his cheek next to Cora's.

She shrieked, pushing him away, and sat forward.

I looked down, noticing that almost their entire section was watching the display. Stephanie's eyes locked with mine and darkened with anger. Her friends whispered to each other, looking from her to me.

"Whoa," Pete said. "What's going on? I'm totally egging Kirk on, and no one's caring . . . except him." He laughed to himself.

Cora rested an elbow on his knee again. "Stephanie Witts and Mackenzie got into it yesterday."

"Got into it?" Nick asked as some people left behind us. He and Kirk had decided to join us, and Nick sat behind me, adding, "More like Mackenzie decided to get in some practice of her own, with Stephanie's head as the ball." He nudged my shoulder with his fist. "Hmm? Hmm? Am I right?"

"Yeah?" Pete grinned. "I remember hearing you wiped the floor with an ex of Ryan's too." He tipped his chin to me. "You the next badass of Portside High?"

I laughed at that. "Badass?"

"She holds her own," Kirk said as he dropped down beside Cora. He nodded to me before turning and shoving Pete off his seat. "Touch what's mine again, and we'll have real words."

"Oh yeah?" Pete was unfazed, scrambling back and pushing his face close to Kirk's. "So Cora's yours now? You claiming her?" It was small, but I caught the smallest wink in Cora's direction.

I studied my friend, and I didn't miss the small smile on her face or the way her head suddenly ducked down. I was starting to wonder if this hadn't been set up by Cora herself. Maybe Pete was doing a little friendly favor for one or both of them.

"I . . ." Kirk was unsure, glancing to Cora. "Well?" He frowned, softening his tone. "Do you—do you want to go out sometime?"

Her head popped up. "Sometime?"

"Tonight."

Nick made a noise.

Kirk corrected, "Tomorrow night?" He winced. "There's a party tonight I already said I'd go to."

Her face was almost bright red. "Oh! Um. Y-yes. Yes."

She beamed, and Kirk nodded. "Cool."

The two continued to stare at each other, having a small moment before Nick punched his cousin in the shoulder.

"Ow!" Pete clamped a hand over his arm and glared. "Honestly. What is up with the physical violence?"

"From what I remember, you hit him the first time I met you." I pointed at Pete and then Nick.

Both cousins froze and then Nick cracked up. "Ha! She got you there." But he swung back and tried to punch his cousin again, only Pete was ready this time. He leaned back, and Nick's arm went in front of his chest, and he grabbed it. Nick retaliated, and the two started brawling right there in the stands.

Kirk grabbed Cora and me, pulling us down a seat, but most of the others around them scrambled out of the way. A few little kids started crying.

"Ah! Stop it!" A middle-aged lady took her purse and began batting at Nick and Pete's backs. "You two. Stop it at once."

It worked, and it didn't.

They stopped wrestling and returned to their seats, but they started shoving instead.

"You guys." Tom had run up the side of the bleachers, using the actual stairs, and he paused at the end of our row. "Kirk." He gestured to the court where some of the basketball players had stopped to watch the scuffle. "They're going to call security."

Kirk groaned, but he started to wade in between the cousins. "I can't take these two anywhere, I swear."

The purse lady gave up and passed her weapon to her husband, who was the only one who didn't seem perturbed by Pete and Nick. He remained almost in the middle of it, sitting calmly and watching the court. I followed his eyes and found his attention fixed on where the cheerleaders were stretching. One had her back to the bleachers, bent over so she could still talk to her friend. Her ass was right there. I didn't think she cared.

Then—smack! I reeled backward, feeling blinding pain on the side of my face.

"Hey!" Kirk yelled, but I couldn't see. I just knew I was falling—falling—until hands caught me, more than one pair of hands.

"Oh, dear." A lady gasped from beneath me, and then an arm came around the back of my waist and lifted me back upright.

"HEY!"

I recognized that chest pressed against mine and started to protest even as I relaxed. "No, no. You're supposed to be warming up."

Ryan's arm tightened around me. His whole body tensed, and he barked again, "Knock it off! NOW!"

He kept me cradled against him with one arm, his other moving around.

The pain started to recede, and I opened one eye enough to see Nick and Pete staring at me.

"Oh no." Nick started forward.

Tom had waded in too, and he made a gurgling sound. If it was meant to stop Nick, it worked because his shoulders dropped dramatically. "That wasn't Pete I hit with my shoulder, I'm betting."

Pete pushed forward. "I'm sorry, Mackenzie. He's sorry too."

Nick hit his shoulder. "I was about to say that. I'm sorry too, Mackenzie."

"Yeah." Pete's head bobbed up and down. "We're both sorry." They looked at Ryan, and if they could've taken a step backward, I was sure they would've. Pete gulped before adding, "Sorry, Ryan."

"Fucker," Ryan grit out, flinging a hand toward the court. "You hit her, and you're causing a scene. Security was coming in before I told 'em I'd stop it." His entire body was rigid, and hearing a threat of violence in his tone, I looked up a little more intently.

I wasn't the only one.

Kirk met my gaze, and I could tell he was also slightly concerned.

I frowned, placing a hand over Ryan's chest to calm him. "I'm okay. Honestly." I blinked my eye open a few times, testing it out. "I can still see."

Ryan didn't respond as he wrapped his arms around me for a hug. He pulled me in tight, dipping his head down a moment. His lips grazed my neck, and then he released me.

He pointed at Nick and Pete. "Sit your asses down, and shut the fuck up." Pointing at Tom, he said, "You. Sit." He pointed on my left side. "Stop hitting on my sister, and if these assholes start fighting, use your face to protect Mackenzie next time."

Ryan glanced at me for a second before leaving for the court. As he went, a few people patted him on the back. One guy pumped his fist in the air. "Bring home the win, Jensen!"

Kirk chuckled once Ryan got back to the floor and turned to Tom, adding, "Or next time just get your ass in here to help out."

Tom sat, but he leaned around us to give Kirk a menacing look. "It isn't my fault these two revert to being nine year olds when they're around each other."

"Hey."

"Hey?"

Everyone ignored Pete and Nick, and Kirk rolled his eyes as we all took our seats again. "You should rethink dating Peach, and you know it. It's going to cause problems with your friendship."

Tom glowered at him but didn't respond, and as if everyone had decided the excitement was done, we all turned back to the court.

A loud alarm sounded, and the players stopped warming up.

It was time to play.

CHAPTER THIRTY-EIGHT

Ryan scored thirty-two points.

Twelve rebounds.

Six assists.

Three steals.

I was starstruck—and ashamed I didn't have a Jensen jersey to wear myself. As the last buzzer signaled the end of the game, I was tempted to ask that lady where she'd gotten hers made.

"Fun, huh?" Cora's eyes were invigorated, but it could've had something to do with her spending the last two hours holding Kirk's hand.

I nodded. "Yeah. Is it always like that?"

She saw the jersey lady going past us down the bleachers and shook her head. "That's a bit much, but it's the first game too. This is nothing compared to state. It's insane then."

Kirk rested his arm around Cora's shoulders. "You need a ride to the party? Are you going?"

I nodded, laughing. "I think I have to."

I'd heard the warnings. I saw some of the excitement leading up to this game, but being there—my eyes were open wide as fuck. Cora's whole heads-up about Stephanie Witts had a new seriousness to it.

"But I know Ryan will drive me."

"I figured, but I still wanted to ask. He and I haven't talked about the party."

Tom had returned to Peach's side after halftime. He'd left for snacks and never came back, slipping in with their crew below.

Nick and Pete had stayed with us, but they were down there, talking with some of Stephanie Witts' friends.

"They're just flirting. You and Cora are taken."

Kirk must've seen where I watched.

"No, I know," I told him. But I'd never felt this emotion before, at least with these guys. It felt a little like betrayal, which was stupid. I knew that wasn't what it was.

Maybe . . .

Ryan's friends are guys. They want to get it on. I could hear Willow rolling her eyes. *Just because they didn't sit the whole time with you doesn't mean they're losing interest in your friendship, and no, Ryan definitely will not. The guy is gaga over you. I'd die from boredom from how cute you two are if I weren't already dead.*

I stiffened. *Willow . . .*

Yeah. Yeah. I can feel your disapproval, but guess what? I'm dead. I can joke all I want. She snorted. *What are you going to do about it? Kil—*

Enough!

I suddenly had to get out of there, and fast. "I'm, huh, I'm going to wait for Ryan down by his locker." I didn't know if they understood me, I spoke in such a rush. But I couldn't take the dead jokes. It was too fresh, too raw.

She told me to remember her, to cherish her, and then let her go. But she was making that difficult. I could still feel her around me. Maybe she wanted to comfort me, apologize . . . I didn't know, but I did not want to hear it. Not right then. It was Ryan's night.

"Mackenzie!"

I heard Nick yell my name, but I pushed past them.

Fuck.

He was standing between Erin and Stephanie Witts, both girls I knew would love to be with Ryan. And there I was, literally running away from a ghost that was in my own head. This wasn't *Supernatural.* I wasn't a medium. Willow didn't exist.

There, Willow! I half-shouted to her in my head, but half-whispered because I still didn't want to hear her response. *You don't exist. I've analyzed myself and decided—you are dead. Make all the fucking jokes you want.* I didn't want to actually hear them.

Going through the doors and into the emptied hallway, I curled my hands into tight fists, waiting for her response. It never came, and slowly, as I approached Ryan's locker, I unclenched my fingers.

I didn't feel her either. She had gone away once more.

Feeling lighter, since she wasn't sitting on my shoulders, I slid down to the floor. My back was to Ryan's locker, and I pulled my knees up, hugging them to my chest.

I clasped my eyes tight, pressing my forehead to the back of my knees.

Even then, I wanted her gone. I wanted all of this out of my head, but I also didn't. I felt less crazy than a few days ago, but I was still halfway crazy. Or one-third crazy. Once that healed, would she really be gone then?

"Planning world domination?"

I started to laugh, lifting my head. My laughter died when I saw Erin standing over me. "You."

She laughed, shaking her head before holding her hands up. "Look. I've given up. I'm laying my flag down, and I think I've done that a few times. You don't have to keep with the hostility."

I sighed. I was already so tired of this conversation. "What do you want, Erin?" Because there was an agenda. She was just one of *those* people.

"Okay. Fair enough." Her hands went back to her side and then she crossed them over her chest. "Look, I never went after your sister, and we both know I could've. You mentioned her twice, and Peach explained." Her head inclined. "She explained better how you and Ryan got to be so close. I get it. I honestly do. He understands your pain, like you understand his." Her top lip curled in a small sneer. She kept going, sounding bitter. "Grief is a great foundation for a relationship, but whatever. I'm not the one fuckin—"

"Get to the point."

If she didn't, I was getting to my point where I'd get to my feet and we'd have a confrontation of a different sort. Maybe. Most likely. Probably not. I'd throw insults at her and leave once I thought I'd given her my best zinger.

Since my physical visit from Willow, the fight in me had dwindled. It might take a bit more to tap into it, but I knew it was there. A good well of craziness.

"—tonight at the party, okay?"

I had tuned her out.

Oh yes, I was such an ace fighter. I got so bored, I only *thought* I might want to fight her.

"What'd you say?"

"Were you listening at all?"

"No."

"Nice. I'm trying to do you a solid, and you aren't even listening."

A second sigh from me, and I leaned my head back against the locker. "I'll listen now. What were you saying before?"

She looked at the floor. "That friend of Ryan's who died?"

"Yeah?" My gut twisted in a knot. I didn't think I was going to like what I was about to hear . . .

She looked up, flicking away a solitary tear. "He was my boyfriend."

"Wait." So that meant—

She was already there. "That's why Ryan and I dated briefly. It wasn't long, and to be honest, it was more just messing around because we both missed him so much. I'd been with Derek for two years when it happened."

It made sense, why Erin was around so much.

"I couldn't figure out why they let you hang out with them," I mused to myself. "I thought it was only because of Peach, but you guys were at the house when Kirk came back."

"Yeah. Derek's cousin. All of us were friends. Then Derek died, and I messed around with Ryan afterward, like a few months afterward." She grimaced, her whole body shuddering. "Want some more honesty? No. I'm not even asking." She plunged ahead. "I don't regret sleeping with Ryan. I just regret the timing of it."

She understood. Somewhat.

"I'm not with Ryan because of my grief."

Yes, I had used him in the beginning, which was something Ryan knew about. Something he understood since he'd used Erin in the same way.

That was why he understood.

"Thanks for telling me." I meant it.

She nodded. "That's the reason I never went after you about your sister, but that's why I'm here. You need to watch Stephanie. She isn't going to understand."

"Yeah." I meant everything I said to her and her friends, but that was before my coming-to-Willow moment. "I heard she's going to make a pass at him tonight."

"She is, and she can be ruthless sometimes. Just watch your back with her. Okay?"

I studied her a moment. Trust her or not?

Erin was the popular girl in her class. Even though she was a grade younger, I knew she didn't need to hang out with Stephanie and her friends. There'd been a divide between them earlier in the year. I hadn't been noticing much at that time, but I had noticed that at Peach's pool party.

"Why are you hanging out with her?"

A fleeting smile was my answer. She started to leave but said over her shoulder, "Because sometimes it's smart to keep your friends close, and your enemies closer." She winked at me. "It's a classic for a reason."

She was leaving as Ryan headed toward me, his gym bag hanging from one shoulder. He glanced at her as she passed him.

"What was that about?" he asked as he drew close to me.

I beamed, feeling the same way I always did.

He pushed back the darkness, sometimes literally.

"Stephanie Witts is going to make a pass at you tonight, and I'm supposed to watch my back," I said, almost upbeat about it. I winked at him. "I heard she's ruthless."

He matched my grin, but didn't respond as he let his bag drop to the ground and then slid down to the floor with me. "You know you have nothing to worry about, right?"

I nodded. "I know." But there were knots in my stomach. I couldn't deny them. "Just . . ." I leaned my head back and turned toward him so we were inches apart. "I don't trust them."

"Yeah. I get that." He dipped down, his lips touching mine and resting there a moment before he whispered, "But I don't want Stephanie Witts. I don't want anyone else." His eyes were hard on me.

My body warmed. A tingle shot through me.

I grinned, my lips curving against his. "You're all I want too."

He pulled back, an uncharacteristic seriousness on his face. No smile. No grin. No smirk. No amusement in his gaze. He was suddenly so serious. "I just want you. I just love you."

My tongue felt heavy.

I should say it back, but I was still hearing Willow.

Pain sliced through me, and I turned away—I started to turn away.

He caught me, his hand touching my chin, and he moved me back to look at him. His thumb caressed my jawline, and his eyes dipped to my mouth. "I couldn't have said this a year ago. I couldn't have said this six months ago, but I can now. It took me that long, Mac. Derek's death fucked me up, so when I say I get it—I get it. But I want to say it."

I needed it.

It was like air to me.

I turned my body, my head holding still, and slowly, I crawled until I was straddling him in the darkened hallway. It was empty, but people were probably lingering just around the corner or by the gym. Two steps—that would be all it would take for someone to round the corner and find us there.

I so wasn't caring at that moment.

I settled down on top of him, feeling him beneath me, and his hands moved to my hips.

I leaned forward, my lips nipping his, and I whispered, "I want to show you what I can't say, not yet."

"Oh yeah?" A small grin pulled at his lips, and he watched me with dark amusement.

"Yeah." I shifted, pushing down with my hips. He was hard for me. His gym pants didn't obstruct him much, and my jeans were a little baggy.

God.

I glanced left and right, but no one was there.

Biting my lip, feeling all the right tingles and pleasure filling me, I knew I should get up. We should take this somewhere else, but I was not caring.

This was reckless.

This was stupid.

This was dangerously intoxicating, and with that last thought—I stopped thinking. My hips pressed against his, and he pulled me in, holding me against him and lifting his hips a little to grind against me.

"Fuck, Mac." He pulled back, his eyes so damned dark I wanted to get lost in them. His left hand slid up my waist, up my arm, around to my front, and lingered between my breasts. They were straining for him, but he didn't go any farther. He just stayed there, feeling my heartbeat and watching me all the while.

He groaned. "You make me feel things I thought were gone."

He seemed tormented by that, and I shifted back a little and slid my hand through his hair. It was half-dry, so there was a tiny little bit of a messy curl to it. I loved how it was chaotic.

"What do you mean?" I asked.

His hand went back to my hip, and he cupped me there, jerking me back in place. He fit right, perfect.

I was having a hard time not moving my hips again, rocking on top of him.

He rested his head back against the locker, watching me. "Derek was my best friend, not Kirk."

"I thought . . ."

He shook his head, his eyes still so dark. "Kirk became my best friend after Derek died, but it was him and me. Even the others— Tom, Nick, and Pete—they knew that. It was me and Derek. Then he died, and God—" He let out an anguished breath, closing his eyes as lines of tension formed around his mouth. "I used to think no one got it. No one understood."

I shifted back even farther.

My gut was sinking. My chest was starting to tear open.

I had a feeling I knew exactly what he was going to say.

He looked at me. "I thought no one would understand what it felt like to hurt so badly that you just wanted to go with that person." His hand smoothed down my hip, stopping on top of my leg, and he looked down at it. "Until you."

He lifted his gaze again. The torment was so real, so haunting, that it hurt me to be there. Every bone in my body started to ache, but not from him. Not because of him. Not in a way that made me want to run from this.

It was an ache because someone else understood.

It was almost as if, for a split second, I got her back. Ryan took Willow's spot. I took Derek's spot, and we were the other's mourned loss for a moment.

Then I gasped, and the feeling left me.

It was back to us. Ryan and me. The ghosts had gone again.

"I didn't know."

He shrugged and went back to watching his hand. He traced it up and down the inside of my leg. "He died before basketball season that year. Some told me I didn't have to participate, if it might be too much for me, but I wanted to. All the others who kept quiet, I knew they were relieved. They wanted me to play. They didn't care about Derek, but it was him and me. We were co-captains on the JV team. I played varsity too, but I don't know . . ."

His eyes met mine. The anguish was back. He whispered, "All I did right away was play ball. It was like I was half-trying to forget him, and half-trying to kill myself. You know?"

I nodded. My heart was in my throat. "Yes."

"But everyone wanted something from me. They wanted me to win. They wanted me to keep going, get faster, learn more drills, learn more tricks. The coaches. The teachers. My friends. My parents—it was all of them. I never got a fucking break. All they wanted was to fucking win. All I wanted was to fucking die."

"Ryan," I whispered, moving back to him. I hurt, but this time, the pain wasn't mine. It was his. I put my hand where his had been, right in the middle of his chest. I felt his heart pounding. It was so fast, almost skipping a beat before going even faster to try to make up for it.

I wanted to say something to calm him, slow his heartbeat, but there were no words.

There was only grief and the silence that accompanied it.

He bent and took my hand, kissing it and holding it tightly. "I gave everything that year, and I was empty after it. I had nothing when the season ended."

"That was when you stopped caring."

"Yeah." He squeezed my hand, resting it against his chest. His other hand went to my hipbone and burrowed under my jeans, his thumb rubbing over my skin. "Kirk and I, we didn't give a damn. Drugs. Drinking. Fights. Fucking." He grimaced. "None of it worked." His hand started up my back, sliding under my shirt. "It took a year and a half, but all of that went away." He stopped, his hand right next to my ribcage. He held me in a gentle embrace, as if I were a delicate treasure. "I get what you feel. I get you talking to Willow. I get you sitting in a dark and empty hallway. I get you leaving the bed to cry in your guest bathroom. I get it. You don't think I do sometimes, but I do."

"Ryan." Tears slid down my face. I reached up, cupping his cheek. "I . . ."

I wanted to say it.

I was feeling it. I was feeling more than just that word, but . . . the words wouldn't form.

His eyes flickered, shuddering a second, and then the agony was gone. He had closed up, returned to being the old Ryan again, and my heart sank because I realized this had been him the whole time.

He had been shut down this whole time too.

"Don't." I leaned forward, catching his face with my hands. I moved so close, my eyes jumping back and forth between his, my lips almost touching his. "Don't do that. Not to me."

"Don't what?"

But he knew. He so knew, and I shook my head.

"Don't shut me out. I'm not them."

His eyes shut again, resting a second, and his chest rose as he took in a deep breath. Then they opened, and I was seeing the real him. He just opened up for me again.

"There." I raised my hands, cupping the sides of his temples, right next to his eyes. My forehead rested against his. "There you are."

More pieces fit together.

Both his hands went to my hips, and he gripped me, just holding me in place.

And then, because it was the right time and a gate had shattered inside me, I said, "I love you, and I love you for loving me."

His eyes closed again, as did mine, and we stayed there, just holding each other.

CHAPTER
THIRTY-NINE

My first warning should've been Erin.

She was standing on the curb in front of Stephanie Witts' house when we pulled in. Peach was next to her, and Tom right behind her, but for some reason, their welcoming party didn't sound the alarms in my head.

It might've been the feeling I was basking in at that moment— telling Ryan I loved him and genuinely feeling it, not feeling all the other baggage inside that had kept pushing it down so I couldn't say it. It felt like a weight off my shoulders.

Or maybe it was because I had a strong feeling I couldn't hold up my promise not to have sex with Ryan again. Though, it wouldn't be sex. It'd be making love.

I suddenly wanted to know what that felt like so bad it was almost worth risking my mom's anger.

Or maybe it was that Ryan hadn't let go of my hand. The only time was when we separated to get into his truck, and he was still holding it as he pulled up to the curb and threw his truck into park.

Of all people to greet us, it shouldn't have been those three.

Peach? Maybe. Tom? Maybe. Both of them together? Terrible idea but still plausible. But Erin? There might've been a temporary truce or a tentative peace between us, whatever we had, but we weren't friends. So yeah, all three of them should've been sounding my alarms at full blast.

We got out. Ryan came around the front and still the trio said nothing.

Tom wore an uneasy grin. As Ryan came to my side, he stepped away from Peach and dipped his head. "Ryan. Mackenzie."

251

Peach shared his uneasiness, biting her lip and looking as if she wanted to reach for his hand. She didn't. She tucked it under her other arm, almost holding herself back, and her head hanging a tiny bit.

It hit me then. Those two were backup for—and my gaze found the girl who'd been my first enemy at Portside: Ryan's ex-girlfriend/fuck buddy.

Then the alarms sounded, tightening my gut. "Erin."

She didn't even look at Ryan. Her eyes were only for me, and I saw the sorrow. It flickered there, but it was strong. It was evident. Her eyes clouded, her eyebrows pinched together, and she frowned, tucking a strand of her hair behind her ear.

"I had no idea," she said.

"No idea about what?"

Ryan moved forward a little, as if he wanted to shield me. "What are you talking about, Erin?"

She still didn't look at him, but his sister did. Peach went to Erin's other side, standing in front of her brother. She held her hand out, saying softly, "Ryan . . ."

He ignored her, barking out, "Erin!"

The door opened behind them. Music, light, and people spilled out.

"Ryan!"

"Mackenzie!"

Kirk, Cora, Nick, and Pete darted down the front lawn.

Cora was unnaturally pale, and her face was streaked with tears. Once her eyes hit mine, she jerked to a stop, and I watched as she sucked in her breath. Kirk stopped too, looking toward her. He frowned and reached for her hand, but like Erin, she only had eyes for me.

She and Erin were both terrified—for me.

The guys were sending nervous looks at me, but they were more wary of Ryan.

Because . . .

Because why?

Why were they concerned about him when the girls were so scared for me?

Me.

Because of . . .

Because Ryan was protective of me, but Erin and Cora . . . the way they were looking at me, as if they pitied me and were horrified at the same time.

It's me.

I jerked backward, hearing Willow's voice like she was standing in front of me.

I swayed, clasping my eyes shut.

No . . .

Yes, Willow sighed. *They're going to use me to get at you.*

I looked again, past everyone in front of me, and I saw her.

She was faint, like a mere reflection in the wind, wavering all around, but I saw her.

Willow was looking right at me, wearing the same dress she had on in the dream. A pink, shimmering dress, but there was no crown on her head. This time, her hair was pulled up into a braid and wrapped around her head, looking like a crown in and of itself.

But she looked alive, so alive that I heard myself exhale a ragged breath.

I blinked a few times, but she was still there.

There were no more words. She didn't come toward me. She didn't point inside, but I knew she was leading the way.

She wanted me to go in, and feeling her courage join mine, I grew calm. I felt ready, and I started forward.

Everyone turned then, and I heard Cora gasp.

"Holy sh—" Kirk exclaimed.

They saw her.

They honest to God saw her.

I almost faltered, my knees buckling, and then she vanished. I only felt her beside me. Her hand touched mine. More strength transferred to me, but there was also peace. Contentment. She was letting me feel everything right along with her.

The door swung open. Someone saw me coming and was ready. The music cut off, and everyone who had been standing around on the walkway turned to watch. Some were smirking.

Some were laughing. Some were sad. And the pity—that seared me the most.

I didn't want anyone's pity, but I was getting it. I gritted my teeth. Whatever was ahead of me, I would show them I didn't need it.

They were in the living room.

The crowd didn't part for me when the hallway forked off to the dining room and kitchen. But it opened to the living room, where people were sitting on the couches. Others were spread out, sitting all over the floor.

They were watching a movie on a large screen. It wasn't even the television. It had been projected onto the wall for maximum effect, and standing right to the side of it was Stephanie Witts, but she wasn't alone.

Zoe.

Gianna.

And next to them? Duke and Willow's ex-best friend, Serena. He had his arm around her. I turned away from them. They didn't even deserve my attention, but Duke dropped his arm as soon as he saw me. His eyes widened, and he jerked forward a step.

"Mackenzie—"

He was already groveling. I heard it in his voice, and I leveled him with a hard look. "Don't. Even."

I didn't need to ask how they got there. I looked right at Stephanie. "What'd you do? Go on my social media? Google my sister's name?"

Her eyebrows went up, and her lips pulled back in a haughty smirk. "You told me to come at you with the worst I could do." She waved at my ex-friends, at Willow's ex-friends. "Here you go. They've been telling me all about your sister—"

I finally looked at the screen, and I tuned her out. She was saying things, no doubt hurtful things, but it didn't matter in that moment.

Willow had been right. It was her. They were watching a compilation video of her winning the championship with that six-foot, papier-mâché dragon. She smiled, holding the dragon in one hand and the purple ribbon in the other. Her trophy was next to her, and she was so proud. She was beaming. Then the video skipped ahead to her nuzzling noses with Duke. Then I saw her and her friends, all in their cheerleading uniforms. Then older pictures of Willow—her school pictures when she was in third grade, fifth, sixth, seventh, eighth, all the way up to what should have been this year's picture.

They showed her senior picture.

I felt tears sliding down my face, but I didn't care.

So many pieces, one after another, connected, and they were strong. Twenty-five. Goddamn twenty-five, and I felt them in me. They were pulsating. They were buzzing. They were firm, cement, and more were coming.

"You guys had your pictures taken right before you moved," Duke murmured, coming closer. "She mailed that back to me. I got it a week after . . ."

She'd sent it before she killed herself.

I didn't respond to him. I wasn't sure if I wanted to yet. The video kept going.

Pictures of Willow and me: she was smiling, I was rolling my eyes.

Pictures of her in her track uniform and me in my soccer uniform.

Pictures of us hugging each other.

Pictures taken of us at school lunch one day. I had a bag of Cheetos, and she was eating a carrot. A goddamn carrot.

Pictures of us before school: Willow was in a dress. I was in jeans.

Willow wore a skirt, and I had holes in my shirt. Willow's hair was always perfectly styled, and mine was pulled into a messy ponytail.

I got the message Stephanie wanted to send, and I looked at her, wiping some of my tears away. "What? Are you going to follow this presentation with your decision that she shouldn't have killed herself, and I should've? That she was the twin who shined, and I wasn't? That I'm drab, and dull, and boring? And she excelled at almost everything?"

I had crossed the living room so my shadow hit the projector. Images of my sister continued to play over my face, but I kept staring right at Stephanie.

"Do you think I don't think of that every day since I found her?" I whispered. "Do you think I'm not haunted by her? By the thought that if I *had*—maybe she wouldn't have?"

My voice broke at the end.

Someone sniffled behind me.

I heard another whisper.

And I felt a presence at my back. I thought it was Willow at first until a hand—a real live hand—touched mine. It was Ryan. He didn't pull me back, though. He was just there for me.

I latched on to him, lacing our fingers together, and he moved a step closer so I could feel his heat against my back. His other hand rested on my hip.

Stephanie's malice had started to wane, and her forehead wrinkled as she began to frown. "I mean, come on." She glanced around for support.

There was none.

I didn't look, but I could feel the somberness creeping over the room. Anyone who had thought this was going to be funny didn't seem to anymore, and if it wasn't because of me, it probably had to do with Ryan, and the whole group that stood behind us.

"It's obvious your sister was popular, and you're . . ." She tried to sneer at me. And like everything else, that too failed.

"I'm what?" I raised my chin higher. "Mourning such a deep loss that I hope even you will never feel anything like it? Healing? Trying to keep going? Forcing myself to go forward because my family needs me? Because I've found people here who love me and support me, and I need to keep going for them? Is that what I am?" I raised my voice, grating out, "Does that somehow make me less than you? Less than anyone else in this room? Or maybe, just maybe, that makes me stronger than you? That makes me a goddamn survivor, when trust me, the thought of joining my sister is sometimes easier than breathing."

I was letting everyone see my insides.

All these months of not talking, and it was spilling out.

I could feel their surprise. It was in the way Ryan tightened his hold on my hand before letting it relax. The way the whole crowd seemed to waver, and the way Stephanie's eyes widened, and the blood drained, finally, from her face.

I turned to my two ex-friends and burned them with the same look of hatred I had for Stephanie. "How dare you come here. How dare you bring that video to a party. How dare you befriend someone you knew wasn't reaching out with my best interest at heart."

Zoe and Gianna blanched, but their mouths opened. I didn't let them speak. I kept going.

"How dare you turn your back on me? How dare you—just, how *dare* you?"

I didn't care why Duke or Serena were there, but I turned to them anyway. "Willow would hate you for this, and you know it."

Serena hung her head, but Duke surged forward again. "It isn't like that. I mean . . ." He gestured to Stephanie. "She said she was your friend."

Zoe and Gianna stepped forward, right behind him.

Zoe tried to smile at me. "We felt bad after you left, Kenz."

"And what Duke said is right. She reached out to us, saying she was your friend." Gianna glanced at Stephanie. "You haven't been on social media. I've been sending you messages almost since you left, but you haven't been getting them."

Because I was using Willow's account.

"We didn't know who you were friends with. Honestly, we had no idea. We aren't here to hurt you." Zoe started crying. "We really aren't."

I shook my head.

Ryan spoke over my head, "You thought showing a video of her sister at a high school party was a good thing?" His tone was hard, biting. "How the fuck do you make that right in your head?"

"We didn't—" Duke started.

"The laughter should've been the first clue!" Ryan cut him off, moving ahead of me. "Her face should've been the second." He jabbed a finger in the air toward Stephanie. "She looked goddamn evil when we first came in. If the other stuff hadn't sunk in, that look should've had you scrambling to turn the goddamn machine off!"

"We—"

Zoe interrupted Gianna, her shoulders sinking down. "We weren't thinking. You're right. We weren't thinking."

"I was hoping it'd all be okay," Duke said. "That's what I was hoping. But I swear, Mackenzie, we didn't come to hurt you. We came to apologize." He glanced to the others before placing his hand to his chest. "Or I came to apologize. You tried to talk to me after the memorial service, and I blew you off." He gestured to Willow's ex-friend. "Serena and I both did."

"It's just hard—"

I nodded, speaking before Serena could say more. "To see her when you look at me? To hear her when you talk to me? Trust me. I get it."

"You didn't expect her to stay, did you?" Erin stepped out of the crowd and folded her arms. She looked right at Stephanie, who had tried to blend in with her friends. "You thought she'd come in, see them, see the video, hear the laughter, and then run away crying? That was what you thought would happen, wasn't it?"

Stephanie's friends melted away, leaving her standing alone. She glared at them before facing Erin and then me. "To be honest, I was going to say everything Mackenzie guessed. That the wrong sister died, that Willow seemed like the better of the two. It's obvious from the pictures. So yeah." She jerked her head higher. "I was going to use the weapon she gave me, and destroy her with it."

She turned to me. "Imagine my surprise when I found out you hadn't been talking to your friends from home, and that Willow's boyfriend and best friend were dating. I mean, you were asking for it." Her eyes trailed to Ryan, pausing a beat before looking away.

"Because of him?" I dropped his hand, moving around him.

"Yeah!" Her head flared up again. "He's ours! He should be dating one of us, not you! Not someone who . . . you're mental! I've heard you talking to yourself in the bathroom. You freak out in the classrooms like you're nuts or something." Her hands went to the sides of her head. "You don't deserve him. You . . ."

My head tilted to the side. "I what?"

"You . . ." She gulped and then shrugged. "You aren't good enough for him."

Her words should've struck me at the core.

They didn't. Not this time.

"You're too late to make that stick. A week ago, I would've agreed with you." A hollow laugh left me. "I wouldn't have left him since I'm selfish enough to need him, but now I think you're wrong." I glanced up, seeing my shadow over my projected self. Willow was laughing, and when I leaned back, moving my shadow and letting the full picture hit the wall, there I was, laughing every bit as hard as she was.

"You're the strong one, Kenz," said Robbie's voice.

"You were the superstar in everything," Willow said. *"You just didn't know."*

"You were what we needed. You were our anchor."

"You're wrong." I looked right at her. "I *am* good enough; I'm better than you'll ever be."

And taking Ryan's hand again, I left the room. He followed. As did Erin. Cora. Tom. Kirk. Pete. Nick.

I was told later that almost everyone followed us out.

Stephanie Witt never had the same clout after that party.

She still had friends, but she wasn't popular anymore.

Erin became more of a friend to me, and somehow she almost took Stephanie's place at school—except for the bullying. I was very adamant that she couldn't do that, and she agreed.

She still somehow managed to rule with intimidation, though.

Cora and Kirk became exclusive after that party.

Nick and Pete hit on Zoe and Gianna before moving on to hit on other girls. There were no more wrestling matches, that night.

And Tom and Peach kissed, blushed, and held hands whenever they could.

The next day, I met Zoe and Gianna for breakfast before they went home. It still hurt that they hadn't been there for me in the beginning, but they'd been a part of my life for so long, and they loved Willow too. Plus, I was trying to be someone Willow would have been proud of. Yes, she'd told me so many times that she was proud of me, but I didn't fully believe her. I was still trying. And that meant meeting Duke and Serena too.

It was harder to talk to them than it was to talk to Zoe and Gianna. They knew Willow in ways I hadn't: as her friend, as her cheerleading accomplice and confidante, as her lover. And seeing them unable to hold back tears unleashed mine as well.

It was an awkward feeling to sit in that booth, first with Zoe and Gianna, and then with Duke and Serena as we all cried. But we were all mourning Willow, and for that I was grateful.

I was surrounded by people who loved her too. This was how it should've been from the beginning.

After that they all went back to Arizona, but I did talk to Zoe and Gianna more regularly.

And as for me and Ryan, well . . .

CHAPTER FORTY

Five months later
Two hundred fifty-three pieces later

With his mouth fused to mine, Ryan pushed me back against the shower wall. Our hands clasped together, and he pinned them above my head before bending to my shoulder and scraping his teeth against my skin.

I gasped as he plunged into me.

He took my weight, and his left hand let go of mine to drop to my thigh. He gripped me there as he sank even deeper inside me.

God.

This guy.

Pleasure built and built low in my belly, and I used my free hand to hold on to him, sinking my fingers into his hair.

The shower beat down on us, but Ryan shielded me, taking most of the water. A slight mist coated my face, and as I drew in oxygen, I drank in some water too.

We had been together for almost a year. In forty-three days, it'd be the anniversary of Willow's death—the same day I'd first crawled into Ryan's bed. I'd gone through hell this last year, but he'd been with me the whole time.

I trailed my fingers down his back, feeling his muscles shifting as he thrust in and out, keeping a steady rhythm.

He bent forward, dropping his lips to my nipple and sucking.

I closed my eyes, feeling desire and the momentum building in me. I wanted him. I wanted him harder, deeper, and in the whole year, that hadn't lessened. If anything, I craved him more and more. Like tonight—we were going to prom later, but I'd stepped into the shower, knowing I had to feel him before we endured a night of mere touches and the whisper of being together.

All eyes would be on us.

All eyes would be on *him*. He'd be voted prom king, which was no shock to anyone. There was a prom queen, and there were rumors it would be me, but I doubted that. I'd only moved there a year ago. It didn't seem right, even though I was Ryan's girlfriend. I wasn't the most liked girl in the grade. But knowing everyone would be watching Ryan made me almost desperate to feel him first. I wanted to remind myself that he was mine, only mine. I wanted to feel him moving inside me, and I wanted to see him watching me the way he did when he took me at night.

I looked up to find him watching me once again.

His eyes were dark, heavy, primal.

Adjusting our bodies, he lifted me higher against the shower wall and began going harder. He was claiming me.

Pulling my hand free from his, I wrapped my arms around his neck, bending forward to kiss his throat.

He groaned, the sound rumbling deep, as his other hand found my hip. He slammed me against the tile, going harder and rougher.

I laid my head back, gasping in more breath as I tried to ride with him, but this was for him. He held me captive as he ground into me. An onslaught of pleasure assaulted me, and I sank into it. Hell, I felt half-drunk from this. All I could do was hold on to him until I felt my climax coming.

"Ryan," I gasped. My fingers bit into his back, my nails scraping his skin. "I'm going to come."

He slowed, grunting. "Not yet. Not." Thrust. "Goddamn." Thrust. "Yet." Thrust, and then he tensed, his hands tightening on me to almost bruising pressure. "Now." And he exploded.

I let go, the climax crashing into me, making my body jerk and shake.

He held me the whole time, waiting until both our bodies had calmed before carrying me out of the shower. My legs remained wrapped around his hips, and I clung tightly to him and rested my head on his shoulder.

He ran a soothing hand down my very wet back and took me into my bedroom.

"Fuck." I sighed as he laid me down and then eased out of me.

He laughed, skimming a hand down my side before following the motion with his lips.

I ran my hand through his hair and then down his shoulders and arms as he moved back up, bracing himself above me. His eyes found mine, still so dark.

"You okay?"

I nodded. "Yes." My hand cupped the side of his face. "I'm good. You?"

He nodded, falling down to kiss me again before settling onto the bed next to me. "Shit."

"Yep."

"I don't want to go tonight."

I laughed, curling on my side and kissing his shoulder. "Ship's sailed on that one, Prom King."

He groaned again, catching my hand and tugging me until I straddled him. "Yeah?"

"Yeah."

I matched his grin, both of us still riding the wave we'd just created in the shower. I was naked, and as his eyes trailed down my body, I tipped my head back. My hair had grown longer over the last year. I didn't have the heart to cut it. Willow always kept hers long, and I wanted it like hers tonight, though mine was darker. I felt the tips of it grazing my back, and it felt nice, but more than that, I enjoyed the feel of his eyes on me.

I knew, even before looking, that they'd be lust-filled, dark, carnal. As if on command, I felt him twitch under me again. He was growing hard, and unable to stop myself, I reached down for him.

"Holy shit, Mac." A guttural moan ripped from him, and he tensed under my hand. His hands went to my hips, but he didn't move me. I had him in the palm of my hand.

I began to rub him, making him even harder. "So if you're named prom king, we both know another girl will probably be prom queen."

He began to pant heavily as I stroked his length. "Can we talk about this some other time?"

"No." I grinned, enjoying the power I had over him. I touched the tip of him, pausing there. "You'll have to dance with this other girl."

"Goddamn, Mac." His chest rose up and down. His eyes were starting to go wild. "I'm going to get you back. You know that."

I was hoping for it.

I kept sliding my hand over him. "And when you dance with this other girl, you aren't going to like it." I held him, squeezing just slightly. "Right?"

He was almost trembling, and he shook his head. "No. Hell no." His fingers sank into me, flexing. "Keep fucking going."

So I did, but this time, I scooted back and bent to take him in my mouth. His entire body paused, his hands in my hair. I could've kept going, but I didn't want to torture him. At least not yet. I'd wait until after the dance, after Kirk's after-prom party when we were alone again. Then I'd torture him all night long.

He didn't wait long. Once my mouth settled over him and I began moving up and down, his hands fisted until he was ripping me away. He flipped me over, and grabbing my leg, he raised it over his upper arm and then slid inside, sheathing himself deep.

I sucked in a breath, letting the air out through my teeth at the sensations. Goddamn. That felt so good.

"Now you were saying?" He smirked at me, pushing deeper in before sliding out, only to go back in.

I sighed, letting the waves of torment roll in, and a half hour later, after he put on a condom, he had me whimpering and biting my lip to keep from screaming. Then my entire body went slack.

Afterward, he curled against my body and kissed my neck. "There's no one else I want to dance with," he whispered, his hand palming my breast. "It's only you." He kissed me again, his thumb grazing my nipple. "Only you, Mac."

I already knew this. I'd known this all year, but it felt good to hear because I felt the same. There'd be no one else.

Closing my eyes, I murmured, "Good, because I love you."

His arms tightened around me. "I love you too."

Thirteen pieces just fit back together, all at the same time.

CHAPTER FORTY-ONE

"Your hair is so much darker now," Cora said, putting her eyeliner down on the counter.

We were getting ready at my house. Ryan had left, going to dress at his place, and he'd texted not long afterward to say the guys were already drinking there.

"Yeah." I pushed up some of the loose tendrils, patting them back into place. It wasn't that much darker, but I had put more brunette coloring in it. There were still some blonde, but I didn't want to look exactly like Willow tonight. I wanted to be me, and as I gazed in the mirror—I was me. I was Willow, but I was me too.

"And Ryan cut his hair short. I can't believe he did that. He's always had it where he could make it all messy."

I didn't smile; I heard the envy in her voice.

Cora was happy with Kirk, but she'd been harping on him to cut his hair too. Once she saw Ryan's new crew cut and how ridiculously hot it made him look, she started in. She hadn't been the only one. Peach had jumped on the bandwagon, asking Tom to cut his hair. Both guys refused, letting their hair grow even longer. Kirk's had grown to just past his ears, and Tom was closely resembling a shaggy dog these days.

Ryan had cut his for the summer. He was starting a new basketball training camp, and he didn't want to deal with too much hair and heat. I'd liked his messiness too. It always looked adorable on him, but I couldn't deny the spark I felt when he got back from the haircut place. It made him seem so much more grown-up, more of a man.

"Erin said Stephanie Witts is hoping for prom queen." Cora lifted her hand, inspecting her nails.

She missed the slight wince I couldn't contain.

It wasn't the prom queen thing. I didn't want it, but it'd become a sore spot over the last month. Erin, Cora, Peach, and all of their friends had been campaigning for me to win. I told them not to, but I knew they kept doing it. So, I started telling people to vote for Cora. She was the one who really wanted it, and after her transformation this year—from being one of the shiest girls in our grade to one of the most well-liked girls—she deserved it.

Not me. That was for sure.

I eyed her lilac-colored dress, the matching dusting of purple eye shadow, and the tiniest bit of glitter on her neck. "Have a speech ready," I told her.

Her eyes opened wide, meeting mine in the mirror. She quickly looked away, focusing on the bathroom counter. "You know that won't happen." But I could see her cheeks flushing.

"Right," I replied.

The doorbell rang, and pounding footsteps told me Robbie was running for the front door.

We looked to the door of my room, as if the guys would appear instantly, and a second later, we heard their voices. We grinned, glancing at each other.

Our men had arrived.

"Mac!" Robbie yelled from downstairs. "Ryan and Doofus are here!"

We heard Kirk grumbling, "It's Kirk, Little Dickwad."

That was another change over the year. Kirk and Robbie had developed this odd friendship. Kirk teased my little brother, and Robbie called him names. Ryan explained one night that Robbie reminded Kirk of Derek, and that silenced any concern I might've had about the situation.

"Ryan and Major Doofus are here!" Robbie added.

"Coming down!" I called back. "You ready?" I asked Cora.

She took a breath, staring at the mirror.

Her hair had been curled and was loose over her shoulders. Her makeup was on point. Everything was done up, complete with the mani and pedi we'd gotten yesterday. I'd had to touch-up my nails after this afternoon, but they were fine.

"Yeah. Ready."

"You look beautiful," I assured her.

"Thank you." She turned, taking me in, and a soft, awestruck expression came over her. I knew she'd been paying attention mostly to herself, which was understandable. She had the nerves, whereas I didn't.

That wasn't true.

I was nervous, just not for the same reasons as Cora.

I wasn't secretly hoping to win prom queen. And I knew she was nervous for Kirk's after-party, but she hadn't confided that in me.

"You look—"

I had to ask, and I reached for her hand. "Are you thinking of having sex with Kirk tonight?"

I noticed a shadow in the hallway at the same time I blurted that out, and I grimaced. But Cora was looking only at me, so she didn't see Ryan pause and then silently retreat.

"I . . ." She was back to picking at the counter. "I don't know. We talked about it."

I couldn't stop my frown. "At his party, though?"

"I know." She shrugged, looking to the side and biting her lip. "He'll be drinking. He's already drinking, but I don't know. I want to. I mean, he does too, but I think I'm just ready to stop worrying about it. If it feels right, I want to."

"Do you love him?"

All the self-consciousness in her vanished at my question. Her head came up. Her shoulders straightened.

"Yes. I love him."

It was the most confident response I'd ever gotten from her.

"Some people wait for marriage," I blurted that out—I have no idea why. "You could wait, if you're one of those people."

"Are you?" Her mouth turned down.

"No. Ryan and I—we already . . ."

"That's what I thought." She lifted her shoulder. "I know why you're saying this, because I do think like that, but I love him. And I don't know. I don't want to get married till I'm in my thirties, and I don't want to wait that long."

"Just—"

Shit. What was my problem? I understood what she was saying. But I felt like I had to say this to her—like I had to say to her what Willow would've said to me. Cora hadn't said a word about sex, but Ryan had said Kirk had stocked up on condoms. It wasn't a big leap for me to go from there.

"Do you regret it? Having sex with Ryan?"

I looked up, but I didn't see his shadow in the hallway. He might've been standing to the side, or he could've gone all the way downstairs, but I didn't lie when I said, "No. I regret not having my sister here, but that's it."

She jerked back. "I forgot about your sister."

My throat burned. "You didn't know her."

"But still." Her gaze lingered on my dress and then moved up to take me in. A wistful look softened her face. "You look really gorgeous, Mackenzie. I can't imagine your sister being more beautiful than you."

I—was shocked, and I couldn't talk for a second.

"And if I do win prom queen, I won't dance with Ryan. I'll dance with Kirk, so you don't have to worry about that." She darted toward me, hugging me and kissing my cheek. "I'll be downstairs." And then she was gone.

I felt Ryan's presence and without looking, I knew he was in the doorway. "You heard all that?"

"Yeah. Now you don't have to worry about the king and queen dance."

I grinned.

He took me in. He looked at my hair, my dress, and lingered on my lips. "She didn't lie. You look really beautiful, Mac."

That nickname.

I'd been in his arms just two hours ago, but a whole new wave of want came over me. I yearned to be in his arms again, to be held by him, to be kissed by him. And there was a whole host of other emotions intertwined there. I thought back to Cora's question, and no. There was no way I could've even considered regretting being with Ryan.

We went fast, but I had a feeling we went exactly the way we were supposed to. Either way, he was staring at me as if I were the most stunning creature he'd ever seen, and my entire body filled up with tingles. My knees were melting too, and my stomach flipped over, but in the good way. I had butterflies in there.

"Thank you."

I wore a shimmering pink dress, one that almost perfectly matched the one I'd seen Willow in. When I saw it at the store, the hairs on my neck had stood on end. Maybe she led me there. I'd been shopping with our mom, and I teared up when I saw it. We bought it immediately, and, like the last night I'd seen her, I put my hair up in a braided crown.

Cora's color was lilac tonight. I knew Peach was wearing yellow, and Erin was supposed to go silver. Not me.

I was pink. It was the most quintessential girl color there was, and it wasn't even my most favorite color, but it was Willow's.

I loved this feeling, seeing how I affected Ryan, but I hadn't dressed for him. I hadn't dressed for myself either.

I'd dressed for Willow.

And with everything feeling all sorts of right, Ryan came forward, his hand curving around the back of my neck as he bent to kiss me. His lips were soft against mine, and I closed my eyes, letting myself get lost in his embrace.

And then we went to prom.

More pieces fit together inside me, but I stopped counting. I didn't need to anymore.

EPILOGUE

"Mackenzie."

I walked into Naomi's office and sat in the same chair I'd been using for the last ten months. I didn't want to do these sessions. I never even wanted to admit that I was doing them, but there I was. I'd promised six sessions to my parents, and this was my tenth. Go me. Pin a star on my file.

I nodded in greeting, folding my hands over each other in my lap.

Naomi took a second, probably evaluating my posture, and she leaned back in her seat. "What's going on?"

I knew what she was referring to, but I still played dumb. I didn't know why. I could've gotten a gold star in stall tactics too. "What do you mean?"

She smiled briefly, nodding at me. "You know."

There was our relationship, right there. She knew I knew. I knew she knew that I knew, and yet I still played the game. And she just called me on it.

I never wanted these sessions, but I'd dropped my wall slowly over the last ten months, even going after I didn't have to. But today was the day. It would be the day I clued everyone in on what was going on with me, because until then, it'd been another stall tactic of mine.

"Okay." She let out a sigh, leaning back in her seat. "For real, what is going on with you?"

I never wanted to talk about Willow.

She'd been the reason my parents wanted me to come to these things—because I'd walked in and found her body first. I hadn't

271

known she was feeling like that. There'd been warning signs, but I didn't know how to read them. I knew that, but it wasn't the same for everyone. I knew that too.

I coughed, clearing my throat. "She had mood swings."

Naomi leaned forward.

"That's one of the warnings signs, right?" I looked away.

"Yes." I saw her nodding from the corner of my eye. "You looked up the signs, or are you guessing?"

I didn't have to guess. "She would go on these tangents, just raging about everything. I thought it was because we were moving."

"Yeah. I can see why you'd be confused."

But I wasn't done. "She withdrew from everyone too."

"Yeah. You mentioned that one time."

"She and Duke broke up, but I thought that was because of the move too. Later, Serena told me she'd stopped talking to her too."

"Serena was Willow's . . ."

"Best friend," I supplied. "I didn't know about that, but Serena told me when they came here a few months ago."

"Right. You mentioned their visit."

I wanted to laugh at that, but no sound came to me. I'd never told Naomi about the night with Stephanie Witts—not to keep it away from her, but because it wasn't something I needed to process. Stephanie Witts never hurt me. She actually helped, and I didn't want to give her any more time in my mind.

"She was sleeping a lot too, and then some nights . . ." Some nights she would be working out. Some days she slept two hours, and some days she slept twelve hours.

"Some nights?"

I shook my head. "I thought she had an eating disorder. I didn't know she was suicidal. She never . . ." My throat was burning again. "Feeling hopeless, thinking about wanting to die, feeling trapped, feeling like being a burden, unbearable pain . . ."

I kept listing the symptoms. The checklist had been engraved in my memory since June thirtieth, last summer.

"I just thought she had an eating disorder, and I didn't take it seriously. I thought they would help her. I just thought . . ."

How do you do this? How do you talk about how it was missed in one person, but it shouldn't have been for another?

Naomi sat forward, leaning down so her arms were resting on her legs. "Mackenzie, I'm confused." Her voice was quiet. It was always quiet. She paused as if she was unsure of what to say, but I knew that couldn't be true. Counselors knew what to say. They understood things the rest of us didn't. They understood us even when we didn't understand ourselves.

Right?

Then Naomi spoke again, her voice still soft and delicate, as if she were trying to trick me into opening up to her. "I haven't pushed about your sister's suicide note, but I know you read it. Your parents told me. It was right next to her when she, when you . . ." Another awkward cough. "When you found her. Your mother told me it was in your hands, but you won't talk about it and acknowledge it. I think . . ."

Yes, Naomi. Tell me what you think. Tell me how I'm supposed to process and grieve, and more importantly, tell me how I'm supposed to tell the truth about the worst day of my life. Tell me, please.

I raged at her in my head, but not one of those words passed my lips. I was a statue, my head turned away, my usual stony expression firmly in place.

Yes, there were cracks. Yes, some of the cuts had healed. Yes, I had a new layer on the outside. My life had changed. It wasn't exactly better. There was no world where I would say it was better without my sister, but it was different.

There were days I felt good. There were days I was convinced I'd already gotten my happily ever after. There were days I felt stronger than before. But then there were days I missed Willow so much I wanted to curl up into a ball and cry. There were days the hole inside me ached so much that I was convinced I'd actually lost a lung or my liver or half my heart. Those were the days when I understood the unbearable pain she must've been in.

But there was still something no one knew. Only Willow.

It was something that tricked me at times—into thinking I was in an alternate universe. If I thought about it, a crack in my foundation would open completely, and everything would fall in. And I didn't know how I would survive if that happened, but I had to talk about it today.

Ten months of counseling. Almost a year since Willow died.

I had healed. I had gotten stronger. I had persevered, but this one thing still haunted me. Maybe this was the real reason Willow haunted me? She wasn't around as much, but I still felt her, and I always knew she wanted me to tell the truth, but it scared me.

My voice would leave me, literally, in those times. It was as if I were too scared to talk about it because I was too ashamed.

"Mackenzie?" Naomi had scooted her chair even closer. "What's going on with you?" Her hand came down on mine. "You're trembling."

"I'm getting better."

"I know you are." I heard the pride in her voice. Her hand squeezed mine. "You and Ryan are good?"

I nodded.

"You went to prom together? I saw pictures in the local paper. I didn't realize they did that, but I guess when it's Ryan Jensen, anything goes, huh?"

"He was prom king."

She lifted her hand and sat back. She was getting comfortable again. "Were you prom queen?"

I shook my head. "Cora was."

"And you were happy for her?"

I moved my head in the other direction, up and down this time. "Yes. She deserved it. She's one of the most popular girls now."

"If I'm remembering correctly, you had a part in that, didn't you? You took her under your wing, like Willow did with you. Am I right?"

God. My throat was searing.

It was never going to go away. I realized it then.

I looked at her, meeting her gaze, and the words choked out of me. "I'm never going to fully heal, am I?"

The sadness in her eyes answered me, but she said, "Losing a twin is like losing a mother, or a father, or a soul mate. I can only imagine that it would be worse in some ways. So no, Mackenzie. I think it's a hole you'll feel for the rest of your life." Her lips pressed together, and she scooted close again, leaning down so she was almost touching my knees. "I don't think this last year was about you healing or getting over Willow's death. I think it was about learning to cope, and I think you've done a remarkable job."

But she didn't know.

No one knew.

Except Willow.

"You wanted to talk about Willow's suicide note?"

Her eyes widened in surprise. I had brought it up, not her. That wasn't how this went.

"Yeah. I wanted to talk to you about it at our last few sessions, but you seemed so much better when you came in, so I didn't push." Her head inclined toward me. "Do you want to talk about it today?"

No. But I had to. "Willow never talked about feeling trapped or hopeless. She never talked about suicide, but those are some of the signs."

"There are others, but yes. The list you mentioned are some of the warning signs, if people are looking for them, but sometimes, it's really hard to see everything the way it is, or for what it is. Your parents were worried about your sister, but they were worried about you too. Moving right before your senior year can be upsetting for any teenage girl. But Mackenzie, you can't beat yourself up for not seeing the signs."

I shook my head. "Willow never talked about that."

"Maybe not, but it was what she was feeling. She talked about being invisible, feeling worthless, of not being able to compare to her siblings. I can tell you that even if she didn't say the words, she was feeling all of those things."

Naomi's tone shifted, and she frowned, looking at the ground for a moment. "I'm confused about the direction of this conversation. It seems as if you don't believe your sister's feelings. It was all in the suicide note." She took my hand again. There was usually a no-contact policy with Naomi. She didn't even like hugs, which I was fine with. I liked touching Ryan, and I liked hugging Robbie, but that was it. No matter my progress over the year, I still held back with my parents and everyone else. It wasn't that I didn't love them or like them; it was just me. It'd been me since Willow died.

I changed that day.

Everything I had been before June twenty-ninth was wiped clean. When I lay down beside Willow, it was as if she took my pain; she took my burdens.

I felt it pressing on me. I knew I would share, but before I did, I needed to make sure Naomi understood.

I murmured again, "She never said anything. Not about that."

She scooted even closer. "But you *are* talking. You *are* saying something."

Yeah . . .

"I'm fine," I told her.

"No, I know—"

She didn't. I had to make sure she did. "Willow died, and I lived. I laugh. I love. I feel happiness, but this year was so hard. I wanted to be with her at times, but I didn't. I couldn't. I had Robbie depending on me. My parents needed me. And I have Ryan. I love him, and I know we'll be fine. We'll be happy. I mean, yeah, we'll have problems, and we'll struggle. Everyone does. Every relationship has ups and down, but we'll be fine. I'll be fine."

"I know." But she still frowned, struggling to figure out what I was telling her.

"I'm not arguing with you about what Willow felt. I know she was hurting. I just didn't know how much she was hurting, and I wish—"

My voice broke. It went back to not working, and I had to wait a moment. One breath, two, three, and then I could speak again. "I wish I had seen more than I had. I wish I had talked to her, but I was wrapped up in myself. I could only see what I was dealing with, and I never thought—"

My voice stopped again. I had to wait longer this time. Thirty seconds, and then, I tried again. "It wasn't supposed to be her. I wasn't supposed to be the one to go on and shine. That was always her role." I repeated again, "She never talked. I am talking now."

Naomi sat up, a look of horror on her face, but I grabbed her hands before she could sit back in her seat, and I finally told her what I'd been hiding from everyone else.

"I don't know how she found it. I don't know why she had it with her, but she didn't write that note. I didn't read Willow's suicide note because it wasn't hers." I let go of Naomi's hands and sat back, finally, finally feeling some peace as I shared my last secret.

"It was mine."

www.tijansbooks.com

Dear Reader:

I have never written a book that changed me.

There were books in my past that changed a part of my life, where they moved my career forward, etc. That's happened. I've had books be so loved by readers, and I've also written books that seemed like a grimace, but I'm always proud of every single novel I write. I grew or learned some lesson with each one.

But *Ryan's Bed* is different.

I began writing Mackenzie's story when I would travel for book signings, and I think there's something so lonely about hotel rooms that it crept into me and then through Mackenzie. I remember writing some chapters and thinking in the back of my head, "Where am I going with this? What am I doing?" And that's how I felt for the first eight chapters, but I didn't want to take the book into a path that I didn't feel was right. I didn't want to be careless with this book because there was something more with Mackenzie and Willow.

I'm glad I waited.

When I started writing it again, I felt Willow wanting a voice and I don't know if she would've had one in the beginning if I just pushed through. And then as the book started to unfold, I heard Ryan's voice more and more and then his storyline unfolded too.

This book was so hard to write, not in the way where I felt like I was taking a chainsaw to a glacier, but in the way where I cried almost every time I wrote it or worked on it.

A friend talked to me about how taboo suicide is, and how teen suicide is even more so, and that conversation really affected me. I agonized over if I should dare write this book. I thought about parents I know who lost a child, friends I know who lost their siblings to suicide, and even the ones I know who have gone. And when I really considered putting it aside, telling people it was abandoned, I couldn't do that. I honestly couldn't. I felt a huge cry inside of me that it was wrong to shove this book back down and ignore it.

I even talked to friends about writing *Ryan's Bed*. I remember having conversations saying that I didn't know what I was going to do with the book, if I would just finish it for myself and not publish it. I was that scared to write this one and publish it, but I kept writing it because there was something in Mackenzie that wanted out.

I know, I know. If you're not a writer or an artist, you may not understand this and it makes me look crazy, but I kept writing this book because I had to. That's the ultimate truth. I felt it was more wrong not to finish it so I started writing it again.

I wanted to respect Willow. I wanted to respect the loss Mackenzie had about losing her twin. I wanted to respect grief itself, acknowledge it, and not have it shoved under a rug. I wanted to write about Mackenzie's relationship with Ryan, but I also wanted to focus on Mackenzie herself.

I always felt something dark with her, something that she was hiding from, even herself. It drove me nuts, trying to figure out what I was feeling from her, until I realized what it was. And even when I did, I was still so scared to address it in this book. If you've read any of my books before, you know that I'm not someone who will shy away from the real issue. I usually go head first into it, exposing it and making you, the reader, sit with it. I wanted to do that with Mackenzie, but I wanted to do it in a different way so if you've stayed with me this whole time, I hope this book will make you think, and I hope this book will sit with you because that's what it's done for me.

No sequel is planned and I left the ending how it is because I hope it will make you think. I hope it will make you reread the book, but see it in an almost totally different way.

Out of all the books I've written, this is the only one that has changed me as a person.

Sincerely,
Tijan

LINKS & RESOURCES

https://www.crisistextline.org/
Text 741741 from anywhere in the USA to text with a trained
Crisis Counselor.

https://suicidepreventionlifeline.org
Call 1-800-273-8255 or if you go on their website, you can chat
online.

For more facts about suicide prevention and warning signals,
go to http://www.211bigbend.org/
nationalsuicidepreventionlifeline
or call 1-800-273-TALK

Made in the USA
Columbia, SC
05 January 2019